I picked up scissors. "I'll slice off one of the threads first," I said.

Amesh was worried. "Be careful."

To my surprise, I was unable to isolate a thread on the bottom of the carpet. I struggled for several minutes, and then moved the scissors to one of the tassels. I tried cutting off a piece of the gold material.

The scissors didn't touch it.

"Sara!" Amesh shouted. "Stop!"

"I didn't hurt it. I don't think I can." I lifted up the lighter.

"Put that away!" Amesh cried.

I ignored him. There was a part of me that felt as if the carpet had thrown out a challenge and that I had to respond. I felt as if it was mocking me.

I flipped open the lighter and pulled the carpet toward the flame. I'm not sure how close I brought it to the fire—half a foot, maybe—before it reacted.

The carpet jerked out of my hands and flew across the room. It landed on the sofa, where it seemed to stretch out comfortably.

Like a human being.

THE
SECRET
OF KA

Christopher Pike

GRAPHIA

Houghton Mifflin Harcourt
Boston | New York

www.hmhbooks.com

The text of this book is set in Centaur MT Std

The Library of Congress has cataloged the hardcover edition as follows:
Pike, Christopher
The secret of Ka/Christopher Pike
p. cm.
Summary: When fifteen-year-old Sara unearths a flying carpet in Turkey, it takes her and her new friend Amesh to the mysterious Island of the Djinn, where she faces terrible creatures and an impossible decision—whether to save mankind, herself, or the boy she is coming to love.

[1. Genies—Fiction. 2. Carpets—Fiction. 3. Arabs—Fiction. 4. Monsters—Fiction. 5. Identity—Fiction. 6. Fantasy.] I. Title.
PZ7.P626Sec 2010
[Fic]—dc22
2009049976

ISBN: 978-0-547-34247-4 hardcover
ISBN: 978-0-547-57729-6 paperback

Manufactured in the United States of America
DOC 10 9 8 7 6 5 4 3 2 1

4500328158

For Christopher,
my brilliant nephew

CHAPTER ONE

AN ENTIRE SUMMER in Turkey alone with my father. When I first heard about the trip I was so excited, I didn't sleep for two days. But now that I had logged the obligatory twenty hours of jet travel that it took to get to the Middle East and another week in Istanbul itself—Turkey's hot and crowded metropolis—I was having second thoughts.

Most of my doubts arose from just two of the above words: *hot* and *crowded*. If I was not in an air-conditioned room, I felt as if my clothes squeezed like a deep-sea wetsuit. And if my room didn't have every window tightly sealed, then my ears ached.

The Turks were so loud! Often I thought the problem was something as simple as mistaking the horn on their cars for the brake. I had yet to master their bus system. Taxis were my main form of transportation, but riding one was like working as a bouncer at a heavy metal concert. I mean, why would any driver use his brake when he could hit the horn and swear?

I had tried running the complaint by my father before he left for work—the only time I ever saw him—but he laughed and said that all foreign languages sound loud when you don't understand them.

"Hell. That's ridiculous," I said.

"Shhh, Sara, don't swear. Remember, you're in an Islamic country."

"*Hell* is a swear word here?"

"Yes."

"Gosh darn, I didn't know," I replied sarcastically. My father frowned but didn't reply. He merely returned to buttering his toast. The truth was, I was annoyed with him. I had not given up my summer to go sightseeing. I wanted to be with him. But after sharing a two-bedroom hotel suite for a week, we had yet to spend a single day together. He had not even picked me up at the airport, but had sent some guy with a turban who worked for him to deposit me at the five-star hotel that had been home for the last seven days.

During that week I'd only seen Dad at breakfast and for a few minutes each night, when he would stumble back to our suite, totally fried. He'd kiss me on the cheek and ask if I'd had a nice day. Naturally, because he looked so tired, I'd smile and say, sure, had a great time. Which made not an iota of sense since I did the same thing each day, which was absolutely nothing.

To put it mildly, by the seventh day, I was going nuts.

Then, finally, fortune smiled on me, and I met Amesh.

I was sitting in the hotel restaurant, eating carrot cake and ice cream, when a cute Turkish guy came pedaling up on a moped. He parked outside the hotel and hurried into the lobby with a package that sported the logo of my father's firm. I was sure it was a Becktar Corporation package and that it was for my father. We were the only foreigners the company had stowed at the Hilton.

I jumped from my seat, gestured to the waiter to put the half-eaten dessert on my bill, and ran to the lobby. The guy was panting as I approached. He had on long white shorts that hid the better part of his muscular legs, and a long-sleeve white shirt—which was odd, since it was over a hundred degrees outside. Then I noticed that his shirt was knotted at the end of the right sleeve—tied so far up his arm, there was no room for anything beneath it.

He was missing his right hand.

The deformity did not bother me. Honestly, I found it intriguing. I wondered if he had lost it in battle. If you could believe my father—and I didn't, really—bloody wars were being waged outside our hotel every night.

But to be honest, his missing hand probably didn't bother me because he was ridiculously cute, though not Hollywood handsome. He didn't look like anybody I had ever met before. His hair was long and black, sort of curly, and he wore it in a ponytail tied with a rubber band.

His features were oversize: large dark eyes, thick lush lips, even his nose was too big for his face. Yet somehow the combination worked, and what we had left was pure babe. Really, back home at my school, if you took a hundred girls and asked if they'd like to get to know him better, all one hundred would have said yes. I felt kind of lucky I had him all to myself.

"Is that package for Charles Wilcox?" I asked as the woman at the desk prepared to sign the guy's form. He had already placed the package on the counter, and he did glance over at me, but I must not have made much of an impression because he turned back to the woman and said something in Turkish. She responded in kind and the two of them went about their lovely business and basically ignored me.

I told myself I should have been relieved. For once, two Turks were having a quiet conversation and not giving me a headache. Nevertheless, I resented being ignored. After all, I was a visitor to their country, and I had suffered to reach their land. They could at least show me some respect by acknowledging I existed.

They continued to babble at a thousand words a minute.

For all I knew, they were talking about how immoral Americans were. It might have been their rudeness, or else I was just in a foul mood, but something inside me snapped. I reached over and grabbed the package.

"I'm going to take this," I said. "See the *Charles Wilcox* spelled out here? That's my father. And see the six red lines over here? That stands for Becktar. That's the company he works for. You don't have to worry about it; I'll make sure he gets it. Bye."

I walked away. I did not get far before I was attacked. Well, maybe that's too strong a word. But the guy did not ask for the package back, in English or Turkish. He tried to yank it out of my hands, which was too bad since the floor was made of very slippery marble.

He sent me toppling. I was lucky to land on my butt, yet I still felt a painful jolt inside my head. But I did not let go of the package. The way he stared down at me, you would have thought I had tried to steal his moped or slaughtered one of his sacred lambs or something.

He was furious! I was furious! We screamed at each other for a whole minute before I realized that he was speaking English. It was only then that I stopped to listen to what he was saying.

"Silly girl, I didn't hurt you," he said, his accent not nearly as thick as those of the other Turks I had met. "You tried to steal my package."

"Your package!" I said. "Where does it say it belongs to you? Huh? And didn't I point out—just before you hit me— that it has my father's name on it?"

"I didn't hit you," he said.

"Are you Sara Wilcox?" the woman behind the counter asked. She was not as upset as I would have expected. Secretly, she was probably enjoying the whole scene.

"Yes. I'm Sara Wilcox," I said. "My father's Charles Wilcox. This package is for him. I was just trying to do you two a favor and deliver it to him. But I can see my help is not appreciated."

He stared at me, puzzled. "Why do you keep sitting on the floor?"

"Because you're too rude to offer me a hand to get up." The words were no sooner out of my mouth than I realized it might sound crass to criticize a guy for not offering a hand when he only had one. But my fear was probably unfounded. He quickly offered me his good hand and helped me to my feet.

"Thank you," I said, brushing off my butt.

"You're welcome," he replied. "Can I have the package back?"

A stroke of genius struck. I suddenly realized that if I played my cards right, I could use this package, and this guy, to get me to my father. After all this time, I still did not know where he worked.

"Don't worry about it. I said I'd give it to my dad."

"But the woman at the counter has to scan it into her computer."

"Sorry, she won't be scanning today," I said as I held up the address slip, which had torn during our fight. "Tell your boss not to worry. My dad will get the package. You have my word."

I walked away. I was not positive he was following until I reached the elevator—I refused to turn around and check—but I was not surprised. The guy was starting to look worried.

"I need it back," he said.

"Trust me," I said. "My dad will get it."

"You don't understand. If the woman at the desk doesn't scan the slip, she won't give me a piece of paper that I have to give to my boss to show I was here."

"Have your boss call me. I'll tell him you were here. I'll even leave out the part where you hit me."

"I didn't hit you."

"You keep saying that. How did I end up on the floor?"

"You slipped and fell."

"After taking a brutal hit." The elevator rang and the door opened. "Excuse me, gotta go." Getting on the elevator, I pushed the tenth floor button. "Bye."

He jumped in beside me. The elevator doors closed and for the first time he looked me straight in the face. He was so interesting-looking, it made me wonder how I appeared in his eyes.

That June, I had just turned fifteen, and my frame was long and lanky. I was five-six, still growing, but I did not have much of a chest. My most formidable assets were my bright blue eyes and long blond hair. They received plenty of compliments, from girls and guys.

My nose was kind of small. My mother had gone through a phase where she called me "Button," as in "button nose"—and she had wondered why I did not speak to her that year. High-priced braces had given my smile some amps.

But what did I have to smile about? I was trapped in Istanbul for the summer. Trapped in an elevator with a cute Turkish guy who didn't like me. Of course, I was the one torturing him. To be blunt, I was behaving badly. It might have been his extraordinary sexiness that had thrown me off. Or else it was my desire to get to my father.

The elevator stopped on the tenth floor and I got off. The guy did not—sigh—and I realized that I was about to lose my excitement for the day. Yet he held the elevator door open.

"What's your problem?" he asked.

"My problem? I have a whole assortment of problems. What's today? Wednesday? I'm usually a monster come the middle of the week."

It was supposed to be a joke. He didn't smile; he didn't even speak.

"Do you work just for Becktar?" I asked, trying to change the subject. "Or do you deliver packages for lots of companies?"

"I work for Becktar. The same as your father."

I suddenly brightened. "You know my father?"

"Yes."

"Do you work in the same place? Out at the job site?"

"When I'm not making deliveries. I'm a gofer. Becktar has another office in town full of executives. That's where this package is from."

"A gofer. Cool. Look, I want to see my dad. But I don't know where your job site is. Can you take me there? Or can I take you there?"

He let go of the elevator door and stepped onto the tenth floor.

"Do I get my package back?" he asked.

I handed him the torn address slip. "This is all you need."

"Thank you . . . Sara."

"What's your name?"

"Amesh. Amesh Demir."

I offered my hand. "Sara Sashee Wilcox."

"Nice name."

"Do we have a deal?"

He stared at my hand before shaking it. "Okay."

"How old are you, anyway?"

"Eighteen."

"Sure," I said.

He stiffened. "How old are you?"

"Seventeen."

"You don't look that old."

"Looks can be deceiving."

"Where are you from?" he asked.

"Raleigh. Know where that is?"

"North Carolina."

I was impressed. "Clever boy. You a local?"

"Yes." He sighed. "A taxi will charge fifty lira to drive us out there. More if I don't argue the price. That's just one way."

"Great. Argue all you want. Just come with me and give the driver directions." I started walking toward my suite. He followed.

"It's none of my business but don't you see your father after work?"

"Look, Amesh, it's complicated. I know I'm asking for a favor, but I'm willing to give one in return. It's boiling outside. You don't want to ride your moped all the way back to the site. Come with me and you can relax in the back seat of an air-conditioned taxi." I paused. "You might even discover that you enjoy my company."

He was interested but hesitant. "Girls aren't allowed where the men work."

"Christ, that's ridiculous," I snapped.

"Shhh, Sara, don't swear."

"*Christ* is a swear word here? Wait, never mind, I'm sure it is. Look, there's got to be some women who work there."

"There are a few. But the site's dangerous. It's easy . . ." He hesitated, before adding, "to get hurt there."

It hit me then that he had probably lost his hand at work.

We stopped in front of room 1026. "If you don't mind waiting, I'll just be a few minutes," I said.

"Okay," he said. It sounded as though he was finally agreeing to my plan.

I hurried inside and grabbed my bag and a wad of Turkish bills from my dad's room. I put on a hat along with my sunglasses.

Before leaving the suite, I placed the package on the night table beside my father's bed and swiped two bottles of Coke from the minibar. When Amesh saw the soda, his face lit up. He had the whitest teeth. I opened a bottle and handed it over.

"Thank you." He must have been thirsty. He gulped down half of it before adding, "I'll take you there, but the taxi has to drop me away from the front gate. My boss doesn't pay me enough to ride in taxis. You have to get yourself inside."

"That won't be a problem," I replied.

Downstairs, he gave the woman at the desk the battered address slip, and she was able to read enough of it to give him the paperwork he needed.

The perimeter of the hotel was always crowded with taxis. One lira, I knew, was worth roughly two-thirds an American dollar. So fifty lira—or thirty-five bucks—was not cheap for a one-way ride. Then again, I wasn't paying for it; my father was. Fair was fair, I thought. He was the one who had locked me up in the blasted hotel for the last week.

Amesh had been right about having to argue with the taxi driver. Since they spoke Turkish, I didn't understand a word they said, but it sounded as if they were insulting each other's mothers. Twice they came close to blows. But finally it was settled, and the driver loaded Amesh's moped in the trunk and we were on our way.

"How much is he charging us?" I asked.

"Fifty lira," Amesh replied.

"You knew that ahead of time. He must have known the price."

"Yes. But if we didn't barter, we would both feel cheated."

The road was hot and dusty. I had to insist the driver put up all the windows and turn on the air-conditioning. He told Amesh that would cost an additional five lira because he would have to use extra gas. This time I spoke up. Leaning forward, I held up fifty lira and said, "Fifty! No more! Understand?"

My tone must have frightened him. He did as he was told. Amesh was impressed. "You must have Turkish blood in you," he said.

"I'll take that as a compliment."

While we drove, I learned a lot about Amesh. He had seen almost every movie I had, but I was shocked to discover he had read even more books. He said he got them at the library. He had a grandfather—his Papi—who had taken over his education at an early age. He had lost both parents in a car accident when he was ten. That's when he had dropped out of school. His Papi needed him to work to help pay the bills, but the old man was determined that his grandchildren would go to college.

Besides his grandfather, he had a ten-year-old sister, Mira. The mere mention of her name caused his face to brighten.

The three seemed to have something my parents and I would never share. They were more concerned about each other than themselves. His family lived together in a one-bedroom apartment. They ate their meals together. Here, I didn't even know where my father worked.

Ironically, I got a call from my mother while still in the taxi. She wanted to talk, but her definition of talking was she made all the sounds and I sat and listened. Yet she did miss me; she had not wanted me to be away from home so long. I felt sort of guilty cutting her off, but I simply couldn't act interested in her boring life with such a cute guy sitting beside me.

"I'm really sorry, Mom, but I can't talk now."

"But you said you're just driving in a taxi."

"That's it, I can't hear you, it's loud. Call me tonight."

"But . . ."

"Or I'll call you. Goodbye, Mom. Love you."

I hung up fast. Amesh was staring at me. I smiled.

"Sorry," I said.

"You could have talked to her."

"No, actually, I couldn't have."

As we took the street that led out of Istanbul, the scenery changed, becoming much drier, more arid. The view of the sea had been the one sight that had helped keep me sane the past week in the hotel. Now it was gone.

We eventually turned onto a narrow road. Dusty hills rose around us. A stiff wind, it seemed, could easily bury the road. Amesh nodded at my unspoken thought.

"During the storm season, this road disappears," he said.

"On days like that, how do you ride your moped to work?"

"I push it. Besides, I don't have to make deliveries in town every day. A lot of the time I just work out here."

"Well, I hope you liked the taxi ride."

"First time I've been in one."

"You're joking, right?"

"No. It's been fun."

He got out a mile later and gave me a quick heads-up on the design of the job site; specifically, where to find my father if he wasn't at his desk. He said my dad liked to get out and get his hands dirty.

We exchanged cell numbers. He said he would give me a call.

I was flattered at his promise. Silly, I know, but my heart skipped.

A twenty-foot gate topped with barbed wire surrounded the complex. I had to go through a security check. Guards carrying automatic rifles stopped me. I showed them my only form of identification—my passport.

The smallest of the guards took my passport and studied it.

"I'm Sara Wilcox, Charles Wilcox's daughter," I said.

"Do you have an appointment to see him?" he asked.

I smiled innocently. "Well, he's my father. I wouldn't be surprised if he's forgotten that he promised to have lunch with me today."

The guard smiled; he seemed a nice man. But he lifted a phone to call in. The half-completed plant must have feared terrorist attacks to take such thorough precautions. Eventually, he handed me back my passport.

"Your father will meet you at the corner of that building." He pointed to a structure. "Tell your taxi to wait for you."

"Why?"

"Talk to your father about that," the guard said.

The taxi drove me to the designated building. He demanded payment before he let me out. I told him that he might want to hang around, that I would probably be going home soon. He just nodded; he was listening to some weird music on the radio.

I finally got my first clear view of the place.

The construction site for the hydroelectric plant itself was immense, and south of the main building was a large herd of oil wells. From what little my father had told me, the wells were designed to pump out natural gas to fuel the engines that would later create the electricity. But the actual oil the wells found—the black liquid stuff—was something of a nuisance. It had to be hauled away in special trucks.

My dad came out of the building a minute later.

We shared the same blond hair and blue eyes, although he kept his hair cut marine-short, and I had yet to see him outside the hotel without his thick shades. His eyes were not a sky blue like mine. They were darker, and he had an intense stare, which he used to good advantage when he wanted to get his way.

I had a feeling I would be seeing it soon.

My father did not like surprises.

At the same time, I steeled myself for a confrontation. I could not let the whole summer slip by and simply bow to his schedule. It had been his idea I come to Turkey. He owed me a certain amount of time, and if he didn't agree, then I was going to remind him there were plenty of planes leaving for America every day.

Yet he disarmed me with a smile and hug. "Sara. This is a pleasant surprise. How did you manage to find this place?"

"There are only so many hydroelectric plants being built in Istanbul. How are you doing, Dad? I was hoping that you weren't too busy and we could have lunch together."

He glanced at his watch—it was close to noon—and

shifted uneasily on his feet. "Lunch sounds great. I just wish you'd given me more warning. I could have arranged things."

I nodded to the rows of what were clearly temporary buildings behind him. "Come on, Dad, there's got to be at least one cafeteria out here. You know I'm not fussy. I'll have what the troops are having."

He frowned at my mention of troops.

"That's the problem. There are only a few female employees here during this construction phase. And the men, when they take a break, they prefer to eat alone."

"You mean, they prefer to dine without females present?" I said, not bothering to hide my annoyance. He quickly held up his hands.

"This form of segregation is practiced in America. Especially when you have a job site where ninety-nine percent of the employees are male."

"Really? When was the last time you worked on such a site?"

"Sara . . ."

"Dad. I just want to have lunch with you and maybe get a quick tour of the place. That's not asking a lot. The hotel is nice but you're the only one I know in this whole country. You know what I mean?"

He considered. I had asked without whining, which was wise. He did not respond well to emotional outbursts. Finally, he nodded and took me by the hand.

"We'll have lunch, and I'll give you a tour. Just as long as you listen to me when I say where we can go and where is out of bounds."

I felt a rush of relief, not realizing how tense I had been about our possible showdown. I leaned over and kissed his cheek.

"I'll follow your orders to the *T*," I promised.

I let the taxi go. The driver looked disappointed when I only tipped him ten lira. What the heck; it was almost seven bucks.

I ended up causing a stir when I entered the all-male cafeteria, but it vanished when I smiled and waved to the men. My charm—or the fact that my dad was one of the bosses—quickly evaporated the tension. Soon we were gorging ourselves on lamb chops, rice, and goat cheese, which I developed an immediate taste for.

The tour of the site proved less successful. My dad found a stripped-down Jeep and drove me around the oil wells and the makeshift office buildings. However, when it came to the main site—where two hundred cranes were performing massive excavation, and thick walls of concrete were being poured night and day—he only let me have a distant glimpse through binoculars. I asked why. He said there were security reasons.

"I'm sorry, but it all seems like a bunch of paranoia to me," I said.

He considered. "Maybe there's a place I can show you that's supposed to be off-limits."

"What is it?"

"A cave."

"Just a cave?"

"It's what the cave leads to. I may be the chief engineer when it comes to this job, but you remember what a hard-core archaeological buff I am. Well, there's this cave that leads to ruins we suspect might be older than anything mankind has ever discovered."

I was getting really interested. "You're kidding me. How old do they think they are?"

"The experts we've hired say seven thousand years."

"But Sumerian civilization . . ."

"Was six thousand years ago. These ruins might be older. Now, I know I can take you to the cave entrance. But getting permission to go inside will be another matter."

I trembled with excitement. I loved archaeology myself. "Please try hard, Dad," I said.

"No promises."

We drove away from the buildings and pit, and down a steep hill to a cave entrance. I was surprised to see Mr. Toval and Mrs. Steward, my father's bosses, hanging out there.

Mr. Toval was from Jordan. He was a Muslim, dark-skinned and tall. The man never seemed to age. I had seen pictures of him and my dad taken before I was born and he looked the same as he did now—at sixty years of age. My father said it was not fair; he was jealous of the guy. Mr. Toval was always polite to me but I nevertheless found him cold.

Mrs. Steward was the reverse. She was from the Midwest and looked like a classic grandmother. She waved as we drove up. She loved talking about New Age topics and had a vast collection of crystals. She occasionally gave me pendants to wear when she visited us in Raleigh. Since they gave me headaches, I never wore them long, but her heart was in the right place.

It was odd how the three were so different and yet they were really close. For years they had worked different job sites all over the Middle East, but always for Becktar Corporation.

My dad parked our Jeep, and Mrs. Steward came over and gave me a hug while Mr. Toval simply nodded hello.

"I assume your dad has told you about our little secret," Mrs. Steward said, pointing to the cave. "Isn't it exciting?"

"I'd be a lot more excited to see the ruins," I said.

"Charles, check with Bill," Mr. Toval said. "Tell him your daughter's here. He's the lead archaeologist on the site today. He has the final say on who gets in."

My father walked toward the cave entrance and disappeared. I stayed seated.

"I thought you guys were in control," I said.

Mrs. Steward shook her head. "We were until we told the government what we found. Technically, we own this land but we can't do whatever we want here."

Mr. Toval studied me. "Sun bothering you, Sara?"

"I'm all right." But no sooner had he asked than I began to

sweat like a pig. It was odd, in the desert, to feel your own sweat. It usually evaporated so fast. Mrs. Steward offered me a bottle of Evian.

"Go ahead, drink," she said.

The bottle was glass, not plastic. It was freezing cold. I feared if I drank too much I would get cramps. I took a few gulps and began to feel dizzy. I told Mrs. Steward as much.

"You've only been in the country a week," she said. "It takes a month to adapt to this heat. Drink more; splash some on your face."

I obeyed her instructions, but most of the water ended up on the floor of the Jeep. My dizziness remained.

My father was a long time returning, and when he did, he said Bill was in a bad mood and wouldn't let anyone in to see the ruins.

"Maybe next week, Sara," my father said as he climbed in the Jeep.

"I don't know if that's a bad thing," Mr. Toval said. "I'm afraid your daughter's showing signs of heat stroke."

My dad was worried. "Are you sick?"

I forced a smile. "I'm fine." I looked around for Mrs. Steward to thank her for the water, but to my surprise she had already left. I told my dad, "I can always see the ruins another day."

We drove back to the entrance and my father called for a taxi. He told me he had to get back to work, that he was sorry he could not stay with me until the taxi arrived.

"It's okay," I said. "I'm just glad we got to hang out together."

"Will you be awake when I get back to the hotel?"

"Sure." I gave him a quick hug. "I'll be waiting for you."

My father left me at the security building, a boxlike structure with no air-conditioning. A half-hour passed and still there was no taxi. I tried calling for one. Unfortunately, everyone who answered spoke Turkish.

I thought of asking a guard for help, but decided to call Amesh instead. He answered right away, and when I explained the situation, he acted angry.

"Your father should have stayed with you until the taxi came."

"I did drop by unannounced. He has work to do. Can you call me another taxi?"

"Yeah. But it might cost seventy lira to get back to the hotel. The taxi has to drive all the way out here to get you."

"I figured as much," I said.

"I'll go to the gate and make sure you get off okay."

"You don't have to do that, Amesh."

"Sara, I don't have to do anything."

It was then I realized he might want to see me again!

He arrived a few minutes later, and this time he was not ashamed to be seen with me. I understood. He could not be seen returning from Istanbul with a girl while he was on the clock. But now our roles had changed. I was simply a visitor who needed help.

His cell suddenly rang. I assumed it was the taxi company calling back to say they couldn't pick me up after all, but as I watched, his face darkened. I knew the news must be bad. He hung up and jumped on his moped.

"What's wrong? What happened?" I asked.

"It's my friend, Spielo. There's been an accident. He fell into the concrete pour."

"Is that bad? Can't they get him out and wash him off?"

Amesh was pale. "You don't understand. They pour the concrete all the time, no stopping, into shafts hundreds of feet deep."

I grimaced. "He hasn't fallen into one of those, has he?"

He was already leaving. "I have to go see. Wait here until I come back."

"I can't just stand here. I want to help."

Amesh shook his head. "There's nothing you can do."

He rode off, leaving a trail that was easy to follow. I hesitated perhaps five seconds before I decided to go after him. I figured I would not get far, that the guards would stop me.

Yet no one bothered me. Several Jeeps sped by in the direction of the main pit where I had to assume Spielo had had his accident. But the men in the vehicles hardly looked at me.

I had walked for twenty minutes and was about to pass out

from the heat when I reached the edge of the hole that was to house the bulk of the power plant. To say it was massive would be an understatement. It looked like a crater that had been formed by a meteor crash. Standing on the edge of it, looking down, I could see the different layers of earth. The deeper it got, the darker red the sand became.

Suddenly a Turkish woman in a veil was standing beside me.

"Impressive, yes?" she asked in a thick accent.

"Yes. But I'm worried. I heard that someone fell into the concrete."

The woman pointed a finger that was studded with jewelry.

"Down there, it looks like a party. He must be okay."

Deep in the eye of the crater, I saw a line of revolving concrete trucks and a cluster of happy men. I assumed they were happy—they were dancing and carrying a young man through the air. That had to be Spielo. I'd missed his rescue by minutes. What relief I felt, for his sake and Amesh's.

"You're right," I told the woman. "He must be fine."

"You seem surprised," she said.

"It's just that a friend of mine acted like no one could survive that kind of accident."

The woman turned and stared at me through her veil. It was black; her face was dark. I could not tell her age.

"True. The boy is lucky to be alive." Then she suddenly handed me a water bottle. "You look tired, thirsty. Come, sit over here and rest."

The woman led me to a spot a hundred yards to the right, deeper in the pit, where there was a row of boulders. I sat and assumed she would join me, but she excused herself.

"I cannot stay," she said, and quickly walked away.

Sitting inside the crater, I marveled at how much richer the red-colored sand was here than on the rest of the job site.

It was then my hand brushed a piece of material sticking out from beneath the ground. It was as red as everything else, but it was definitely cloth. The more I pulled on it, the more came out. Finally I yanked it free—a thick sheet, about seven feet long and four feet wide. It was so completely coated with hard red dirt, I was surprised I recognized it at all.

Yet the instant I held it in my hands, my fingers trembled.

I knew it was a carpet. A very old carpet.

CHAPTER TWO

THE HIKE TO THE CRATER, and the effort I had spent digging up the carpet, had exhausted me. I did not want to interrupt Amesh during what was surely a joyful time, but I needed a ride back to the entrance. Particularly if I was going to carry the carpet. With all the dirt on it, the thing weighed at least forty pounds.

I took out my cell and dialed his number.

He sounded happy to hear from me. He sounded happy, period! Spielo was alive! Yet whatever joy he felt over his friend's rescue vanished when he finally caught up with me and saw what I was carrying.

"You're crazy! You can't take that with you!" He and his moped were covered with red dust from the celebration in the bottom of the pit. Again, I was struck by how well muscled his legs were.

"Why not?" I asked innocently.

"It's dirty! No taxi's going to give you a ride with that thing."

"We'll wash it off. It'll dry quickly in this heat."

"Why bother? It's just a piece of old cloth."

"Amesh, get a clue! It's a carpet! It might be a really old carpet."

He gave it a closer look, but was not impressed. "If it is a relic, then there's no way you can take it. The guards at the gate will stop you."

"I already thought of that. I have a plan."

"No plan. No way either of us is going to jail."

"Would you at least listen to what I have to say?"

He wiped the sweat from his brow. "Say it."

"Help me wash it off and I'll tell you," I said.

Only a handful of men were heading back toward the entrance. Most were probably still in the pit. Amesh was able to stow the muddy carpet on the back of his moped—he had a fair-size basket—but there was no room for me. I had to hurry to keep up. No one gave us a second look.

Not far from the gate, he veered behind an office building that stood beneath an elevated water tank. The tank's hose was as thick as a fireman's. Indeed, it was probably there in case of a fire. The nearby office building had no windows. We appeared to be alone.

Amesh tried shaking the dirt off the carpet, but it was too much a part of the material. He ended up laying the carpet on the ground and turning the nozzle on full strength. I had to stand on one end of the carpet to keep it from washing away. We worked on a strip of asphalt that could have fried eggs, it was so hot. The cool water felt fantastic on my bare legs.

"Turn it over, Amesh!" I shouted. The "old cloth" was magically taking on color, and I was not the only one who was seeing it in a new light. Excitement began to show on Amesh's face. "Let's lower the water," I said. "I don't want to damage it."

"We need the water on hard to wash it clean," he said, ignoring me. There were no two ways about it—Turkish boys didn't like American girls telling them what to do. I knew we weren't going to get the carpet out of the complex without a fight.

When he was done hosing it off, I laid it on a dry piece of asphalt. The instant the scalding heat and damp material touched, a wave of steam rose.

One side of the carpet was almost supernaturally black. The material was so dark it seemed to absorb light. The other side was navy blue, decorated with an assortment of stars, planets, and dozens of tiny figures—some human, others myth-ological.

"I want to take it back to the hotel," I said.

"If you're right and this is a relic, then it belongs to the government. We have to report it. Otherwise, it will be stealing."

I called his bluff. "Fine, call your boss. Hand it in."

He blinked. "What? I thought you said you had a plan."

"That was before you accused me of being a thief."

"I didn't accuse you of anything."

I snorted. "You just said I was trying to steal it."

"Tell me what your plan is."

"Not unless you apologize."

"For what?"

"For the mean thing you just said."

He simmered. "I'm sorry. Now what's your stupid plan?"

"Never mind. You're right; it is stupid. The carpet belongs to your government."

"The smart thing to do is hand it in," he said.

"Whatever. I'm too hot to argue. Go ahead and call your boss."

He took out his cell. "All right."

"But be very careful which boss you call," I added.

He stopped. "What do you mean?"

"If this is a relic, then it's worth a fortune. Whoever you give it to—they'll probably keep it for themselves, at least until they can sell it on your black market."

"What do you know about our black market?" he demanded.

"I know it exists and that many relics are sold there."

Amesh shook his head. "This is Turkey. We don't have the corruption you have in America."

"I was just going by how your taxi drivers behave."

"Huh?"

"You had to fight with the last one so he wouldn't rip us off."

"If you think all Turks are liars and thieves, then you don't know us."

"You're right, what do I know?" I muttered.

"We're a Muslim nation. People have high morals here."

"Call Mr. Toval. He's your boss, right? Tell him about the carpet."

"That's true, but . . ." Amesh considered. "Maybe we should call your father."

"Why?" I did not want to call my dad. He would never let me study it. He would hand it in immediately.

"He's well respected. He'll know what to do," Amesh said.

I shrugged. "You can do that if you want, but I have to warn you, my father's an engineer. He doesn't like to get involved in administrative affairs. He'll probably give the carpet to Mrs. Steward, and she's not even a Muslim."

Amesh looked as if I had just punched him in the gut.

"I don't want some rich American stealing it," he swore.

I was sympathetic. "The carpet would probably make her super-rich."

Amesh stopped and studied me. "Do you really think it's worth a lot of money?"

"If it's been buried beneath this desert for thousands of years—then yes, it's worth a fortune. Look at it; it's in perfect shape."

Amesh looked puzzled. "How can it be so old and look so new?"

"The dry sand mummified it. That doesn't just happen to dead bodies. If it was buried deep enough to escape the rain, then I'm not surprised it kept its original colors."

"But you dug it up near the surface."

"I dug it up after tons of heavy machinery brought it to the surface. Amesh, for all we know, it was buried near the bottom of the pit."

"I see what you're saying." He frowned, worried. "But if we try to smuggle it out of here—that would be like stealing."

It would not be *like* stealing; it would *be* stealing, but I didn't bother to point that out to him. "I don't plan to keep it," I said, not sure if I was being 100 percent honest. "I just want to check it out, you know, back at the hotel."

"Why?"

I reached down and touched it. It was incredible. Already, in the short time we had talked, it had begun to dry. "There's something strange about it. It feels almost magnetic."

Amesh reached down and touched it. "I don't feel anything."

"That's because you're tired and you've been working all day."

He wiped his sweat away. "Okay, what's your plan?"

"I'll call another taxi and leave the site. I'll wait for you on the other side of that sand dune we saw when we drove up."

"So you want me to sneak it past the guards?"

"Yes."

"They're not going to let me take a carpet out of here."

"No. But they will let you take a nicely wrapped FedEx package out of here."

"Is that your secret plan?"

"Yes. And it's a good one."

"That's what you think. I don't know if we have a FedEx box that can hold something this big."

"It doesn't have to be an official FedEx box. Just put lots of FedEx stickers on it. Heck, you're their number one gofer. You're always running around with packages. Do you forget how we met?"

"I usually deliver smaller packages."

"Like the guards care. They see you every day. They'll take one look at you and wave you through. Also, remember, you're leaving the job site, not trying to enter. Security is tighter on the way in than on the way out."

"Who told you that?"

"No one! It just makes sense."

Amesh considered. "We can ride back to your hotel together?"

"As long as you can get out of work."

"I can make up some excuse." The logic of my plan was slowly changing his mind, but Amesh continued to stress. He began to pace back and forth. He was starting to make me nervous. "If I get caught, it'll be my life on the line, not yours," he said.

"I doubt they'll take you out and shoot you."

He glanced back toward the pit. A shadow crossed his face. "They could. When it comes to stealing, Turkey is more strict than America. You have no idea."

The change in him was dramatic. He looked scared.

It made me wonder, just a tiny bit, if I was being reckless.

"If you get caught, I'll tell them it was my idea," I said.

He shook his head. "You say that now . . ."

"I mean what I say. That's one thing you've got to learn about me."

"If I get it out of here, then I'll own a bigger piece."

Boy, did my blood boil then, in two seconds flat.

"Gimme a break! I'm the one who found it!" I yelled.

"You found it by chance. It doesn't belong to you. You're not even from this country. You're . . ."

"Go ahead and say it: I'm just a girl. An American girl."

"That's not what I was going to say."

"Liar."

Amesh frowned. "If we do end up selling it, then we'll have to be clear about who owns what."

"Fine. If I decide to sell it, I'll pay you a ten percent commission for helping me get it out of here."

"That's crazy!"

"Why?"

"Because I'm taking all the risk! I should pay *you* ten percent!"

I reached over and squeezed his good arm. "Amesh?"

He shook me off, he was so heated. "What?"

"If we get it out of here, we'll both own it equally. And if we decide to sell it, we'll split the money."

He began to cool down. "That's fair."

"But I have one condition. In the end, I get to decide what we do with the carpet."

"No way!"

"For the last time—I found it! Now we've talked enough. Do we have a deal? Yes or no?" I stuck out my hand.

He shook it. "All right. But you have to promise not to do anything with it without first talking to me."

"Agreed." I handed him my cell. "Find a taxi that will come out here, then go wrap up the carpet."

"For someone I just met, you're asking me to trust you an awful lot."

"It works both ways," I told him.

To lure a taxi to the work site, we had to promise to pay a staggering eighty lira. I was being exploited but there was no helping it. We had to keep moving forward.

The carpet took only fifteen minutes to dry in the boiling sun. But a minor miracle occurred when I went to roll it up. The carpet practically shrank. I folded it in two and it lay down perfectly flat. Then, I rolled it up, and it was like handling a deflated air mattress. The more I folded it, the smaller it got. By the time I handed it to Amesh, it was two feet by one foot. Plus it was so light—five pounds max!

Amesh didn't notice the miracle. He just nodded. "Good work."

"Thanks," I mumbled, staring at it with awe.

While Amesh went off to wrap it, my taxi arrived. The guards had it wait outside the gate. Before leaving the job site, I decided to give Amesh a quick call. I was worried about his nerves. Turned out, I was right to be worried. He sounded scared. I warned him to stay cool.

"That's easy for you to say," he complained.

"I'd take the risk if I could," I said, but I wondered if that was true. Swiping something this important in a foreign country was no laughing matter.

"You can," he said. "I can give you the package. Then you can have your taxi pick you up inside the compound and leave with the carpet already hidden inside the taxi's trunk."

"It won't work. My taxi's already here. The guards know I'm leaving. They have no reason to let my cab through the gate." I paused. "Look, if you can't do it, I understand. Hide it in the building you're in and I'll find another way to sneak it out."

"Yeah. Then you'll own it a hundred percent."

"Well, yeah."

Amesh sighed. "Wait for me. If I'm not there in fifteen minutes, then it means I got caught."

He hung up. Getting in the cab, I smiled and waved goodbye to the guards. They waved back. This particular taxi driver did not have his radio on, nor did he complain when I stopped him a mile from the job site. I held up a ten lira note and repeated the Turkish sentence Amesh had taught me: "A friend's coming on a moped." The guy did not complain. He turned off the engine and quickly pocketed the cash.

Amesh did not show for twenty minutes—the longest twenty minutes of my life. When he finally did appear, he acted nonchalant. He let the driver stick his moped and the package in the trunk, and soon we were on our way to Istanbul.

"You're as cool as James Bond," I teased when we were both seated in the back.

"This had better be worth it."

I saw he was serious. "Did the guards give you a hard time?"

"For the first time ever, they wanted to know what was in the box. I told them I didn't know, just that my boss told me to deliver it to FedEx. I said I wasn't allowed to open it."

I patted his leg. "You did good. I'm proud of you."

"Just remember our deal."

The ride back to Istanbul proved uneventful. We were so weary from the heat and stress, we both passed out. In fact, I did not wake up until we reached the hotel. I must have been growing accustomed to the traffic noise. The taxi driver got out to help Amesh unload his moped, but I was up fast to grab the box. He had done an excellent job wrapping it.

The driver took his fee and left. A security guard at the hotel parking lot let Amesh lock his moped beside an assortment of bikes. When we were finally alone, I told him to wait downstairs for ten minutes before coming up to my room.

"Why?" he asked, suspicious.

"We might draw attention to ourselves, being seen together."

"More like you're ashamed to be seen with me."

"I would say the reverse is closer to the truth."

"Or else you plan on stealing it the moment I turn my back."

That hurt. I threw the carpet at him. He barely had a chance to raise his good arm and catch it. "Hold it if you don't trust me!" I yelled.

He was ashamed. "I'm sorry, I shouldn't have said that. It's just . . ."

"What? All Americans are thieves?"

"No, no," he said quickly. "It has nothing to do with that."

"Then what is it?"

"Last summer . . ." he began, but stopped, his expression pained.

"What about last summer?" I asked.

He shook his head. "Forget about that; it's not important."

"Amesh. Come on, what are you saying?"

He shrugged. "This is a rich hotel. I don't know how much Becktar's paying for you and your dad to stay here, but it's a lot. I don't know how much money you have—and it's none of my business—but whatever it is, compared to what I have, it's a fortune."

"What does this have to do with the carpet?"

For one of the few times, he looked me directly in the eye, and I was struck by how beautiful his eyes were. He spoke in a soft voice.

"We live in different worlds. This carpet fascinates you. You find it beautiful. You might think one day of hanging it on the wall of your house. But to me it's something that could change my life and the life of my family."

"*If* we establish that it's old and worth a lot of money," I said.

He nodded. "And if we can sell it on the black market."

I considered his words carefully. Up until now, I had wanted time alone with the carpet so I could study it. He was right—it intrigued me, but in ways I could not explain to him because I could not explain them to myself.

I simply felt drawn to it.

But I was not a thief. I had not truly considered selling it in Turkey or trying to smuggle it back to America. In the end, after I had fun playing the archaeologist, I figured I would tell my father about it and we would turn it over to a museum.

Yet now I saw how the idea worried Amesh. He was trying to say he was not a crook either, but the carpet might be an unexpected windfall that could help his family. I could appreciate that. Money was good, especially when you didn't have any.

Unfortunately, it was too early to make any promises concerning the carpet. We did not know enough about it. I tried telling Amesh as much—I thought I was reassuring him—but the more I talked, the more unhappy he looked.

He handed it back to me. "You carry it. I'll knock in ten minutes."

"Give me fifteen. I want to take a quick shower and change."

He glanced uneasily around. "I'll wait across the street."

"You can't wait in the lobby?"

"They'll ask what I'm doing here. They'll probably throw me out."

His remark was so simple, and so true, it made me sad.

In my room, I did not bother to unwrap the box, but jumped in the shower. I wanted to wash and blow-dry my hair before Amesh arrived. Like I needed a dryer in this climate. I could stand on the balcony in the breeze that blew off the sea and my hair would dry in the same length of time. Yet I was hoping to give it bounce. Yes, I admit it, I was still hoping to get this cute Turkish guy to like me.

It was half an hour before he knocked. Perhaps he had given me extra time, afraid he might catch me in the shower. It would have been just like him; he was so shy. But all I had on when I answered the door was a tank top and shorts. It's what I wore most of the time since I had arrived in Istanbul, but somehow, right now, it felt kind of mischievous. I mean, he noticed how little I was wearing. It was like he was afraid to look.

I think it was my belly button that got him.

He looked hot from the sun so I offered him another Coke, which he took gratefully. I gestured to the bathroom.

"You can take a shower if you want, cool off, I don't mind."

He quickly shook his head. "I'm fine," he said.

I smiled as I picked up scissors and moved toward the package, which was sitting on a table not far from the flat-screen TV. "I feel guilty opening it after you did such a nice job wrapping it up," I said.

"Be careful you don't cut it," he said.

"I hear ya." I sliced off the tape without penetrating the cardboard. In minutes I had the carpet in hand and was about to unroll it on the floor. Then I ran into the bathroom and returned with four giant towels. The floor was clean but not clean enough for me.

The first thing I noticed was that we had done a great job hosing it down. There was not a spot of dirt on it. Amesh made a similar observation.

"It was this clean when I wrapped it," he said.

"Did anyone see you wrap it?"

"No. I was alone."

"Good," I muttered, because my eyes were growing larger with each passing minute. Again I was amazed at how black the bottom of the carpet was; it looked like a rectangular window into deep space. It was made up of an incredibly dense forest of one-inch fibers—that stood up so straight, but which bent so easily—I could not for the life of me figure out what they were made of.

"It almost feels like hair," Amesh said.

"Very stiff hair, and at the same time, very soft."

"Can something be stiff and soft at the same time?"

"No, not really. But this is unlike anything I've felt before."

"Turn it over," Amesh said.

We flipped it, and our puzzlement deepened. There were no individual fibers that we could see, but the reverse side was extremely soft and smooth.

"It's silk," Amesh said.

"It's not silk."

"What is it?"

"I don't know."

"How can you be sure it's not silk?" he asked.

"Because it's like it's all . . . one."

"One what?" he asked.

"I don't know, one piece. Let's study the design."

The predominant dark blue color was rimmed on all four sides with an inch of bright gold. In the center was an ill-defined black circle, two feet across and filled with stars.

Around the star field flowed a group of characters set against a series of exotic backgrounds. The carpet seemed to tell a story.

At the top, there was a garden filled with two types of beings—humans and what might have been angels. The latter walked with the people, but were taller and brighter. Most wore silver gowns, while the humans wore simple animal skins.

The scene flowed by a dragon, or some kind of monster. It glowed a sober red and as it pressed upon the soft green of the garden, the monster transformed it into a desert.

On the lower half of the carpet were the humans; the angels, who had lost height as well as luster; and a third species, who were taller than the other two. They were an unpleasant brownish gray and had flat, almost featureless, faces. The bottom showed these three groups at war with each other. But then the dragon reappeared and crushed the life out of the angels and the other mysterious creatures. In the end only the humans remained.

At the top and bottom of the carpet were gold tassels. There were nine on each end. They were woven from some kind of thread, but I hesitated to say what it was. I tugged on them to reassure myself they were real. Staring at the mysterious images had left me feeling spacey.

I sat back on my knees. Amesh sat on a chair beside me.

"Wow," I whispered.

"It's amazing," he agreed, before frowning. "Sara?"

"Huh?"

"Do you feel all right?"

"Yes. Why?"

"You're pale. And your voice sounds funny."

I shook myself. "Staring at those scenes hypnotized me somehow."

"The artwork is amazing. The person who made this carpet had skill. Maybe a team of people worked on it." Amesh tried to keep his voice casual but failed. "So do you think it's a relic?"

"Definitely. It almost looks as if it were made by . . ."

"What?" he asked when I did not finish.

"People who know a hell of a lot more about carpets than we do."

"Please, Sara, don't swear around it. It might be a holy item."

"Sorry."

"What should we do next?" he asked.

"The smart thing would be to photograph it, download the pictures onto my computer, and send them out to experts all over the world. We could contact a handful of universities and museums."

Amesh shook his head. "Then everyone will know what we have."

"True." I realized I was staring at it again. It was hard not to. "Do you feel its power?" I mumbled.

"What do you mean?" he asked.

Slowly, I got to my feet, walked toward my father's room.

"I want to try an experiment," I said.

"What?"

"You'll see."

In the room I found a lighter. My father liked a cigar after dinner, but was polite enough to smoke on the balcony. The lighter was low on fuel but was still able to produce a decent-size flame. When I returned to the living room and Amesh saw the lighter, he jumped up.

"You're not going to burn it," he said.

"I'll separate out a single thread from the bottom."

"And do what?"

"Burn it."

"No! You might light the whole thing on fire!"

I picked up the scissors. "I'll slice off one of the threads first," I said.

Amesh was worried. "Be careful."

To my surprise, I was unable to isolate a thread on the bottom of the carpet. I struggled for several minutes, and then moved the scissors to one of the tassels. I tried cutting off a piece of the gold material.

The scissors didn't touch it.

"Sara!" Amesh shouted. "Stop!"

"I didn't hurt it. I don't think I can." I lifted up the lighter.

"Put that away!" Amesh cried.

I ignored him. There was a part of me that felt as if the carpet had thrown out a challenge and that I had to respond. I felt as if it were mocking me.

I flipped open the lighter and pulled the carpet toward the flame. I'm not sure how close I brought it to the fire—half a foot, maybe—before it reacted.

The carpet jerked out of my hands and flew across the room. It landed on the sofa, where it seemed to stretch out comfortably.

Like a human being.

CHAPTER THREE

FOR THE FIRST TIME in my life, I knew what it meant to "go into shock." I underwent a total brain wipe. I was sitting in the room, Amesh was standing across from me, and the carpet was lying on the couch. These three facts I knew—nothing else.

The carpet should not have been on the couch, which was fifteen feet from where I was sitting. It had been in my hands seconds ago.

"What just happened?" Amesh asked, looking pretty stunned for someone who was asking such an ordinary question. I didn't answer; I couldn't. I just stared. He tried again. "What's wrong?"

I shook my head, realized I was shaking, tried to stop, failed.

"Sara? What did you do to the carpet?" he asked.

I cleared my throat. "Nothing," I said.

"But you threw it . . ." He searched for the right words. "You acted like it bit you."

"It didn't bite me."

"Then why did you throw it on the couch?"

"Did you see me throw it on the couch?"

He hesitated. "Yeah. I mean, there it is."

"There it is," I agreed. "But I didn't throw it anywhere."

"What are you saying?"

"You saw it with your own eyes. The carpet flew over to the couch."

Amesh grinned, and it was a stupid grin because it was so obviously forced. "You're saying it's a flying carpet?"

"Maybe," I replied.

"Those are just stories. My Papi used to tell them to me when I was a kid, when I had trouble falling asleep at night. My Papi reads all the time—he knows all the old tales. He'd be the first person to tell you there's no such thing as flying carpets."

"Okay." I nodded toward the carpet. "How did it get over there?"

"Maybe you bumped the flame and your arm jerked and you let go of the carpet and—"

"Did you see any of that happen?" I interrupted.

He hesitated. "It all happened so fast."

"Yeah. In the blink of an eye." I stood, lighter in my hand, and walked toward the carpet. Amesh stepped in front of me.

"You're not going to burn it again."

"I didn't burn it the first time. It didn't let me. It jumped out of my arms." I struggled to get past him. "Get out of my way!"

"This is silly, Sara."

"Then why are you so scared?"

"I'm not scared."

"You're sweating."

"It's a hot day."

I shouted at him. "This room is air-conditioned! You're sweating because you're scared."

"Scared of what?"

"Of this carpet!"

"It's just a carpet!" he yelled.

"Then get out of my way and let me prove if that's true or not."

He finally stepped aside. I approached the carpet with a vengeance. Picking it up from the couch, sitting down, I flipped open the lighter. The orange flame burned like a tiny sun. Outside, the sun must have gone behind a cloud. The flame cast flickering shadows in the gloom as I brought the lighter near the carpet. Of course, the shadows only shook because my hand was shaking.

The flame touched the tip of a gold tassel. The carpet did not react. It did not "fly" away. But it did not burn either, not even when I placed the entire tassel right over the flame.

"Allah save us," Amesh whispered, his eyes huge.

"That's blasphemy," I said. Amesh shook his head and pointed a shaky finger at the carpet.

"It's cursed! It belongs to a demon, a witch! We have to get rid of it!"

"Why do you automatically assume it's evil?" I put out the lighter and felt the tassel. It was room temperature.

"The carpet must be protected with a spell. We can't fool with it. It's too dangerous."

"I thought you didn't believe in magic."

"I didn't. I don't."

"Amesh, you can't have it both ways. It's either a magic carpet or it's something else."

"What else could it be?" he asked, a hopeful note in his voice.

"Have you ever read any books by Arthur C. Clarke?"

"No."

"He was a science-fiction writer. He's dead now, but he had this line where he said, 'Any sufficiently advanced technology is indistinguishable from magic.'"

"What's that supposed to mean?" Amesh asked.

"It means this could be an advanced tool built by an advanced race."

"Who?"

"I don't know."

"A tool to do what?"

I shrugged. "To fly on, maybe."

"There you go again, saying it's a magic carpet. I told you, they don't exist."

"Sure. They don't exist. Not like demons and witches and curses."

"Sara, stop." Amesh put his left hand to his head. "You're doing it again. You're giving me a headache."

"Would you like to lie on the carpet? Maybe it will heal you."

He paled. "I don't even like you holding it. Leave it there on the couch. Come over and sit beside me."

This time I obeyed. I needed to get perspective on our situation, but I couldn't while holding the carpet. However, as I spread it out on the couch, it seemed to arrange itself so it was more comfortable. All the while, Amesh talked.

"It's probably not old at all. Someone must have made it out of fireproof materials."

"It doesn't absorb heat," I muttered.

"Your Discovery Channel's popular in my country. I remember they did a special on insulators where they took a tile off a space shuttle and burned it with a torch. Then they put their hands on it right away, and it didn't even feel hot."

"That's what I said. Advanced science can appear magical."

Amesh began to relax, the idea of demons and curses fleeing from the room. Or hopefully leaving his brain alone at least for a few minutes.

"It might be a secret part of the hydroelectric plant that got accidentally lost and buried," he said, thoughtful.

"Ridiculous. No one would accidentally misplace something like this."

"I guess you're right."

I studied him. "Have they discovered something out in that desert that I don't know about?"

"No. I mean, if they have, they don't allow . . . They don't tell grunts like me about it."

"What don't they allow you to do?" I asked.

"I don't know what you're asking."

"When I was out there, my father took me to this secret cave. It was like he wanted to show me something inside but then suddenly changed his mind. Or else he got ordered away."

"But your father is one of the bosses."

"I know. That's why I thought it was so strange."

Amesh was definitely uneasy. "I don't know anything about that cave. Anyway, we're talking about the carpet. What was the last thing you said?"

He was hiding something. He knew a lot about that cave.

"Nothing," I muttered.

"Sara?"

"What can I say? It's a complete mystery. That we're nowhere near solving."

"That's a big help," he said.

"When you don't know, it's better to admit you don't know."

We had reached an impasse. We fell into a tense silence. But at last I knew why he was so scared. He was a lot more superstitious than he wanted to admit.

"What time does your father get back?" he finally asked.

"Late. You don't have to worry about him." I noticed Amesh eyeing the menu on the table that stood beside the main balcony, where I usually had breakfast with my father. "Hungry?" I asked.

"No."

"Get off it, you told me you missed lunch. You must be starved. Let's order room service."

He hesitated. "Room service?"

It was nice, finally, to talk about something I was an expert on.

"That's where they bring the food to your room. Here, I can order for you." I picked up the menu and room phone. "What would you like?"

"What do they have?"

"Pretty much anything you can imagine. Do you like lamb? Chicken? Steak? Turkey? Fish?"

He licked his lips. "Is the steak expensive?"

"Amesh, it's all free! Or at least, Becktar's paying for it. Don't worry about the cost. How do you like your steak cooked?"

"They cook it special ways?"

"You can have it any way you want."

"How do you usually get it?"

"Well done; I don't like it bloody. And I love a baked potato with it."

"That sounds good. But . . . would you eat some of it with me?"

I reached for the phone. "We'll split it. How about dessert?"

"They'll bring all that to one room?"

"You'll be amazed," I said.

Besides the steak and potato, I ordered french fries and chocolate cake and cheesecake, plus ice cream: vanilla, strawberry, and coffee. While waiting for the food to arrive, I convinced Amesh that a shower wasn't going to kill him. It was cute how careful he was to lock the bathroom door before turning on the water.

The truth was that I wanted some time alone. I had a brand-new PDA—a BlackBerry—my mother had bought for my birthday. I had gotten so used to texting friends and looking stuff up on the Internet, I kept it with me 24/7. It was addicting.

My fingers danced over the tiny keyboard. In minutes I scanned a half dozen sites on magic carpets. I clicked on a few and was amazed to find the historical existence of magic carpets was treated as a genuine possibility by real scholars—men and women with PhDs, not just New Age freaks.

Certain documents described how the carpets seemed to appear and disappear over big blocks of time. It was as if the knowledge of how they were made was found and then somehow lost. Some records were Egyptian, over five thousand years old. Many were half that age; they dealt with the period of King Solomon. He was a central figure when it came to magic carpets. He was supposed to have had dozens under his command, plus a team of alchemists who knew the secrets of how to build them.

On another site, I read a document that dealt with the Library of Alexandria. It stated—the image was almost comical—that the library had been so big, the stacks of books so high, it was normal for patrons to use magic carpets to browse. And I thought the Internet had spoiled me! What a way to do research!

"Who built you?" I asked it as it lay on the couch. It was odd how we kept calling it a flying carpet. It had not really flown. So far, it had only bolted across the room and calmly withstood a withering flame. Before closing my files, I scanned for information on "how to fly a magic carpet."

It was then I found out about "ley lines."

I memorized as much as I could so I could tell Amesh about them.

The food came while he was still in the bathroom. From the sound of it, he was taking a bath, not a shower. Signing the bill, I scooted the waiter out the door, preferring to set up the dishes myself.

"Amesh, the food's here!" I called. "Hurry, the steak will get cold." Which was not exactly true. Like at many fine hotels, the hot meal came with its own miniature heater.

"Coming!" he called back.

"There are bathrobes in the closet. Grab one and let your clothes soak in the sink with a little soap. After dinner, we can rinse them out and spread them over the balcony."

Amesh sounded uneasy. "It would be an insult to your father to use his robes."

"They're not his robes. They belong to the hotel."

"Why do you want me to wear one?"

"They're super comfortable. They come in a variety of sizes. There are big ones, baggy ones."

I was trying to tell him—without saying so—that he could wear a robe and still cover his stump. He seemed to get the message.

"They're nice," he called through the door.

Minutes later he appeared. I was not surprised to see he had chosen a large robe. The end of his right arm was completely covered. He spread his shirt and trousers on the chairs on the balcony.

I had already put the carpet in my bedroom so its mystery would not haunt us while we ate. Amesh appeared to appreciate the gesture. His eyes were riveted by the amount of food. I let him have the bulk of our steak and gave him the baked potato. I was content with the fries. He laughed as I drowned them in ketchup.

"You won't be able to taste them," he said.

"Fries are just vehicles for ketchup and salt. Didn't you know?"

"We prefer to put vinegar on them."

"Ah. You take after the British."

"They take after us." He took a bite of steak. "Oh Allah," he blurted out before he could stop himself. We both laughed.

"You like it?" I asked.

He cut off another bite. He used his stump to keep his fork steady, then sliced the meat with his left hand. He was surprisingly smooth. If I hadn't known he was missing a hand, I would never have noticed his handicap from watching him eat.

"I've never eaten food that tastes this good," he said. "Do the hotels in America cook such delicious meals?"

I did not have the heart to tell him that the Hilton was an American hotel.

"Our food's almost as good," I said.

While we ate, the inevitable happened. Even though his bathrobe was large, the material was bulky, and it had probably not been easy for him to tie the end of the right arm. I don't think he had even tried, and at one point the sleeve slid up and his stump was exposed. Even though I averted my eyes, I was not quick enough. He saw that I saw, and he lowered his head in shame.

I didn't know what to say, but felt I should say something.

"I'm sorry," I said.

He was a long time responding. "Why are you sorry?"

"I'm sorry for . . . prying."

A note of bitterness entered his voice. It was not aimed at me, I knew, but it made me sad nevertheless. "I'm not ashamed of it," he said.

"Why should you be?" I gushed.

"I was not born this way, you know. I lost the hand in an accident."

"I know," I said.

He looked up. "How do you know?"

"I mean, I assumed you did," I said. "It's hardly noticeable."

"It was the first thing you noticed about me."

"Not true. The first thing I noticed about you was that you liked knocking me to the floor."

"You were trying to steal my package."

"I was trying to get to know you."

He blinked, startled. "Why?"

"Because you looked interesting."

He shook his head. "You just wanted me to lead you to your father."

"That was just an excuse. The main reason I ran over to the counter was to . . . to say hi."

"You have a strange way of saying hi, Sara."

"Thank you." I sat back on my knees. "Now tell me how you lost your hand."

"Why?"

"I want to know. I want to know you, Amesh. In case you didn't notice, we're in the middle of a strange adventure together. And I have a feeling it's going to get stranger before it's over."

"There was an accident at my job. I lost it. What else can I say?"

I put my right hand on his left knee. "That's fine; you don't have to say any more. But I wish you would. I wish you'd tell me exactly what you went through. Because I know it hurts, what happened, and if we're to be friends then I should know what happened."

He looked away, out at the calm blue of the sea, then back at his plate. "Can I finish my supper first?" he asked.

"Sure." I returned to my seat. "You have to finish all the desserts, too."

"All right," he muttered, returning to his steak.

It didn't take as long as I thought it would for him to finish everything. Okay, I helped with the cheesecake and ice cream. But soon Amesh was telling me what happened to his hand, and when he was done I went out on the balcony to check on his clothes. They were virtually dry, holding on to just a few drops of moisture, which would help with the ironing. And I felt I had to iron them; I had talked him into washing them and now they were all wrinkled.

The ironing board was not in the bathroom or living room. I searched my bedroom and found it in my closet. It was only while I was stepping back into the center of the suite that I realized something was wrong.

I panicked. "Amesh!" I cried.

He was beside me in a moment. "What's wrong?"

I was close to tears. "The carpet! It's gone!"

His dark eyes scanned the area. Then he relaxed. He pointed outside the sliding glass door that led to my private balcony. It also overlooked the sea, although it faced south rather than west. Like the main balcony, it was equipped with two lounge chairs.

One was occupied. By the carpet.

It seemed to be relaxing beneath the evening stars.

We took a step closer and realized it was doing more than that.

"Allah . . ."

"God . . ."

We both whispered in awe.

CHAPTER FOUR

THE FEW STARS in the evening sky were causing the stars in the center of the carpet to glow with a soft light. In some mysterious way, the carpet was tied to the heavens.

Plus, the carpet had climbed off the bed, strolled onto the balcony, and made itself comfortable in a lounge chair. With each passing miracle, the case grew stronger that we had discovered something truly magical.

When we showed the carpet to the world, we'd be famous. We'd probably be on the cover of every magazine in the world.

Yet, the odd thing was, the more I contemplated how rich

and famous the carpet could make us, the less wonderful I felt. Indeed, I started to feel sick to my stomach, and I quickly identified what the problem was. We had to keep the carpet secret. I just knew it. Call it intuition, call it paranoia, but I didn't want anyone to know about it.

I worried about how I could make Amesh understand.

We were still on the balcony when he turned to me. "I don't think we should try to sell this for money."

I felt a wave of relief. "You feel the same way I do. It has to be protected." I paused. "We have to keep it totally secret. I swear I won't tell my father about it."

"I swear I won't tell my Papi about it."

"What about Mira?"

"What about her?"

"Amesh!"

"I share everything with Mira. We're practically the same person. I'm not kidding; even if I don't tell her about it, she'll know. She can read my mind. She'll know something's up."

"Let her know something is up. Just don't tell her it's a magic carpet."

Amesh hesitated. "All right."

"I'm serious. I need you to swear on Allah's name."

He shook his head. "I told you, that's blasphemy."

"It's blasphemy when you use Allah's name for something trivial. This may be the single most important discovery in the history of the human race. Swear to Allah that you'll keep the carpet secret. At least until we both agree it can't be kept a secret any longer."

He paused. "All right. But you have to do the same."

"Fine. I swear on the holy name of Allah that I'll never . . ."

"Stop!"

"What's wrong?"

"You're not a Muslim. You can't swear to Allah."

"Why not?"

"He's not your God. You have to swear to Jesus."

"But I don't go to church regularly."

"You don't? Why not?"

"I don't know. Why don't you pray to Allah five times a day?"

"I do."

"Gimme a break. I haven't seen you pray once."

"I do it when you're not looking."

"You mean, you were praying in the bathtub?"

"Yes."

"Didn't you get water up your nose when you bowed down?"

"Don't make fun of our prayers."

"I'm sorry. Let me start over. I swear to the Father; and to the Son, Jesus; and to the Holy Spirit, that I'll keep secret the unique and mysterious qualities of this carpet."

"Why don't you just say you'll keep the *carpet* secret?"

"I would but there's a good chance my father will see it. I'm going to tell him it's just something I bought."

Amesh shook his head. "You're not keeping it here."

"What are you talking about? Of course I'm keeping it here."

"It would be safer at my house."

"Your house? I don't want to hurt your feelings, but from what you've told me, your neighborhood's not that safe. Besides, you're gone all day at work."

"That's why Mira . . ."

"Mira's ten! She can't be trusted with a secret this big! Plus you promised not to tell her!"

"All right, you can keep it here." Amesh lowered his head. "I swear on Allah's holy name to keep the carpet secret."

"Thank you." I gave him a hug. I had not known him long but somehow trusted that his word was good.

His body was pretty good, too. I let the hug linger; he did not push me away. I rested my head near his collar, on the left side, where I could hear his heart beating.

Like mine, it was pounding.

But it was no time to fool around. He would have been too shy, anyway. Not that I wasn't feeling shy, too. Sad to say but I was fifteen and had never been kissed.

We turned back to the carpet. It was still acting like a mirror of the heavens. The darker the sky got, the brighter the carpet's stars became.

"While you were in the bathtub, I read up on magic carpets," I said. "They're historically connected to genies, or what you guys call *djinn.* Did you know the djinn are mentioned in the Koran? It speaks of them like they're real."

Amesh hesitated. "My Papi said something about that. Did you find out anything about how to operate the carpet?"

"Many magic carpets are controlled by spells or incantations. If you know the secret words, and repeat them three times, then the carpet lifts into the air."

"A lot of good that does us," he grumbled.

"I felt the same way until I discovered another technique listed on two sites. They said magic carpets don't fly just anywhere, but follow what are called ley lines. Have you heard of them?"

"No."

"I hadn't either. The British are the experts on them. Ley lines deal with lines of magnetic energy that cover the earth. There are legitimate scientists who have mapped them throughout England. Stonehenge, for example, is supposed to be a focal point of dozens of ley lines. That's why it's considered a place of mystical power."

"We're not taking the carpet to England."

"We don't have to! I'm just saying the British studied them. There are probably as many here as there are there. We just have to find them."

"You think the carpet will fly on such lines?"

"It's possible. We know the carpet has twice tried to fly in this suite. But it's never really taken off. Maybe it can't without a ley line to float on."

"Did these sites tell you how to find one?"

"Just hold a compass in your hand, and when you cross a ley line, the needle will dance."

"Dance?"

"It will start spinning like crazy."

"Why?"

"A compass is sensitive to magnetic fields, and ley lines give off strong fields. From what I've read, the lines are all over the place. We shouldn't have to go far to find one."

Amesh was surprised. "You want to look for one now?"

"Why not?"

"It's getting late. Your father will be home soon. My Papi will be waiting for me. Let's look for one tomorrow, during the day."

"You're working all day tomorrow. Even if you call in sick, it's too hot to go hiking when the sun's up. You might be used to this climate, but I'm not."

"I can look for one while you wait here."

"Listen. There are other reasons I want to do it tonight. The carpet came alive as soon as it got dark. The stars at the center might have been glowing before, and we just didn't notice, but I don't think so. It's possible the carpet only flies at night."

"What's another reason?"

"Common sense. If we do find a ley line, and we're able to use it to ride the carpet, then no one can see us. Since I got here, I've been hiking in the evening by the water." I pointed. "The beach is usually deserted, and I have the place to myself. There's lots of room. I wouldn't be surprised if that's where we find a ley line."

"Does your dad know you hike there?"

"Of course not."

"You shouldn't go out after dark."

"I know, I might be killed. What is it with you males? I feel as safe here as I do in any American city."

Amesh hesitated. "Do you plan to ride the carpet over the water?"

"If that's the direction the ley line goes."

"Do you have a compass?"

"One. But maybe we can buy another in the hotel shop. That way we can search together."

Amesh glanced at the carpet and smiled. "What are we waiting for?"

CHAPTER FIVE

BEFORE WE LEFT THE ROOM, I changed into jeans and a long-sleeved shirt. Then I packed a bag of supplies: bottles of water, binoculars, protein bars, candy bars, a flashlight, a map of Turkey and the surrounding area, a jacket. I also left my father a note explaining that I had been invited to a slumber party by a girl named Rini.

Rini was a real girl. I had mentioned her to my father before. In fact, he had met her; she worked at the hotel as a maid. He wouldn't worry if I was hanging out with her, even during the night. But he would still be annoyed I hadn't called and asked his permission.

"You think we'll be gone that long?" Amesh asked as he watched me prop up my note.

"Best to be prepared. You should call your Papi and tell him you might be staying overnight with a friend."

He looked uncomfortable. "He wouldn't believe that."

"Why not?"

"I don't have many friends."

"All you need is one. What about Spielo? Wouldn't he back you up?"

"Spielo's still in the hospital," he said.

"Is he okay?"

"They say he's going to be fine."

"Then use another friend."

Amesh fidgeted. "Let's not worry about it."

"All right," I agreed, going against my gut feeling.

The sun had completely set by the time we reached the beach. The night was as black as the bottom of the carpet. Amesh carried our supplies while I held our prize. Once again, I was amazed by its weightlessness. It was as if holding it to my chest made me feel lighter.

The night was warm and dry, but a faint breeze stirred over the water, adding a salty flavor to the air. I felt its coolness on my neck as we took out our compasses and figured out which way was north. I double-checked the accuracy of our tools by following the cup of the Big Dipper to the North Star—a trick

I had learned from my dad. Both compasses were working. Now all we had to do was find a spot—no, a line—where they didn't work.

We walked near the water. I took off my shoes and let the foam wash over my bare feet. Amesh preferred to stay on the dry sand. The beach was deserted. The glow of the stars embedded in the carpet did not waver. There was no denying it—the carpet was reacting to the nighttime sky.

"I wonder why," I muttered.

"Sara?" he asked.

"Why the carpet likes the stars."

"You would have to ask the man who made it."

"How do you know it was a man? Maybe it was a woman."

"Maybe it was a team of men and women."

"Ha! The boy is finally learning to be diplomatic."

"Don't call me a boy."

"How old are you really?" I asked.

He did not answer and I thought he was embarrassed to admit that he had lied earlier. I couldn't see him very well in the dark. I certainly couldn't read his expression. But I saw his hand shaking.

"Sara!" he cried. "It's spinning!"

"The pointer?" I asked, checking my own compass, which was still pointed north.

"Come look." He stopped and swung the compass around his body. He took a step back. "It's strongest here."

I ran to his side. Studying his compass, I saw that he was not exaggerating—the arrow was all over the place. Then I realized mine was spinning, too.

The carpet fluttered against my chest!

"I think we've found one!" I exclaimed.

"But we just started looking. How is it possible?"

I did not answer, but since I had found the carpet—especially since it had begun to jump around the hotel room—I had wanted to take it down to the beach. To this beach in particular, almost as if I knew the spot was special.

We wasted no time spreading the carpet on the sand. Then . . . nothing happened, it just lay there. I could hear the disappointment in Amesh's voice when he said, "Maybe it needs a spell to work, after all."

"Not so fast. We were about thirty feet apart and walking parallel with each other when your compass began to dance. But my compass didn't react until I moved to where you were standing."

"So?"

"What if this ley line doesn't run toward the water? For all we know it runs down the beach. It might be important to find exactly where it's headed and align the carpet in that direction."

Amesh nodded. "Good idea. We'll scan the area."

Leaving the carpet as a focal point, we walked up and down the beach, trying to find where our compasses spun the most.

We finally decided that the ley line led farther down the beach—away from the hotel—but at a slight angle that would eventually take it out over the water.

We hurried back to the carpet and aligned it as carefully as we could. The change was instantaneous. I felt a magnetic charge in the air.

Yet the carpet—although it quivered on the sand—did not float into the air. Amesh and I knelt beside it, and for the first time I took out a small flashlight. In the light we saw that the central three tassels were standing straight up. The same was true of the rear of the carpet, which meant all together six tassels had come alive.

I stared at Amesh across the carpet.

"Are you thinking what I'm thinking?" I asked.

He nodded. "They look like controls."

I turned off the flashlight—I did not want to disturb the carpet's reaction to the stars—and sat on the front of the carpet that faced the water. My taking charge annoyed Amesh.

"I think I should be the first one to fly it," he said.

"Why?"

"I know how to drive a car."

"So do I." My dad had given me a few illegal lessons. "But I don't think that's going to help us fly this baby."

"Sara, you have no right . . ."

"Amesh, get on the back and relax. I know what I'm doing."

"How can you know?" he asked, reluctantly obeying.

"It's just a feeling I have."

I pulled back on the front middle tassel—one of the three on my end of the carpet that were standing up—and the carpet immediately stiffened and gently bobbed off the sand. Still, it went no higher than an inch, not even when I pulled all the way back on the tassel. It was only when I pulled back on the tassel to its right that we began to gain altitude.

"Glory be to Allah!" Amesh gasped.

I laughed. "Amen!"

When we were six feet above the sand, I eased the central tassel forward, but nothing happened. It made me wonder if the tassels worked together like the clutch and gears in a car.

I experimented a minute and discovered that the central tassel was the clutch. It caused the tassels to the right and left of it to work. The right tassel was for lifting the carpet. And the left tassel . . .

I pushed the left tassel slightly forward.

Suddenly we began to glide!

"Whoa!" Amesh cried.

We were flying at maybe ten miles an hour, a fast run.

Laughing, I pushed the left tassel further, and we picked up speed.

"This is so cool!" I screamed.

The sensation of speed was exhilarating, of course, but even more striking was the feeling that I was one with the carpet. I was an eagle, the sides of the carpet were my wings. I felt so powerful.

"Can we go higher?" Amesh asked.

"Do you want to go higher?"

He looked down. "Not if we're going over the water."

I had my back to Amesh, and to the circle of stars as well. I asked if there was any change in the star field. "You won't believe this. I think they're moving," he said.

"Moving? How?"

"Around and around," he said.

I twisted my neck to see. "Around what?"

"I don't know. Maybe you shouldn't sit on them."

"I'm not," I protested.

"Your butt is."

I shuffled forward and tightened my crossed legs. The carpet was long enough for me to easily avoid the star field.

"Can we go faster?" Amesh asked.

"Just a second," I replied, giving the left tassel a shove. In an instant our speed doubled. That scared us both; there's a huge difference between twenty miles an hour and forty. As the dark sand swept beneath, the wind blew in our faces and roared in our ears. I pulled back on the tassel and we quickly slowed.

I suddenly noticed the tassels on the far right and left were standing straight up. Now five on my side appeared to be active.

"This is fast enough!" Amesh called.

"I hear ya!" I shouted.

In a minute our course took us away from the sand and over the water. Fortunately, the sea was calm. The swells beneath us were less than a foot. The air was thick with moisture—a huge change from the dry desert air that gripped the city.

"Have you tried turning right or left?" Amesh asked.

"No. But I'm pretty sure the tassels at the edges will let us do that."

"They're standing up?"

"They are now."

Amesh glanced toward the shore. Already we were more than a quarter of a mile from the beach. If we were to get dumped now, it would be a long swim back, although not an impossible one. For me. With his missing hand, he might not make it.

"Try it, before we get too far out," he said.

I hesitated. "If we jump off this ley line and there isn't another one beside us, we might end up in the water."

"The ley line should be wide enough to let us turn," he said.

"I checked it on the beach. It was only ten feet across."

Amesh sighed. "We're going to have to turn around at some point."

"Do you know how to swim?" I asked.

"Yes. But I'm not a fish."

I understood. With each second we allowed the carpet to take us away from the shore, we increased our risk.

"There's another set of those things, the tassels, sticking up behind me," he said. "I'll try to use them to take us back to the beach."

"Don't you want me to try to stop the carpet first?"

He hesitated. "I'm not sure. If we stop, we might sink."

"It beats flying away from the ley line."

"All right, give it a try. But be careful," he said.

Slowly, I pulled back on the left tassel. We immediately began to lose speed, until we came to a dead stop. The carpet felt less stable floating above the water than it did flying over it.

Behind me, Amesh turned so his back was to me.

"You just pushed the central tassel forward?" he asked.

"No, it's more complex than that." I explained how the three central tassels worked together. Then I left him alone to try to make it work.

A few minutes went by. We continued to hover in place. Below, the surf lapped with a soothing hypnotic sound. Overhead, more stars became visible. I turned sideways so I could watch the stars at the center of the carpet move. They appeared to rotate around an invisible point.

"It's not working," he finally said in disgust.

"Maybe only women can fly magic carpets."

"Or maybe your controls got locked in place because they were the first ones we used."

"I suppose," I said, although I thought that sounded silly.

Amesh turned to face me. "Now that we've stopped, we might be able to turn the carpet around without leaving the ley line. Grab that tassel on the right and bend it to the right. See what happens."

"We might tip over."

"We have to try. We can't float here all night."

I reached for the tassel. "We should have experimented more with the controls while we were still on the shore."

"We should have done a lot of things. Turn us around."

He knew I was stalling. The sense that the carpet didn't want to go back plagued me. I could not explain why. Still, I did what he said, and slowly the carpet rotated. In seconds we were facing the shore. Far off, the lights of Istanbul beaconed. There lay safety, I thought, security. But out here on the carpet was magic, and I didn't want to give that up so soon.

"Take us back at a slower speed," Amesh said.

"Aye, Captain." I reached for the central left tassel to restart our silent engine. But the second I did so the carpet rotated back out to sea. I wondered if it was responding to what I wanted, instead of obeying what my hands were doing.

"Why did you do that?" Amesh demanded.

"It did it on its own. Maybe it wants to keep going."

"You talk about it like it's alive."

"What if it is."

"Don't be silly."

"Amesh, I feel something coming from it. Like you can sense another person's feelings. It's like it's telling me it wants to go farther."

"Where? All we have in front of us are miles of ocean."

"Aren't there islands off this coast?"

"Well, technically, we're in a really huge bay. But everyone calls it the Sea of Marmara. If we keep going, we'll either run into the Gallipoli Peninsula or fly through the Dardenelles Strait. That's a narrow strip of water that connects this bay with the Aegean Sea. But no way are we going that far."

"Why don't we go just a little farther, then make up our minds. I don't think it's going to dump us in the water and run off."

Amesh was not happy with the plan. "You can't be sure of that."

"I have faith in the carpet."

The words just popped out of my mouth, but they were true. Not only did I feel the carpet was alive, I felt it was a friend. An ally, at least.

I bent the left tassel forward until we reached a speed of about fifteen miles an hour, which proved to be easier on our nerves. The night air continued to brush my face but it was a gentle breeze.

To my surprise, the farther we went, the calmer the ocean

grew. Soon the sea was as still as a mountain lake and utterly quiet. The lights of Istanbul faded to a faint glow. We were able to see the band of the Milky Way, along with a million more stars. Glancing over my shoulder, I could see the center of our flying machine was thick with stars.

And my friend's breathing had grown long and deep. He was out cold! At first I was stunned. Who could sleep at a time like this? I pulled him away from the carpet's edges so he wouldn't fall off, and he still didn't wake up.

My thoughts turned to what Amesh had told me in the hotel, the story of how he had lost his hand. It had happened only a year ago, the previous summer. He was still healing from the blow, he admitted, emotionally as well as physically. But losing a hand—maybe that was something he would never get over.

He had described the accident to me briefly, almost as if he were reading from a prepared card. He was working a circular saw that was used to cut long steel cables that provided a framework for the tons of concrete the company poured daily. The machine was a powerful band saw—it had the power to reshape diamonds. He wore goggles while he worked to protect his eyes, and a mask to block out the fine particles of metal the saw threw into the air.

One day a smoldering shard of metal flew off a cable he was cutting and struck his goggles. Ordinarily that would not have been a problem, but the shard was exceptionally large and hot. It melted through the goggles and filled the interior with scalding steam. Afraid the metal was going to reach his face and maybe put out an eye, he panicked and fought to get the goggles off. Unfortunately, in his haste, he swept his right wrist in the path of the band saw.

He said he didn't feel his hand get cut off. There was just a sharp tug, no pain, followed by a wave of dizziness. He probably fainted; he was never sure. Fellow workers picked him up and took him to the hospital, which was where he woke the next day.

"Why weren't they able to sew your hand back on?" I asked.

It sounded to me like it could not have been removed more cleanly. But he shook his head and said his hand had landed on a pile of recently cut cable that was still smoldering. The flesh was too badly burned. The doctors could do nothing with it.

"Why don't you wear a prosthesis?" I asked.

The question troubled him. He told me the hospital kept offering him lots of prostheses, but he couldn't find one that was comfortable. He would get sores and blisters where the synthetic material touched his skin. He was beginning to think he was better off without one.

"Did you sue the company?" I asked.

He didn't sue anybody; his boss had convinced him that the accident was his fault. They covered his medical expenses and paid his salary while he was at home healing. But he was never given money for his pain and suffering.

"Why didn't you hire a lawyer?" I asked.

The question angered him. This was Turkey, not America; people did not go around suing each other. He was lucky the company gave him another job. It happened; it was an accident, he said. It was Allah's will.

I did not know what else to say, so I gave him a hug and told him he was very brave. That, at least, made him smile. Why was he brave? For being clumsy?

"No," I said. "Because you're not a whiner."

That was the end of our discussion about his hand.

Now, flying over the water on our magic carpet, halfway to God knew where, I reflected on his story and realized it had all been a lie. There were too many convenient details. A burning shard had hit his goggles and melted into them. He worked with the band saw every day, but rather than taking a step back to get his bearings or turning it off, he swept his hand directly in its path. Then, his hand just happened to land on the one spot where it could be destroyed.

Who cared if it was Turkey? He was working for an American firm. He should have been able to sue for big bucks.

Plus, who would have given a teenager such a skilled job in the first place? The fact that Amesh was now a gofer made sense. Making deliveries was an ideal job for a young man on a moped. But cutting critical cables to within a fraction of an inch? Gimme a break—that was a job for someone with years of experience.

Amesh continued to sleep. Scooting around, I saw the knot on his right sleeve was loose. His stump was visible, although it was only a shadow in the dark. Taking out my flashlight and cupping my palm over it to reduce the glare, I decided to take a closer look.

"Forgive me, Amesh," I whispered.

I had to be sure I was right. I lifted his sleeve several inches.

Amesh had not lost his hand with a single clean cut. The skin on his lower right arm was heavily scarred. A number of scars reached past his elbow. The discolored flesh on his stump was particularly bumpy. The surgeon who had sewn it together had done a poor job. Or perhaps he had not had much to work with.

The wound had been no accident.

It was as if Amesh had been hacked with a sword.

CHAPTER SIX

THE FACT THAT AMESH had fallen asleep did not stop me from eventually passing out. Perhaps the carpet was casting spells, or else I simply stopped worrying about falling into the water. It had been a long day and I was totally exhausted.

When I woke up and checked my watch, I discovered it had stopped. It read 10:35 p.m. That would have been an hour after we'd left Istanbul.

It was an expensive watch. Waterproof. Shockproof.

The battery was fresh. It should not have stopped.

I didn't have time to worry about it. It was no longer dark, although we were light years away from a sunny day. The carpet had transported us to an eerie fog bank, where there were no stars or sky. And it had lowered us to within three feet of the water. Our speed had also decreased; we were creeping along.

The fog was neither cold nor warm. It did not even feel damp. I might have mistaken it for smoke, but I smelled no odor. I could not tell from which direction the light was coming. There was no wind and yet the fog moved, forming brief-lived spirals that spun up from below. As one swept over me I felt a distinct chill. They looked like ghosts.

The stars in the center of the carpet had disappeared. In their place was a gray-green circle—the same color as the water.

I had lost my desire for adventure.

I wanted to go home.

Amesh sat with his chin resting on his chest, breathing heavily.

"Amesh," I said, then louder, "Amesh!"

He did not wake up. I tried shaking him. He slumped to the side; he almost fell off. Still, he did not regain consciousness. "Amesh!"

I was terrified. He was breathing; he was alive. Why didn't he wake up? Was there something about this place we were traveling through that was keeping him asleep? Of course I blamed the fog and not the carpet, although the reverse could just as easily have been true. I felt it was a mistake that I had woken up in this place. I wished I hadn't.

Not long after, I blacked out again.

When I awoke next, Amesh was softly calling my name. I sat up with a start. I had passed out sitting in his direction, and as soon as I saw him I gave him a quick hug. "You're all right!" I gushed.

"Of course. Why wouldn't I be?"

"Because . . . never mind, I was just worried." I realized our surroundings had changed again. The creepy fog had lifted and the sky was back, along with the stars, although a rising sun in the east was chasing them away. Yet in the opposite direction, near the horizon, was a weird red glow. The color seemed angry; a bloody red. It was shrouded in mist and I could not tell if it was caused by a single star or planet. At the same time it was sinking below the horizon.

I mentioned it to Amesh but he had no idea what it was.

"I woke up just before you," he said, gesturing in the direction of the sunlight. "I can't believe we slept the whole night."

"Maybe we didn't." My body was stiff from sitting for so long, and yet I knew I had not been asleep seven hours. But how could one argue with the heavens? It was a brand-new day. And now my watch read 6:30 a.m. I said the time out aloud. Amesh's expression suddenly turned glum.

"My Papi's going to kill me," he said.

"I won't tell you I told you so."

"You just told me."

"Well, that's beside the point. Where are we?"

Amesh frowned as he scanned the area. The carpet had climbed once more to ten feet, and it was traveling at about ten miles an hour. The color of the water had returned to normal, but the red glow was not the only thing that troubled me.

Like I said, my dad had taught me a few things about the stars, but I was not an expert when it came to astronomy. Still, I did not recognize a single constellation. I tried to explain my difficulty to Amesh. He brushed me off.

"The sun's coming up. There aren't that many stars to go by."

"There's that weird red glow, too. We can't just ignore it."

"I'm not ignoring anything; I'm just trying to figure out where we are. If the carpet stayed at this speed for eight hours, we could be two hundred kilometers from shore."

A kilometer was about two-thirds of a mile, I reminded myself. He was saying we were about 140 miles from Istanbul.

"You said if we kept going, we'd run into the Aegean Sea. Isn't that full of islands?"

"Sure. We're bound to run into one. But there's more chance we'll see one in the distance. We should keep the binoculars handy and practice turning the carpet. If we see one, we'll want to head straight for it."

"You don't want to retrace our path home?"

Amesh yawned and stretched. "I can't sit here another eight hours. Let's find an island. They'll have boats heading back to Istanbul. It's the biggest port in the area."

The red glow vanished as the sun rose higher. We decided to have breakfast. Protein bars, candy bars, and bottled water. Amesh chewed the peanut butter bars with relish.

"I thought you were nuts when you packed all this stuff," he said.

"It goes to show how good my intuition is."

"You've been right about a lot of stuff, Sara."

I blushed. Just the way he said my name, it got me.

"A lot of lucky guesses. Usually my batting average is lower."

"Batting average?" he asked.

"Like in baseball."

"Oh. I'm serious. You were right about the carpet, how to fly it, the ley lines. Everything."

"Does this mean you'll be my slave from now on?"

"I feel like I already am. Why don't you use your intuition and figure out how to turn the carpet?"

"Okay," I agreed, although my intuition was still telling me to do the opposite and keep going. The carpet knew where it was heading and we would know when we got there. But there was no point in saying that to Amesh.

Especially since we had a more pressing problem.

"I have to pee," I told him when we were done eating.

He turned red. "So do I."

"Why are you blushing? You can just slide up on your knees and pee off the side into the water."

He turned a deeper red, if that was possible. "I can't do that."

"Don't be embarrassed. I won't look. I'm the one with the problem."

"Why?"

"Duh! I'm a girl!"

He looked away. "I'd rather not talk about this."

"We have to talk about it. I can't hold it much longer."

"Why not?"

"Because I'm a girl and Allah made us inferior to boys. What do you mean, why not? My bladder's about to burst."

"You shouldn't have drunk so much water."

"I was thirsty! Besides, you drank twice as much as I did."

"I did not!"

"You drank half a bottle! And you ate three protein bars!"

"Well, why didn't you stop me?"

"You were hungry. But forget that. Are you going to go or not? There's no reason for you to suffer just because I am."

"In my country, males do not urinate in front of females."

"Like it's a big sport in America! I'll turn around and put my fingers in my ears so I can't hear you."

He did not respond. He was simply too embarrassed.

Fortunately, ten minutes later, when I was on the verge of stripping and hanging from the back of our glider, we spotted an island. It appeared small, devoid of trees and grass, although there was an array of low-lying hills that blocked a clear view of the far side. I was learning not to make snap judgments. For all we knew, it might be miles across and have a hotel on the other end.

The carpet took us beyond the shoreline before it slowed and began to lose altitude. A moment later we were sitting on a sandy beach and staring at each other. A wind howled against the stone cliffs and in our ears. The sun was bright in the sky. The stars in the center of the carpet had stopped moving. They faded until they were no longer glowing.

I was the first one to shake myself and stand. "Get up," I said.

"What's the hurry?"

"You know."

"You don't have to take the carpet with you."

"We have to keep an eye on it at all times. We don't know anything about this island." The second he was off the carpet, I knelt and rolled it up.

"All I'm saying is I can watch it while you—"

"I like carrying it," I interrupted, holding it close. I did not know why I felt so possessive of the carpet. Especially here, of all places, it wasn't as though he could steal it from me. "I'll be back in a few minutes."

"I'll meet you here in five!" he shouted after me.

Not far from the shore were plenty of boulders, which offered many places to pee. Honestly, I could not recall having ever felt such relief. When we met back at the beach I was in a much better mood, although Amesh was puzzled.

"What's wrong?" I asked.

He gestured to the island. "I don't recognize this place."

"You told me there were plenty of islands out here. Why should you recognize it?"

He frowned. "Let me see that map you brought."

I reached in my pack and gave it to him. As he studied it, his frown deepened. "Well?" I said finally.

He sighed. "I don't know where we are."

"Can you make an educated guess?"

He handed back the map. "I suspect the carpet picked up speed while we slept and flew us deep into the Aegean Sea, maybe close to Greece."

I almost mentioned the fog we'd passed through but something held me back. I didn't like thinking about it, never mind talking about it. Plus, he'd never believe I couldn't wake him up.

"That's good, right? The Greek islands are crowded with tourists. We should be able to hitch a ride back with someone."

Amesh nodded, although there was doubt in his eyes.

"We'll be okay," he said.

We debated sticking to the shore and heading right or left, but felt that hiking straight inland would bring us to civilization faster. I favored the latter course for another reason. I worried about our water supply. We had four one-liter bottles. With our dozen protein bars and eight candy bars, we could do without real food for a while. But we would be dead in two days—three at the outside—without water. I hoped we'd stumble upon a stream soon.

The wind disappeared as we left the beach behind. But there were problems with hiking inland. First, there were no paths and the ground was loose and rocky. Gravel kept seeping into my shoes. I had to keep stopping to empty them. Second, the hills that looked low and gentle from the sea were nevertheless hard to climb. I had always hated walking uphill. While Amesh coasted along, I panted heavily.

The temperature increased rapidly as the sun rose higher.

But the biggest problem was, we didn't know where we were going. At least if we had tried circling the island, staying by the shore, we would have had a clear direction. But even with our compasses, we couldn't plot a course because we would no sooner crest a row of hills than discover another row behind it. Just as I had guessed, the island was much larger than it appeared from the sea.

After three hours of hiking, Amesh called for a halt. I was grateful. My throat was parched and I had blisters forming on my feet. Amesh opened another bottle of water. He had greater endurance and was carrying more weight—he had our backpack and the bottles on his back—but he was going through the water faster than I was. Naturally, I carried the carpet.

"Careful," I warned. "We only have two bottles after that one."

He gestured to some tired-looking grass and a few low-lying shrubs.

"There has to be water here for this stuff to grow," he said.

"I wonder. They look pretty thirsty. Maybe they live off the rain."

He shook his head and handed me the bottle. "We have no choice. We need to drink to keep hiking, and to find water, we have to hike. Unless you want to find some shade and take a long nap and wait for someone to rescue us."

I accepted the bottle and took a hearty slug. "That idea's not as silly as it sounds. Not the rescue part, but the waiting until dark. Then we might be able to find another ley line and explore the island from the air."

"You wouldn't use the carpet to take us home?"

"I'd like to take a look around first." Amesh did not look happy with my answer so I added, "Well, I don't think it took us here to die."

He snorted. "There you go again, speaking as if it were alive."

"Maybe it is."

He threw his hands in the air. "That's . . . that's blasphemy!"

I was suddenly angry. "How can you say that? The carpet has proven its worth. It can fly! It can fly because it's a magic carpet."

"If it's so magical, why can't it fly during the day?"

Not long after peeing, I had tried to get the carpet off the ground with the sun up, but nothing happened. It either needed the stars for power, or else we had lost our ley line. I told Amesh as much but he was unimpressed.

This was the first time I had seen him get mad at the carpet. I supposed it was because he was hot and tired.

Amesh continued. "Last night you kept saying, 'It knows where it's going.' Well, we tried it your way and now we're stuck on a deserted island without water."

"You just said we're bound to find water. And earlier you praised my intuition. Your opinion of me, the carpet, and the island keeps flip-flopping."

Amesh was weary. He plopped down on a boulder. "I'm sorry. I should have insisted we turn back when we were floating offshore."

My anger eased up and I smiled. "We're not dead yet. And you have to admit, the carpet's taken us to a pretty mysterious island. We can't even find it on the map."

He grunted, dug a candy bar out of the backpack, and then put it back.

"Amesh, when I say the carpet's alive, I'm saying there's an intelligence about it. And if my gut feeling is worth anything, I feel like it brought us here for a reason."

"So you're not anxious to get off this island?"

"I'd like to discover something first."

"What?"

"I don't know. Something magical."

Amesh laid his head back and closed his eyes. "I'd rather find a nice cool pond of water and take a bath," he mumbled.

I lay down and closed my eyes, too. We rested for over half an hour. Then Amesh was shaking me and saying it was time to get going. The sun seemed to be higher in the sky. It felt hotter. I wished I'd had the foresight to have brought shorts and sunscreen. My jeans and shirt were soaked through with sweat. I didn't have sunglasses or even a hat.

As we hiked, the terrain changed. The ground firmed up; there was more grass and shrubs to give it stability. That was good. Unfortunately, the hills got bigger and steeper. Up and down, up and down—there seemed no end to it.

Yet the ravines were not as deep as the rises. Which meant we were climbing. So we never got a clear look at where we were headed.

As my legs turned to rubber and the burning cramp in my shoulders swelled to encompass my entire back, I began to believe the island had been purposely designed so that anyone foolish enough to try to cross it on foot would not be given a glimpse of what they were in for. At the same time, I began to think Amesh was right. I was looking for mystery in a place where there was only misery.

God, I was tired! I did not want to just rest. I wanted to lie down beneath a tree—which we had yet to discover—and not wake up for twelve hours. My parched lips were cracked. The blisters on my feet had already popped. Now they were bleeding.

Without asking Amesh, without warning him, I sat down and took another break, even though we had taken one an hour ago. He walked on another fifty yards before he realized I was no longer by his side. He called from the hill.

"Are you all right?" he shouted.

"Great! Any other stupid questions?" My sarcasm was unfair and uninspired. If anything, I was feeling guilty for having dragged him to the island. But it was easier to complain than to apologize.

He stumbled back down the hill and sat across from me. Then he pulled out a chocolate bar and looked at me like a hungry puppy. I nodded and he opened it, took a bite, and offered me the rest. But I gestured for him to keep eating. He didn't argue.

"You know, I haven't seen you pray once since we left Istanbul."

"We generally don't pray in front of—"

"Infidels?" I interrupted, teasing him.

He frowned. "Non-Muslims. But I'll pray later." He paused. "What time is it?"

I checked my watch, stunned at what it said. "Six thirty!"

He nodded. "The sun will set in an hour."

"I didn't know it was that late." But as soon as I spoke, I saw how long the shadows between the hills had grown. All we had to protect us from the elements was a magic carpet. It was funny in a sick sort of way, I thought.

"Should we camp on top of a hill or down in a valley?" I asked.

He considered for over a minute. "I don't know."

"You don't know? You're a guy; you should know something like that. Weren't you in the Boy Scouts?"

"The boy what?" he asked.

"Never mind. Do we want to be up where we can see someone approaching? Or do we want to be down low where no one can see us?"

"We could fly around on your carpet all night," he said.

My carpet, I thought. "In the dark? We'd smash into a hill."

"It's hard to say where to camp without knowing if there's anything dangerous on this island." He took a last bite of his candy bar and looked sad that it was gone. "What does your intuition tell you we should do?" he asked.

"Order room service and watch TV."

"That sounds like fun."

"What do Mira and your Papi like to watch?" I asked.

"The classics. They're big Hitchcock fans."

"I love them already. Tell your Papi I want to be adopted."

My remark was meant as a joke but Amesh took it seriously.

"He would never do that. You have a nice father."

I forced a smile. "A nice father I never see."

Amesh studied me. "You're an only child. You must be close to your parents."

The smile on my face slipped away despite my best efforts. Suddenly, there was a tear in my eye, and it was silly because I did love my parents and I knew they loved me. It was simply that I could not speak of them the way Amesh spoke of Mira and his Papi. I felt ashamed to tell him they were divorced.

Amesh asked if there was someone I did feel close to.

"My Aunt Tracy," I said, and this time I could not keep the smile from my face. "She's fantastic. I can talk with her about anything going on in my life. No matter what I say, she never lectures me."

"She doesn't judge you," Amesh said.

"Exactly! I don't know how she does it."

"She loves you. She can't judge you. It's like with Mira. We take care of each other. We don't worry what other people say about us."

"You must fight with your sister sometimes."

Amesh nodded. "Mira can get mad at me, especially if I try to do something she thinks is dangerous. For a little girl she can really yell. But no matter how much we fight, it doesn't matter. We respect each other. She's ten years old but she has the wisdom of an adult." He paused. "Will you be seeing your Aunt Tracy this summer?"

For a moment there—I don't know how, maybe it was the island—I had almost forgotten what had happened to Tracy.

"No. Not now." I paused. "She's dead."

Amesh was stunned. "I'm sorry, Sara."

"There was a car accident. A hit and run, we never did find the driver. It was four . . . no, five years ago. She suffered serious head injuries and was in a coma forever. That summer we drove to visit her all the time. But come fall, my mother and father decided to pull the plug. But they didn't tell me; they did not ask my opinion, not until they had disconnected her from life support and had her remains cremated. I remember planning this trip to visit her at the hospital where she was staying. I had the whole bus route mapped out. I had already bought the ticket with my own money, without telling my parents. I was leaving the next day when suddenly they showed me this urn filled with ashes and said this was all that was left of her."

I stopped talking then; I didn't know what else to say. Yet suddenly Amesh did something very sweet. He came over and put his arm around me. And when I began to cry, he didn't wipe away my tears. He just let me be.

I wanted to kiss him then. I prayed that he would kiss me. Maybe a part of him heard my wish because he touched his lips to my head. I felt a soothing warmth as he pressed his cheek against my ear. There was a wonderful moment when I heard his heart and mine beat together.

He held me until my sadness passed and I took a deep breath and felt strong enough to climb the final hill. We had decided, after all, to camp up high rather than down low.

The sun was about to set when we reached the top of the peak. It was the highest one we had encountered all day. But we were well rewarded for our effort—at least that was what we thought when we saw the last orange rays of sunlight play over the ancient marble, transforming a network of temples and pools into a heavenly vision.

Amesh stopped and nodded toward the carpet, which was still pressed close to my heart. He did not have to say it; we both knew.

This was the reason the carpet had brought us to the island.

CHAPTER SEVEN

FROM A RIDGE, staring down into a valley, we counted six individual temples. They stood at the points of a massive six-point star. The star looked as if it was made of some type of white stone. At the center was a circular pool of clear water. It was as large as the six structures combined. Grass grew between the spikes of the star, and long oval pools of water stretched from the central pond toward each temple.

Naturally, we were in a hurry to get a closer look.

I tried using the carpet, searching for a ley line, but couldn't find one.

We had to walk, which was okay; our adrenaline was pumping.

But with the fall of night, we had to carefully wind our way into the basin. At last our feet stumbled upon a path that circled the valley, running along a gorge that seemed to shield the temples and pools from the rest of the island.

Yet the path was in ruins. It was made up of an assortment of stones that had probably once been as effective as a modern sidewalk, but which now had lost the glue that held them together. A few times I came close to spraining an ankle.

"Who could have built all this?" Amesh said.

"The Greeks?"

He shook his head. "It looks more like something from the time of the Ottoman Empire."

"Then the Turks must have built it. Be proud."

"But look at these temples. They haven't aged."

"I know. But this path has; it's weird."

"It's magical," Amesh said seriously.

The pools of water we had spotted from above were connected to the central pond, and almost touched each temple. I called them temples for lack of a better word, yet their designs were simple. They were patterned after six basic geometric shapes: a square, a triangle, a circle, a rectangle, a pentagon, and a hexagon.

The roofs were flat, except for chimney-like protrusions that mimicked the shapes of the building themselves. These were located at the center of each roof and stuck up more than ten feet. But our view of the roofs was cut off as we neared the valley floor. The temples blocked our view; they were at least two stories high. The size of it all made my head spin.

Using the lines of the star as a sidewalk, we headed for the central pool. We were both thinking how nice it would be to bathe in it, but when we touched the water, we quickly changed our minds. It was freezing.

"An underground stream must fill it from below," he said.

"You mean an underground glacier," I corrected.

"At least now we don't have to worry about dying of thirst."

I knelt and studied the material that made up the six-pointed star. We had been in such a hurry to reach the central pool, I had not bothered to give it a close look before. It appeared to be made of marble. Yet it showed no signs of wear.

We retreated to one of the oval pools, on our way to the square-shaped temple, and tested the water. It was not as cold as the liquid in the central pond, but it was close. Amesh wanted to know if it was safe to drink. But he was not in a hurry to test it himself. I scooped some water into my hand and touched my tongue to it.

Immediately, I threw myself down and began to roll on the ground. "Help!" I cried.

Amesh rushed to my side. "Sara! Are you in pain?"

"It burns!"

"Allah save us! You shouldn't have drunk it!"

"I thought you wanted me to! Amesh! Help me!"

"You have to spit it out! Oh, Sara! How can I help?"

I shook my head wildly. "I'm poisoned! I'm dying! Oh, God!"

He grabbed my hand. "No, Sara! You won't die! I won't let you die!"

I couldn't take it anymore. I burst out laughing.

"That's so sweet of you," I said. "Now tell me exactly how you're going to keep me from dying."

He leaped up in disgust. "That wasn't funny!"

I sat up, still giggling. "You're right; it was hilarious!"

"Don't ever do that again! Or I'll . . ."

I stood. "Or you'll do what?"

"Leave you."

"You'll never leave me. You like me too much."

He shook his head. "You're dangerous."

"Of course. I'm an American babe. By the way, the water tastes delicious. But it's super cold. Let's fill our empty bottles with it and let them warm up in the night air. If we drink it the way it is now, we'll get cramps."

Amesh paused. "How do you know all that?"

"I used to be a Girl Scout," I lied.

"There's that *scout* word again. What does it mean?"

"It means you're lucky to have me as your partner." I

pointed to the temple at the end of the pool. "Should we have a look inside that door?"

Amesh hesitated. "It might be better to wait until daylight."

"Don't tell me you're scared."

"I'm not scared."

"Sure you are. You'd be crazy not to be," I said, walking over to it. "But it looks like we're going to spend the night here, and it will probably be more comfortable inside than outside."

Too bad; the door to the temple was locked. There were rows of what appeared to be stained glass windows on all sides, but they were closed as well, and up high, out of our reach.

The doors to the other five temples were also locked. As we tugged on the handle of the last one, and it refused to budge, I felt a wave of frustration. To have come so far and to have learned so little!

But I kept coming back to my belief that the carpet had brought us to the island for a purpose. It couldn't be just so we could stand and stare at pretty buildings. We had to get inside the temples; I was determined.

If I could have found a ley line, I might have been able to take us into a temple through the roof. Yet the valley appeared magnetically dead.

We were exhausted. We decided to arrange our jackets like pillows and plop down on the thick layer of grass that grew between the marble star spikes. By then it was eleven o'clock.

Amesh wanted to rest on the carpet itself, but that was something I just couldn't allow. The way I snapped at him when he suggested it annoyed him. But I apologized, and a few kind words seemed to go a long way with him.

We drank what was left of our water, and to celebrate the success of our adventure, we treated ourselves to two protein bars each. It was cute to listen to Amesh talk about how we were going to get our pictures on the cover of *Time* magazine once the world learned about all we'd discovered.

But at the same time, I was worried.

"We'll be rich and famous," he kept saying.

"Aren't you forgetting one thing?"

"What?"

"The carpet. It was the carpet that brought us here."

"So? This place is more important than the carpet."

"I wouldn't be too sure about that. Even if we tell the world about this island, we can't say how we got here."

"People are going to ask."

"I know. We'll tell them, I don't know, we took a boat."

"Why shouldn't we tell them the truth?" he asked.

"Because then we'll have to give up the carpet."

"We don't know that. We're the ones who found it."

"I found it, Amesh. As you've already pointed out, I found it on Turkish soil, at a place where I didn't belong. Your government will try to claim it for itself." I paused. "And that's not going to happen."

I felt him stiffen in the dark. "I thought we agreed to share whatever money the carpet brought in," he said.

"We already agreed not to sell the carpet! It's not just an artifact. It can fly! It knew to bring us here. God only knows what else it can do."

"What are you saying? We're not going to tell anyone what we've found?"

"I haven't decided yet."

"*You* haven't decided? Don't I get a vote?"

I realized I was sounding like a megalomaniac.

"Of course you do. All I'm saying is that the situation's changed since we first found it. The carpet's more important than we could've imagined."

"It's more important to you. That's what you mean."

"That's not fair."

"No? Have you noticed the way you treat it? Like it was your child."

"So? It's natural I should want to protect it."

He rolled on his back and stared at the sky.

"Nothing about that carpet is natural," he mumbled.

Those were his last words. A minute later he was snoring. Despite my exhaustion, I felt relieved to have time alone to think about our situation. Our argument about who was in charge was more dangerous than I wanted to admit.

In two days we had become friends. I trusted him more than I trusted most of my friends at home. Yet trust could be defined in different ways. If I were in danger, I knew he wouldn't hesitate to save me, even if it meant risking his own life.

The reverse was also true. Long before we'd found the ponds, I had decided to give him most of the water, even though it meant I might die of thirst first. I was proud of myself for that.

Unfortunately, even though we joked about the differences in how we had been brought up, they were real. He did not see the world the way I did. No matter how much I teased him about his belief that men were superior to women, he honestly thought it was true. When the final decision had to be made concerning the carpet, I feared he might try to take over.

Then there was the financial issue. I could try to imagine what it meant to live with as little money as Amesh and his family possessed, but it was just that—my imagination. I had grown up spoiled. Whatever I wanted I pretty much got. I just had to look at the way he dressed and the condition of his moped to know he owned next to nothing. The promise of the money the carpet could bring must have been weighing on him constantly. And that weight had no doubt doubled with the discovery of the temples.

What was wrong with that? It wasn't like his desire for money was bad. Money and fame were what most people in the world wanted.

But they weren't what I wanted. I didn't need money. And

what about fame? Like all teenagers, I daydreamed about being a rock star or a movie star. Yet when I placed that desire beside the mystery of the carpet, it paled in comparison.

The carpet opened doors I had not known existed. The carpet filled me with wonder. And that was a sensation I wasn't willing to give up.

"I was the one who found it," I mumbled as I lay on my back and stared up at the sky.

It took me a minute to realize there was still something wrong with it.

Like this morning, I did not recognize the stars; or rather, I did not recognize their positions. Vega was a bright summer star. During June and July, right after sunset, it was always straight overhead. And there was Vega, high in the sky, only it was forty-five degrees south of straight up.

The other night I had used the North Star to test the accuracy of our compasses. Now I could not find it. I tried using the cup of the Big Dipper to locate it but failed. Because I could not find the Big Dipper.

It was gone. Yet that was crazy. Stars did not simply disappear. They burned for billions of years.

Plus that weird red star—that glow—was back. Since we were nestled in a deep basin and surrounded by hills, neither of us had seen it rise. However, now that it had crested the eastern hill, it was obviously brighter than any other star in the sky.

Yet such a star did not exist.

The mystery made me restless. Suddenly I did not feel sleepy. I kept wondering how the stars on the carpet were reacting to the stars in this weird sky. Also, I was still anxious to find a ley line in the valley. We had looked for one before but it had been a hasty search.

Not that I planned on flying anywhere without Amesh.

Picking up the carpet, I headed toward the second temple we had tried to enter, the triangular-shaped one. I was not interested in trying to break in; I just wanted privacy. As I neared it, I felt a familiar charge in the air—the same charge I had felt on the beach.

I laid out the carpet and let it soak up the sky. Almost immediately I saw the tassels on the ends of the carpet stiffen and knew it was on top of a ley line. I could take the carpet for a ride if I wanted!

I was about to wake Amesh when the carpet's central stars caught my eye. They were not moving like they did when we flew the carpet, but they were much brighter.

"I wish you could talk," I told the carpet. The words were barely out of my mouth when several stars brightened while others dimmed. The effect was not subtle—something was happening at the center of the carpet. Certain stars were moving to make a shape. No, that was not precisely true. I still had to connect the stars—like one had to connect the dots.

The only problem was, it was not an image I recognized.

I stared at it for a long time before inspiration struck.

Was it a letter? Had the carpet responded to my question by creating a letter in an unknown alphabet? My heart pounded wildly at the prospect. If that was true then it meant the carpet was trying to talk to me!

"Stay cool," I told myself. "You don't know anything yet."

I reached for my BlackBerry and was surprised when it failed to turn on. It made no sense; I had just charged the battery.

This forced me to stare at the stars more. There was nothing else to do. But it was like the carpet sensed my frustration. The object it had formed with the stars broke into two pieces and then reformed.

A minute later, I shouted out in glee.

I saw two letters! An *H* and an *I*!

The carpet was saying hello to me.

"Hi!" I said back.

More stars joined the two letters.

They formed an exclamation point!

I leaned close to the carpet. "Do you speak English?"

The star field formed a *J* and an *A*.

"Ja," I muttered to myself, momentarily confused, before I burst out laughing. *Ja* was German for *yes*. As I watched, the star field spelled out three more letters: *O . . . U . . . I. Oui*, French for *yes*. It was playing with me.

"My name's Sara," I said. "Do you have a name?"

It switched and spelled out entire words, one at a time, but quickly, as fast as I could read them.

"No name now."

"You don't have a name now? Did you have a name in the past?"

"Depends."

"It depends? On what does it depend?"

"On who asks."

"But I'm asking. Who am I speaking to?"

"Mystery."

"Am I capable of understanding who I'm speaking to?"

"Not yet."

"Will I be capable of understanding in the future?"

"Depends."

"What does it depend on?"

"On whether you survive."

Talk about getting a chill. Someone didn't just walk over my grave, as the old saying went. They took a shovel and began to dig it up. It was saying I might die soon. My voice trembled as I asked if that was true.

"All life ends in death."

"All life ends in death," I repeated. "Sure, I know that. It's more a question of when, don't you think?" The carpet didn't respond. I tried another approach. "Is this island dangerous?"

"This island is magical."

"Were we brought here for a purpose?"

"You were."

"What about Amesh?"

The carpet did not respond.

"Why was I brought here?"

"To know."

"To know what?"

"What needs to be known."

On the surface, one might have thought the carpet was playing with me again. Yet as I read the message, a sense of purpose stirred inside. What I needed to know was important, not for myself but for everyone. I asked if that was true.

"Yes," it said.

"Can you tell me what I need to know?"

"Hint."

"You can only hint?"

"Yes."

"Because I have to discover most of it on my own?"

"Yes."

"Was I meant to discover you?"

"It depends on who you ask."

I was asking the carpet! Didn't it know that? I tried another tact. "Was I meant to discover the carpet?"

"Yes."

Why did it answer one question with a simple yes when it gave such a cryptic response to the other question? The questions were almost identical.

Except the second time I had asked, I had identified the *you* as the carpet. Maybe I was not really speaking to the carpet at all.

"Am I speaking to the carpet now or to someone else?"

"Someone else."

"Are you connected to the carpet and yet separate from it?"

"All are connected to the Carpet of Ka."

"The Carpet of Ka," I whispered, feeling power in the words, the beauty. The name was not unfamiliar. I had heard it before, somewhere.

"Should I address you as Ka?" I asked.

"No."

"I feel power when I say the word. Why?"

"Certain words are words of power."

"Can you teach me them?"

"Your intuition knows them when they are spoken."

"How do I know how to fly the carpet?"

"Intuition."

"Can you explain in more detail?"

"Knowledge is in the blood."

"What's special about my blood?"

"Lineage is ancient. Royal."

That made me feel pretty good about myself. "Are you saying I used to be a princess?" I joked.

"Lineage," it repeated.

"Someone in my past was a ruler?"

"Many Kalas in your past."

"What is a Kala?"

"Kala is the name of your lineage. It is what you aspire to be. Just as a student who practices healing might one day become a doctor, he or she who bonds with the Carpet of Ka and comes to this island hopes to become a Kala."

"How long have the Kalas existed?"

"They existed before mankind remembers."

"Is the Carpet of Ka older than mankind's recorded history?"

"Yes."

"Can it be damaged?"

"No. It protects."

"It helps protect me?"

"Yes."

"From what?"

"Evil."

I stopped to take several deep breaths. We were getting heavy here, especially since I was sitting alone in the dark.

"You said this island is magical. Is there evil here?" I asked.

"Good and evil."

"What makes this island magical?"

"Djinn."

"Djinn." My heart shook with excitement. "Are you saying there are genies here?"

"Djinn."

"God," I whispered. "Where are they?"

"Here."

"Are you saying they're all around but I can't see them?"

"Yes."

"Can they see me?"

"Some. They see you when you enter their temples."

"Is that what these temples are? Djinn temples?"

"Yes."

"Are the djinn evil?"

"Most are ambivalent when it comes to humans."

"Are you related to the djinn?"

"No."

"Was I brought here to contact the djinn?"

"Perhaps."

"Would it be dangerous to contact them?"

"Always dangerous. But . . ."

It did not finish. "But what?" I asked.

"Perhaps necessary."

"How can I protect myself if I try to contact them?"

"Don't tell them your full name."

"Why not?"

"Names have power."

"My name has power?"

"To you it does. That power can be used against you."

"Is it important that I learn the name of any djinn I meet?"

"Your intuition serves you well. The name of a djinn is key."

"How else can I protect myself from them?"

"Learn the Three Laws of the Djinn."

"What are the Three Laws of the Djinn?"

"First wish, the djinn must grant for free. Second wish, one owes the djinn. Third wish—"

I did not get to hear what happened with the third wish. Amesh was suddenly nearby, looming over me like an angry lion.

"What are you doing behind my back?" he shouted.

CHAPTER EIGHT

HE STARTLED ME, and his tone made me feel guilty, although I had done nothing wrong. So I instinctively lied, saying, "Nothing."

He crouched beside me, his head an outline in the dark. I did not need to see his expression to know his mood.

"I heard you talking to it," he said.

"Talking to what?"

"Don't play dumb. The carpet. It was talking to you."

I did try to play dumb. "You heard it talking to me?"

He pointed at the central star field, which no longer displayed any words. "You were bent over it, staring at that spot," he said.

"I was trying to study how—"

"You were talking to it!" he interrupted.

"I don't know what you mean."

"What you mean is you don't know how long I've been standing in the dark listening to you."

I tried acting hurt, anything to deflect his anger. Why was he so mad? He was scaring me.

"You were spying on me," I said.

"Spying? I wake up and suddenly you're gone. I got up because I was worried about you. Then I find you off with the carpet trying to learn stuff behind my back."

"I didn't find out anything."

"Really? The Carpet of Ka didn't tell you any secrets?"

Damn, I thought. He had been listening for a while. I had not only asked the questions; I remembered repeating many of the carpet's answers aloud. But I couldn't remember exactly which ones. He brought his head closer in the dark. I could feel the heat of his breath.

"What did you learn about the djinn?" he asked.

I sighed. "I thought it was spelling out words, using the stars. But it might have just been my imagination."

"You were having a conversation with it. You knew exactly what it was saying." He paused. "Is this the first time you've spoken to it?"

"What kind of question is that? You've been with me since I found it."

"I wasn't with you all the time in the hotel room. And you said I fell asleep last night before you did. For all I know you talked to it all night."

Sarcasm was an old ally of mine, particularly when I felt cornered. "You're right. We plotted against you. It told me the best way to murder you in your sleep."

He stood and stared off into the distance. "In a way I'm glad you're sticking with your lies. From the moment we found the carpet I've had a bad feeling in my gut. I thought I was being paranoid. But now I know you're not who you pretend to be."

That hurt.

"I'm sorry," I whispered.

He turned back to me. "What are you sorry about?"

"I'm sorry I lied to you," I said.

"You're just sorry you got caught."

"I only took it away from where you were sleeping so I wouldn't wake you. I had no idea it would start talking."

He pointed at the carpet. "How does it work?"

"I ask a question and certain stars brighten while others dim. They spell out words."

"Show me."

"Okay, I'll try talking to it," I said hastily, turning toward the carpet. "Can you tell us more about who made you?"

The star field did not change.

Amesh crouched beside me again. "Ask it more about the djinn."

"It said the djinn are dangerous."

"Ask!"

"Can you tell us more about the djinn?"

Again, the stars did not change, and I knew why. There was too much tension in the air. Besides, I sensed it didn't want to speak to him because it knew he was not of the same lineage as me.

"It's not working," I said.

"Why not?"

"I don't know."

"Is it because I'm not royalty? Like you?"

Oh God, I thought, he had heard so much!

"Amesh, please, I apologized. I was wrong not to tell you at the start that I spoke to it. But you startled me and . . ."

"You automatically lied to me," he said.

I leaned over to gather up the carpet. "Fine. Be angry, I don't care. I'm going to sleep."

He grabbed my arm. "We're not sleeping tonight!"

I shook free and shoved him in the chest. Hard. "Don't touch me!"

I could not believe the trust we shared had collapsed so quickly. Yet I felt in no mood to repair it, not now. He was behaving like a madman.

He seemed to realize that. He bowed his head, softened his voice.

"I'm sorry, I shouldn't have yelled at you like that."

"Unlike you, I accept your apology."

He nodded. "I accept yours, too."

"Well, I'm no longer offering it. I had a right to talk to the carpet if I wanted to. I'm glad I was successful. And it's not my fault if it doesn't want to talk to you." I turned away. "Now I'm going to rest."

He blocked my way. "Sara, please, you have to see my side. When I woke up and you were gone, I got really scared. We're on a strange island. I thought maybe someone had taken you away. I called out your name and you didn't answer. And then, when I saw you laughing with the carpet, talking to it, all my fear just turned to . . ." He didn't finish.

"Rage," I said.

"I got angry. I said I'm sorry."

"You're only sorry because you want to fly into one of these temples and summon a djinn."

What I said was true, but it was also odd. His whole attitude had changed since he had heard about the djinn. He was supposed to be the cautious one. He had not wanted to take the carpet across the sea. He had even been reluctant to enter the temples.

This was an Amesh I didn't know.

Even in the dark, I could sense his pride returning.

"What's wrong with that?" he asked.

"Amesh. The carpet said the djinn are dangerous."

"You spoke to the carpet for a minute about them. And you're from America. How many Americans even know what a djinn is? But they're a part of my culture. And the one thing I know for certain is a djinn has to grant the wish of the person who frees it."

"Earlier, you said your Papi said there were no flying carpets."

"I never said that."

"Yes, you did. You said—"

"Who cares!" he interrupted, excited. "The djinn are something else! We have to try to summon one. Just one. So we can make one wish. There can't be any danger in that."

He was being very persuasive, and I feared it was because I continued to feel guilty about having lied to him, never mind having shoved him. I had never struck a guy before.

His outburst had not erased my feelings for him. I wanted to please him. And the carpet had said I had been brought to the island to contact the djinn. If we were very careful . . .

I pointed to the temples. "We tried the doors. They're all locked."

He pointed to the stiff tassels. "We didn't try going through the roof because we couldn't find a ley line. But you've found one."

"It might not be safe, taking the carpet up as high as these roofs."

"Less safe than flying across an ocean? I don't think so." He knelt beside the carpet. "Please, Sara?"

I gave in. I could list all the reasons why, but one stood out in my mind. I realized how jealous I would be if the roles were reversed. If the carpet obeyed him and ignored me. I would have been crushed. To not do him a favor now—when he was begging for one—just seemed cruel.

We decided to head for the triangular-shaped temple. It was nearest. The ley line felt powerful. We had barely sat on the carpet, and I had only touched the tassels, when we lifted off the ground. We rose faster than we had on the beach, and I discovered I *could* steer the carpet by using the side tassels. In seconds we were floating above the temple.

The height made me dizzy, but at Amesh's prodding, I steered toward the three-sided chimney. I intended to land beside it, check it out from above first, but he saw no reason why we should stop on the roof. He wanted to fly directly into the temple.

I could hear frustration in his voice as he told me where to go. He tried to hide it but failed. Again, he had tried the tassels but they hadn't responded to his touch. There was no hiding the truth—the carpet was in my control. He was just along for the ride.

As we descended through the opening in the temple ceiling, an orange glow sprang to life beneath us and scared me half to death. Had we tripped a sensor by entering through the roof? As if by magic three tall white candles—located at the three corners of the temple—suddenly lit. It might have been the extreme darkness inside the temple but they appeared to shine with exceptional force.

Beside the candles there was an altar in the center. It was also shaped like a triangle. We landed near it and quickly stood. It was made of gold and silver, although across its top was spread a red cloth that seemed to be made of silk. In a way it reminded me of the material of the carpet. It did not look old or dusty.

Indeed, there was a feeling of timelessness inside the temple that was difficult to describe. The place was ancient; I had no doubt. And it was a place that was probably best left undisturbed.

What looked like the handle of a sword rested in the center of the altar. Around its top curled a long green emerald fashioned in the shape of a serpent. Its mouth hung open at one side, its sharp teeth waiting for God only knew what.

I wanted nothing to do with it.

Amesh studied it without touching it. He asked an odd question.

"Do you have your BlackBerry with you?"

"I have it in my day pack," I said.

"Open it, turn it on. Search for *djinn artifacts.*"

"It's not working."

"Why not?"

"Beats me." I pointed at the serpent. "This isn't a lamp—that's plain enough."

"You don't know everything about our culture. Djinn don't have to be imprisoned inside lamps. They can be bound to all kinds of objects."

"Really? Then why did you want me to look it up?" I asked.

"I was curious if there might be a reference to this object."

He was still wary of it. Good; I wanted him to be afraid. The last thing we needed was to unleash a djinn into our dimension. Let them remain invisible and hidden—in a realm where they could do us no harm.

While Amesh studied the green serpent from every angle, I took the opportunity to check out the stained glass windows. There seemed to be numerous battle scenes. They reminded me of the story that was laid out on the carpet, except these were much more detailed and far more bloody. But I still couldn't see much of them in the dim light. I would have to look again during the daytime.

While prowling the temple, I discovered I could push the door open from the inside. I propped it slightly open with some nearby rocks.

I wondered if Amesh had heard the first two laws of the djinn. Had I really repeated everything aloud? What if he didn't know the exact danger?

I might have told him about them right then but he appeared to tire of the sword hilt—although he had yet to touch it—and told me to take him to another temple. I wanted to argue, but we were still in our first "make-up phase." I did as he asked.

The carpet lifted off effortlessly and floated out the opening in the ceiling. We flew over the length of the pond in the direction of the square temple. I suspected if we stayed above the icy water and headed toward a specific temple, the carpet would stay afloat. It did.

We entered the square-shaped temple through the roof. Once more, a candle in each corner sprang to life and we had enough light to park beside an altar that bore an uncanny resemblance to the first. Except this one was square, and a black box rested on top.

"Don't open that!" I blurted out even before we had stood from the carpet. Amesh jumped up and laughed at me.

"Why not?" he asked.

I stood. "It looks like Pandora's Box."

As if daring me to stop him, he reached over and poked it.

"It's not very heavy," he said as it slid a few inches over the altar. The box was a foot on all sides, and yet it had a distinct impression in one side—an inch shy of the top. It looked like a lid.

"Amesh," I said. "I'm not sure what you heard the carpet tell me. But there's one thing it made clear—after you make two wishes you owe the djinn. We shouldn't mess with their . . . stuff."

"That's dumb. It goes against all my people's stories about the djinn. Our tales are clear—the person who frees a djinn has total control over it."

"Has it occurred to you that your stories might have gotten distorted over time?"

He stopped and stared at me. "It bothers you, doesn't it?"

"What?"

"That I have the courage to free one."

"It doesn't bother me; it scares me."

Amesh made a dismissive gesture, and as he'd done in the other temple, he began to study the box from every angle. This time I kept my eyes on him, which might have been a mistake. He clearly wanted to show me that he wasn't afraid. He finally picked up the black box.

"Amesh!" I cried.

"Don't be such a coward." He slipped his nails in the indentation. He was about to pull off the lid.

"Stop!" I cried.

"Would you please shut up for a minute!" he said. The lid

was frozen in place. He could not get it off, not with one hand. Relief washed through me. There would be no djinn knocking on our door tonight. But he didn't give up. He tugged at it until he was blue in the face. The poor guy tried gripping it with his thighs, with miserable results.

Yet he did not ask for my help. He was too proud.

"I can help you," I said. He didn't respond, so I added, "But if I do, then the djinn will probably end up obeying me."

It was just a joke. I was teasing him, trying to lighten the mood. It did not work. His jealousy remained. Just his luck, he had to find a magic carpet that liked girls instead of boys. Plus he was stranded on an island swarming with invisible djinn, and he couldn't find one to grant him a single wish.

Too late I realized that he might have misunderstood my last remark and felt I was making fun of his handicap. He threw the black box down on the altar.

"Take me to another temple!" he growled.

"Amesh," I said gently, putting a hand on his good arm. "Let's call it a night. We hiked, like, twenty miles today. We just had our first fight, and it was stupid, like all fights, but it happened because we're both exhausted. We need to sleep. Really, I don't know if I can fly the carpet any farther."

He stepped away and sat on the carpet. "I just need to make one wish," he said sadly. I sat beside him.

"Is that true? Do you promise only to ask for one wish?"

He gave me a puzzled look. "What does it matter to you?"

"I tried to tell you. It's because of the Laws of the Djinn the carpet told me about. One wish isn't dangerous. But after that you owe them something."

For the first time since he had caught me talking to the carpet, he appeared to listen. His dark face looked beautiful in the candlelight. Had I been more experienced, I believe I would have leaned over and kissed him. I felt a wave of love for him wash over me. Who cared if he wasn't royalty? He was special to me.

"I'll just make one," he promised.

I did not ask him what his wish would be. I knew he was desperate to get his hand back. How could I deny him that? After all he had suffered?

I smiled wearily. "Let's try one more temple."

Again, I propped open the temple door before we left. I hoped to study the interior of all of them at some point.

It was ironic that as we flew into the circular temple we saw a bottle that closely resembled a genie's lamp—at least the way lamps were portrayed in cartoons. We landed and walked toward it. The lamp was polished ebony, smooth and shiny, a wide bulb on the bottom that tapered into a narrow stalk at the top. Of all the artifacts we had seen, it looked the most harmless. Yet as Amesh tried to lift it, he staggered on his feet.

"It weighs a hundred kilos!" he exclaimed.

"Put it down!" I said.

My order was unnecessary. He dropped it on the altar.

The round temple was better lit than the others. There were more candles against the walls. They were red candles. For some reason, these candles did not burn with orange flames. The wicks shone with red fire; they filled the temple with a deathly shimmer. The color made me uneasy. Their fire was powerful enough to give me a glimpse of the images in the stained glass windows.

What I saw did nothing to soothe my nerves. The images were even worse than in the first temple. The scenes depicted one battle after another. There were soldiers in armor. Steel swords held high and corpses lying low. Blood everywhere.

I suddenly felt it was a mistake to be in the temple. Everything we were doing suddenly felt wrong. The carpet had said the djinn were dangerous. Why wasn't I listening?

It was because I had lied to Amesh, and now I was trying to make it up to him. It was a foolish reason. The lamp might have been difficult to lift, but all it had on top was a simple wooden cork. It would be easy to open. Amesh said as much. Still, he made no move to open it.

"What are you waiting for?" I asked.

"I keep expecting you to stop me."

"I wish you would stop. Do you really want to confront a djinn?"

"Do you really think one is going to pop out?"

I shook my head. "I don't know."

"But if one does appear, you said it was safe to make a wish."

"One wish. If you make two wishes, you owe it."

"I know, I know. What if you make three wishes?"

"I think something bad happens."

"What?"

"I'm not sure," I said miserably.

My uncertainty seemed to give him confidence. He circled the lamp. "If a djinn does come, I'll talk to it. You keep quiet. Okay?"

"Okay."

"You understand why?"

"Because I'm a girl and you're a boy."

"I don't want there to be any confusion about who freed it from its prison." In other words, he wanted it to obey only him.

"I'll keep my mouth shut," I said.

"Good." He reached for the lamp, then paused. "I might need help."

That was the last thing I wanted to do. The thought of touching it made me feel ill. Yet that desperate note had returned to his voice. How could I say no? Still, my legs felt heavy as I moved to the altar.

"You want me to hold it down?" I asked.

"Yeah."

"It's so heavy, it shouldn't move."

"The cork might be in tight. Can you just hold on to it?"

"Okay," I said.

I clasped the neck of the lamp. The black bottle was hot, while the room was cold. It made no sense, unless there was something inside that burned to be set free. I tried to stay calm.

"Amesh," I whispered. He was only four feet away, on the other side of the altar, his left arm already outstretched.

"What?" he said.

"Let's not do this. Not now, not tonight. Please?"

"Why not?"

"Because I'm afraid."

He gave me a sympathetic look then, and I was sure he was going to listen and stop this madness. Then his hand brushed the cork and his face suddenly hardened. He sucked in a sharp breath and his fingers closed around the cork.

"I have no fear," he whispered as he yanked on the cork. I expected a popping sound, but instead I heard a scratching noise, like nails being raked across metal. The noise grated my nerves and I let go of the lamp without thinking.

It didn't matter. It was done.

The djinn did not appear to me; it was visible only to Amesh. That was my first surprise. Yet I was instantly aware of its presence. As Amesh turned to the left to stare at it, I sensed an invisible shape swelling before him. Somehow I was aware of its weight. It was more than a ton, and I suspected it could crush us if we lost control of it. No, I corrected myself. If Amesh lost control. He had set it free. He was the only one who could master it now.

"It's magnificent," Amesh whispered.

He was talking to me; I assumed he wanted me to respond. Yet I had promised to remain silent. Best to be safe, I thought. Keep quiet; don't draw its attention. Let Amesh get his hand, and then hopefully the djinn would return to its bottle and leave us alone.

A voice spoke. The words did not emanate from the direction of the invisible mass alone. They came out of the walls. They were inside my head, too, an echo of a sound so old it could have existed before the earth. Words both soft and oppressive, definitely sly. It was clever; its life had been long. It would be difficult to fool.

"What is your name?" it asked.

Amesh opened his mouth to speak. I abandoned my vow of silence.

"No!" I shouted. "Demand to know its name."

Amesh tried to look at me, but the thing had him hypnotized.

"Why?" he mumbled.

"Your name will give it power over you. Tell it to reveal its name."

Amesh swallowed, struggling. "Who are you?" he asked.

Now I felt the djinn stare at me. It did not want to give out its name. Plus, it was angry that I had helped Amesh. I sensed it saw me as an enemy.

Yet a part of me felt that was not necessarily bad. The djinn were not there to make friends. They were forces of nature. They possessed power, and apparently they craved power. Amesh could use it as an ally to get what he wanted. But then he had to break the bond.

I felt as if the carpet were still talking to me, telling me these truths. But I wondered if it was not something else. The carpet had spoken about my intuition. But I felt as if talking to it had been the real jolt that had awakened a hidden part of my mind.

"Don't just ask. *Order* it to reveal its name," I told Amesh.

He coughed weakly. "Tell me your name," he muttered.

His voice lacked authority; another mistake, I knew. The djinn's gaze swung between us. Amesh had set it free. However— and it was as if I could read a piece of the djinn's mind!—it was suddenly curious about me.

The djinn wanted to know my name!

Even more than Amesh's. It wanted his name so it could get mine. It was fortunate I was in the temple to guide Amesh. At the same time, it was a pity I had not had a chance to learn more from the carpet before I had to face a djinn. I was not sure why it was interested in me.

"Be forceful," I urged Amesh.

"I demand that you tell me your name!" he said, finally showing some strength. The attention of the djinn swung back to Amesh.

"Darbar Aloya Ta," it replied. "Now your name."

Amesh went to reply.

"Ignore it," I said. "Make your demand."

"Should I ask for my wish now?" Amesh asked me.

"First invoke its name. Then make your wish an order."

Amesh nodded at my instruction, which had just popped into my head. Frankly, I felt as if my mind was not my own. I felt like the carpet was still trying to warn me about the djinn, while the djinn was still checking me out.

As Amesh focused on the djinn, he flashed a cocky grin. That worried me. Cockiness and mastery were not identical. In fact, they were usually opposites.

"Darbar Aloya Ta," Amesh said firmly. "I demand you grant me great riches of jewels. A treasure chest full of them."

"Huh?" I gasped. He was asking for money when he should have been asking for a new hand! Money could always be earned; only magic could fix his handicap.

A red mist formed at Amesh's feet. A wind blew, taking the mist and twisting it into a spiral that spun before him, giving off bright sparks, changing into a pillar of fire. I heard a loud popping sound, and a gold chest appeared at Amesh's feet. The jewels inside it sparkled with exotic beauty. The pillar vanished.

I knew I had to get over my shock and watch closely what Amesh did next. The entire night had led to this moment. He had made his wish. It was not the one I had hoped for but it was done. Now he had to return the djinn to its cage and walk away.

But Amesh had fallen to his knees. He was running his fingers through the jewels, lifting them to his lips, kissing them, spilling them over the floor. His eyes were drunk with joy. He looked so happy—I scolded myself for being judgmental. His wish had not been my choice but it had been . . . his.

All along I had been wrong. He wanted wealth more than anything. Now it was his. Now he could buy his Papi and Mira whatever they desired. From what I could see, the gems the djinn had given him were priceless. I suspected the richest men in the Middle East would sign over their fortunes to possess them.

Possess. The word haunted me for some reason.

"Do you see what I have! Sa—"

"Don't say my name!" I interrupted. "Not in front of the djinn!"

But the djinn had heard. I heard it whispering to itself.

Sa . . . Sa . . . Sa . . .

Amesh made a dismissive gesture. "Don't worry, I'm the one who freed it from the bottle. It owes me. You can't hear everything it's telling me. You can't see it, can you? It says you can't."

"No, I can't see it. But I can hear it, and I know it's telling you what you want to hear. For one thing, it doesn't owe you anything. It already granted you a wish. Remember the laws I told you about. If you make another wish, you will owe it."

Amesh plucked a large ruby from the chest and stared at it hungrily.

He giggled. "What are you talking about? I'm its master. That's why it told me its name. It's under my control. You saw how it obeyed me."

I took a step toward him. Yet I was afraid to step between him and the djinn. I suspected the creature would not allow that.

"Please," I said. "You promised me you'd make just one wish. We have to put the djinn back in its bottle. We have to get out of here."

"Why?" he asked, the silly grin still on his face. He was not hearing everything I said. The djinn had its own dialogue going on inside my friend. It did not want me messing with its plans. No doubt its plan was old, tried and true, for whoever opened its bottle. It probably kept giving the person whatever they wanted, as long as they kept making wishes . . .

I worried Amesh would make a second wish.

I was terrified he would make a third.

"We're in danger!" I pleaded.

He laughed and stood, shoving a few prized gems in his pocket. He held out a huge pearl to me, which was encircled with a diamond-studded gold band. It was a pendant—the pearl dangled from the end of a gold chain. Amesh came near.

"This one's for you. Take it. It's my gift to you."

He was close enough to slap. I felt I had to knock some sense into him. Mental telepathy, the ability to dominate a person's will—these were not powers I had expected the djinn to have. I realized I had been a fool to go along with Amesh, to help him get even a single wish. Because all of it had just opened a door—the djinn's front door.

I pushed his hand away. Unfortunately, he dropped the pretty pearl, and it bounced over the floor. He took a step back, stunned that I would reject him so blatantly. I wanted to shock him back to his senses.

"Keep your stupid jewel," I said.

His grin was gone, but something else had also vanished. There was a flatness in his gaze I couldn't quite understand. It was as if his inner light had been extinguished.

"What's wrong with my jewels?" he asked. "Not good enough for the proud princess?"

I tried to grab hold of him, to get him to focus on me.

"They belong to you, not me," I said in a clear voice. "They're what you wished for. That's fine; you're rich now. Let's leave this place with your riches. It's time to go." I paused. "Order the djinn back in its bottle."

He blinked at my last remark. I knew why. My words were not jiving with the words he was hearing inside, words he believed were his own thoughts. Yet I could pick up enough of them to know they were coming from the djinn.

Make another wish. Another wish. Don't stop. Make another wish . . .

Amesh believed he was in control, when he was really the puppet. He staggered back as if drunk and pointed an unsteady finger at me.

"You don't want my jewels because you think I'm a freak."

"That's not true. I think you're a great guy," I said.

"Right!" he shouted. "A great guy who has only one hand! A guy who can hardly dress himself in the morning! Yeah, you admire me, all right."

"It's true. What happened to your hand doesn't matter. You are who you are." I lowered my voice, desperate to reach him. "I never told you this before but it looks like a war wound to me. It makes you look kind of sexy."

He blinked again, this time with interest. "Really?"

I nodded vigorously. "I almost told you that when we met."

But I had gone too far. Doubt crossed his face as his internal war intensified. Again, I heard what the djinn said inside his head.

Hand. Wish for hand back. Hand will impress pretty girl.

Amesh shook his head and took another step back.

"I'll always be ugly in your eyes," he said.

I opened my arms wide. I reached for him, to hug him. I opened my heart. I did everything I could to pull him back from the abyss he was racing toward.

"Don't be silly. You're the cutest guy I've ever met."

"Sara . . ."

"I have a crush on you, Amesh," I said.

He heard me; I know he did. Because for an instant he smiled, and it was real. I sensed he was on the verge of sharing his feelings for me. Sure, it was a strange moment to share intimacies, but I didn't care. I just needed him to be safe.

Then I heard the djinn speak loudly in his mind. With power. The power we'd just given it when we'd both accidentally given it our first names.

Amesh. Wish for hand back. Amesh. Get hand back for Sara.

Amesh turned away from me then and was lost.

"Darbar Aloya Ta," I heard, as he began to make his second wish.

CHAPTER NINE

WHEN I AWOKE the following morning, I had the sun in my eyes and a throbbing headache. As I sat up, a bone in my back cracked. The morning was warm. The air was still and dry; the vast basin was as silent as a tomb. For a long time I just sat there, staring at the pond, the temples, the oval pools, and our bottled water.

I corrected myself: it was no longer our water; it was *my* water. That jerk, Amesh, was gone; my carpet was gone. He and his djinn had taken it and flown back to Istanbul. I was alone. Alone and stranded on an island swarming with invisible djinn where I might die.

I couldn't have been more furious! I wanted to kill him! But I also couldn't help missing him. I was so worried about him.

I let these intense and opposite emotions burn inside me. I had no choice; it was as if they had a life of their own. To hate someone and to miss someone—all at the same time. It was too much for my brain to process.

The time was 10:35 a.m. I had slept seven hours.

Finally, I calmed down enough to check my supplies. The candy was finished. I had six protein bars left. It was time to ration, I decided. I'd eat just two bars a day, max. It was not as if the island had demonstrated that it could support human life.

Was there any reason to explore farther? An argument could be made for staying where I was, conserving my strength and food.

The marble sidewalk that stretched between the temples did not appear simply new. It was extremely clean. In other words, it looked as if someone was maintaining the site.

Yet it went against my nature to just sit around and hope for someone to rescue me.

Amesh and I had approached the valley from the east, and seen no one. However, north, south, west—each offered an equal promise of running into someone. It was sad but true— those who kept the basin tidy might be less than a mile away, but if I chose the wrong direction to hike, I could walk until I died.

I slowly chewed on a protein bar, in between sips of water, while I contemplated my dilemma. In the end I decided to hike up the ridge and make a thorough scan with my binoculars before I chose a course. Who knew, I thought, I might discover a village on the far side of the western hills. We had entered the basin in the dark yesterday, with our eyes focused on the pools and the temples. It was possible I was not as alone as I feared.

It was hard to stand, harder to get my feet moving. The previous day had destroyed my muscles. Yet before I hiked out of the basin, I revisited the three temples Amesh and I had entered and made sure the rocks I had used to prop open the doors were still in place. Indeed, I added more rocks to each one. It was always possible that I might be forced to flee to a temple for shelter—for protection not just from the elements, but from wild animals, or even more dangerous creatures. And the more choices I had, the better.

I ignored the cobblestone path as I exited the valley. It was too rocky for my taste, too long. Using my compass, I faced west and hiked straight uphill. In my pack were my four bottles of water. They were heavy but I was not worried about their weight. I would go through them quickly.

Straight up was steep. I had to stop and rest several times before I reached the ridge. No "surprise town" waited for me on the other side of the hill. But I was careful to study the terrain before deciding on a course. Due west did not look inviting.

There was a range of hills taller than the one I was on. It stretched out of sight, to the north, another direction I was not thrilled about. Its hills looked like mountains. South had the fewest obstacles, and so south it would be.

My heart was still heavy. My emotions kept swinging— missing Amesh, cursing Amesh. But, to be blunt, I cursed him far more than I missed him.

I set off at a steady pace, hoping the exercise would distract me. The first part of my journey took me downhill, and I was not walking long when I noticed a change in the terrain. Most of it was caused by the addition of a new type of shrub that was dark green and had red berries on it. The fruit was unlike anything I had seen before.

It looked like raspberries, strawberries, and blueberries all put together. I wished I could look the fruit up in my BlackBerry, but it was still dead. Just my luck, I thought. The berries were probably poisonous.

Breakfast had been only an hour ago, and I was already starving. I decided to try one. Picking out what looked to be a ripe specimen, I bit into it carefully.

The juice that flooded my mouth floored me. Not only was it sweet, it had a taste that went straight to my brain and rang the pleasure bell. Without thinking, I stuffed another three in my mouth, chewing hungrily.

"Stop, Sara!" I said aloud. I needed to wait an hour. If I got sick, I'd have no one to take care of me.

I washed down the berries with water before grabbing several handfuls and stuffing them in my pack. Storing them was probably unnecessary. As far as I could see, my path was littered with the bushes. But I figured it was better to be safe than sorry. The fruit gave off a delightful aroma; it seemed to give me energy. I felt stronger than when I had left the basin.

Psychologically, the discovery gave me a boost. I wasn't going to be able to live on the fruit forever, but at least now it would take time to starve to death—if I didn't get sick. Hopefully Amesh would be back soon . . .

"I wouldn't count on it, Sister," I told myself.

My late start proved a handicap. I was not far from the basin when my watch read two o'clock—normally the hottest part of the day. To lighten my load, I was purposely drinking lots of water. Two bottles were already gone. Yet now I worried that I was making a mistake. With all the hiking I had done so far, over both days, I had not seen so much as a trickle of liquid outside the mysterious basin.

I wondered if the strange temples and pools took water from the rest of the island. A perfect question to ask my carpet.

My vow to wait on the berries did not last. Taking another break, I ate about a pound and enjoyed every mouthful. A part of me didn't care. If the berries were poisonous, at least now I would die quickly.

While I was sitting and digesting my lunch, a big sheep

walked over and casually licked my berry-stained hands. The creature showed no fear, which told me it was familiar with humans. Plus its wool was not that thick. It had been sheared in the last month.

Talk about a morale boost. I felt like dancing!

"Where did you come from? Can you take me to your master?" I asked the sheep as I petted it. The animal stared at me with soulful eyes and licked my face. I laughed; I took that as a yes. When I stood, the sheep began to walk in a southwestern direction. Naturally, I followed.

Unfortunately, my companion was in no hurry to go home. It stopped every few minutes to eat. It liked the berries as much as I did, and enjoyed the leaves that surrounded the fruit as well.

Near sunset I came upon a herd of sheep. The herd was a fair size—I counted at least fifty beasts. A dozen goats mingled with the crowd. On the whole they were not as friendly as the sheep, except for one.

This girl—there was no mistaking her gender—came over and nuzzled me. Lowering my gaze, I saw why. Its huge teats were swollen with milk. A pity I was a city girl—I didn't know a thing about milking animals. But the goat refused to accept that. It made a loud baying noise and tried to bite me.

"Hey!" I shouted, shoving it away. "I'm not dinner."

The sun went behind the hills; the light grew dim. Still, I had yet to meet any people. Luckily, the herd finally took note of the time. With the goats leading, it set off due west at a brisk pace. I kept to the side of the animals and tried to avoid their droppings.

It was dark when I finally saw three torches burning up ahead. They were attached to a well, which stood between two buildings. Left of the well was a large wooden barn with a triangular roof. It looked like it had been painted brown. Its doors were wide open, and the animals jostled happily toward them.

The design of the house was different from the barn. The exterior was made of stone. It was hard to be certain in the dark, but it seemed to weave across the side of a hill. The hill itself was rocky, too. Perhaps because I was exhausted, but it was easy to pretend that the house had grown out of the hill. While the barn looked like a recent addition, there was an old feeling to the house.

No one appeared to greet me. I walked toward the front door. Light flickered through glass. I assumed there must be someone inside. My heart pounded but I felt more tired than scared. Besides, I had no choice but to knock and wait.

A large man answered. His expression was kind, yet it had power, strength that only came from having lived a hard life. I saw it in his eyes; they shone a bright blue. His skin was ruddy. He had only a few wrinkles but his skin seemed as coarse as the material he wore.

His clothes were from another time and place. I wanted to

call his garment a robe, but it was probably closer to a kilt. It reached to his knees and was beige, held up by a woolen rope.

He had an impressive belly, and a white mustache and beard, which he kept neatly trimmed. His age was a mystery—he was sixty, maybe older. Everything about him was oversize. I imagined I looked like a mouse to him.

He did not act surprised to see me.

"Ha talpa sang," he said in a sweet voice.

I shook my head. "I'm sorry, I know only English."

"Engleesh?"

"English." I paused and pointed to myself. "American."

"Amaren." He gestured for me to enter.

He thought my name was Amaren. I tried to point to myself again, to correct the misunderstanding, when a second person appeared. She looked nothing like the man. Her hair was long and curly, a delightful cross between blond and white. The white was not from age, I realized. It was her natural hair color. She was at most thirty-five.

She wore a beautiful maroon robe made of sheep's wool. Like the man, her eyes were blue, but darker, her gaze more intense. It was as if when she looked at me, she saw nothing else.

I felt out of place in my blue jeans and T-shirt.

I pointed to myself. "Sara. My name is Sara."

The man gestured to the woman. "Aleena," he said. He ran a finger across his lips and then pressed his palms over his ears.

I took a moment to understand. He was saying that she could not speak or hear.

I nodded to her. "Aleena."

She nodded back, probably reading my lips. She smiled.

The man patted his hard chest. "Hara," he said.

I offered my hand in greeting. "Hara."

We shook, my fingers vanishing in his massive palm.

Their language was a mystery, but to my surprise, it didn't matter, at least not that first night. Aleena and Hara were both warm and kind and so comfortable to be around that talking was unnecessary. Only later did this strike me as odd.

I suppose it helped that they fed me dinner.

We ate as a family, and although the food was simple, it was like being treated to a feast. There was lamb, naturally, marinated in a spicy sauce that had me drinking glasses of juice. What was this secret beverage? It tasted like wine, apple cider, the berries I had discovered on the trail—a delicious combination.

There was also goat's milk and cheese, and a type of bread that reminded me of Indian naan. I wondered if they grew their grains or plucked them wild. The parts of the island Amesh and I had explored had been barren. But the more I ate, the less I cared where the food had come from. I just felt happy to be welcomed into their home.

I felt at home with strangers who did not speak my language. With a woman who could not speak at all. Again, I did not puzzle too deeply over my reaction; I merely let myself enjoy it after the strain of the previous two days. Not for an instant did I sense any danger.

Hara ate plates of food; he urged me to eat more. Aleena nibbled. I noticed that beneath her robe she was extremely thin, yet there was nothing frail about her movements. She was not a vegetarian—she ate the lamb—yet it was clear she preferred the bread and cheese. She was adept at hiding how little she ate. She spent most of her time serving me.

Guilt gnawed at my stuffed belly. Had I eaten food that had been meant to last them through hard times? With a series of clumsy gestures I tried to ask, and was relieved when they smiled. They might have been putting on a show for my benefit, but they acted as though this was a normal meal.

Especially Hara. With a twinkle in his eye, he patted his big belly and pointed to my small one. They did everything they could to put me at ease.

But they did not take me on a tour of the house. Instead I was led to a room not far from the kitchen, where they indicated I would spend the night. They lacked indoor plumbing but Aleena brought jugs of heated water, and I was able to take a bath in a large metal tub she rolled into my room.

The toilet was outside. It was not as comfortable as those at my five-star hotel, but it was sufficient. It reminded me of the outhouses at my father's job site, except it was made of wood instead of plastic.

I worried about what my father was going through right then. Unless Amesh had contacted him to say I was okay—"Sara's fine, Mr. Wilcox, just hanging out on an island that's not on any map"—he would be frantic. What could I do?

My bed was firm, narrower than I was used to. I was given a small pillow for my head. It didn't matter. I was totally exhausted. I suspected I would sleep deeply.

Yet as I began to drift off, my thoughts turned toward Amesh and the djinn and I could no longer relax. My friend had left the island after making two wishes. He had departed with two hands. He had left after promising to return, but he had also left after swearing vengeance upon those who had wronged him. It was the last statement that troubled me the most. Because it meant my guess had been right, and someone *had* cut off his hand. With Darbar whispering in his head, how long would it take before Amesh made a third wish to destroy that someone?

I sensed the third wish would be the most dangerous.

His djinn knew it was. It was why the creature had volunteered to take up the carpet and fly Amesh back to Istanbul—free of charge, so to speak. The djinn was sly. It knew it had but to bide its time. It didn't matter how much I had told Amesh about the danger. His hatred for those who had hurt him was too powerful.

Hot tears rolled over my cheeks and stained my pillow. Yet I refused to accept that Amesh was lost. I had spent half the day cursing him, but I swore I would not rest until I had saved him.

I fell into a restless slumber.

CHAPTER TEN

THE NEXT MORNING I awoke to pure silence. It was remarkable how still the house felt, inside and out. I could have been all alone, the only one on the island. For a long time I lay there thinking about how much my life had resembled a dream since I had found the carpet.

But I had to get up; I had to pee. I ran into Aleena on my way to the outhouse. She had on a plain blue dress that reached almost to her ankles. She gestured to her mouth, and for me to follow when I was done with my business. I assumed I was going to get breakfast.

After last night's feast, the meal was light: yogurt flavored with the island's berries, thick brown bread and butter, and pears. It was odd but the water struck me the most. Ordinarily I would have said water had no flavor, but this liquid tasted like the water that flowed around the temples. It was cold and yet it had power. I was not particularly thirsty but I drank two glasses and felt more alert afterward.

Hara appeared in blue pants and a short-sleeved shirt and had breakfast with us. Aleena had yogurt and nothing else.

Then it was chore time. They did not ask for help; it was assumed I would give it. Hara hiked away from the house—west, a direction I had yet to explore—while Aleena led me to the barn animals. The female goats needed to be milked. Aleena pulled up two stools, placed them behind a goat with an udder as large as a five-gallon bottle, and gestured for me to sit. Shaking my head, I pointed to a broom and dustpan.

"Goats aren't really my thing," I said. "Can't I clean up?"

Aleena shook her head, pointed to the stool. Her politeness remained but there was a firmness to her bearing. As if she was saying, Sit, girl. I sat.

My first milking. I would love to say it was messy at first, but I soon found my rhythm and enjoyed myself.

Not!

Aleena demonstrated. I was supposed to close off the teat from the udder, then squeeze the teat starting at the top and move the squeezing motion downward, pushing the milk out. It looked simple when she did it. A nice warm spray of milk flew into her bucket. But when I did it, I must have pinched too hard. Before I could even get to squeezing its teat, the goat growled and kicked my shin.

"Ouch!" I cried while Aleena laughed silently. A kick from an annoyed goat might sound like a minor problem. It is not; my leg hurt. I moved my stool back to leave, but Aleena would have none of that. She pulled it forward and demonstrated again. Slide hand over nipple, move up to swollen breast, squeeze, then yank down firmly and quickly.

"Okay, I'll do it," I said. A minute later, my other shin was sporting a bruise, and I made a vow not to touch that particular goat again, except maybe to eat it. Ignoring Aleena's protests, I moved my stool behind a smaller goat and tried a third time. You know what they say about the third time being the charm? I did not get a thick stream of milk, but I got something, and the goat didn't kick me, which was all I really cared about.

I ended up milking three goats—Aleena did twenty in the same amount of time. When we were done, my back ached from bending over. It was then Aleena handed me the broom and dustpan. She chased the animals out and gestured for me to sweep up. Yes ma'am. Now I understood why they had been so happy to see me the night before. I was their new slave.

Before we ate lunch, Aleena led me to a stream not far from the house, where I was able to wash and cool off. The sun was straight overhead and the temperature was warm. Aleena was tactful and left me alone, and I stripped off my clothes and washed them as well. Leaving them to dry on some rocks, I floated on my back in the stream and stared up at the sky. It looked a much deeper blue than I remembered.

Lunch was more interesting than breakfast. I was starving from all the hard labor, and Hara had returned with several rabbits, which he appeared to have caught in traps. I helped Aleena peel potatoes, so I wouldn't have to watch Hara skin the animals. But once they were roasting outside over the fire—the smell made my mouth water—I forgot all about where they had come from. I was pleased to find they tasted almost identical to chicken.

During the day, for a time, I'd forget about Amesh and the carpet and the djinn. Then the feeling of being stranded would return, and the danger of my predicament would crash down on me. How was I to escape this island?

Aleena wanted me to take a nap after eating. I said I was not sleepy, and tried exploring the remainder of the house. That was the first time I saw her face darken. She showed me three closed doors that led to the rest of the house, and indicated that I was not to pass through them.

"Why not?" I asked.

Aleena shook her head. For a moment I swore she was reading my lips. But she did not speak English. Or did she? Hara did not.

"Are you keeping other kids hostage in there?" I asked.

Aleena frowned and shook her head. So she did understand me! Why would one know English but not the other?

"Is that where you keep their skeletons?" I asked.

I was just joking, but Aleena threw up her hands and led me outside.

On the far side of the house, beyond the barn, they had a garage of sorts. Not for cars or bikes—or even horses, which would have been nice—but for tools where Hara did carpentry work and Aleena molded clay and painted.

Aleena took her hobbies seriously. She had several pottery wheels that she drove with her feet, and a kiln where she fired her pots to make them hard as rock. She showed me her work and I was dazzled. Not just because of her great skill, but because her style reminded me of the art on the carpet. Same color scheme, same lines, identical creatures and people.

It was like one had inspired the other.

Was it possible the carpet had led me to her?

Aleena wanted to teach me how to make a pot. The task was infinitely more appealing than milking a goat. I watched attentively as she lifted a lump of clay onto the wheel and sprinkled it with water, then massaged it into a circular mass. She did this before she moved the wheel an inch.

I was stunned to see how much water the clay absorbed, and gestured for her to pour the water on it and get it over with. She shook her head. That wouldn't work. I did not really appreciate that fact until she kicked the wheel into motion and I saw what she could do with the clay.

The power for the wheel came from twin pedals, one on either side. They duplicated the motion of riding a bicycle. But she had to lean forward to stay above the clay while she worked it.

Then the magic began, right before my eyes. She dug her right hand into the center and the clay spread out. Just as quick, her left hand stopped it from expanding, and she pushed upward until a bulge grew in the center. It took Aleena three minutes to create a pot.

Yet she wanted more from her design. Whether it was because she wished to teach me or because she needed a tall container for the kitchen, she continued to add pieces of damp clay until the pot grew into a vase. She coaxed the bulge higher and higher. Soon it floated near the top.

I was amazed. I tried to tell her.

She smiled and pointed to the wheel beside her. To the clay.

Pull up a chair, girl, and get to work, she was saying.

I dove in, and I was a disaster. A small pot seemed a wise way to start, but Aleena insisted I use a fair amount of clay. Not as much as she was using, but nearly five pounds' worth. Naturally, I rushed the preliminary steps. I was anxious to get the wheel spinning, and because I didn't take time to moisten the clay—to let the material absorb the water at its own pace—it refused to respond to my touch.

Actually, it responded too much. Once I had it spinning, I had only to place a finger on it and it would assume one grotesque shape after another. Yet Aleena was happy with my progress. She did not like the way I milked goats, but seemed confident that I could make pots.

So went my first full day with Aleena, and my third day on the island. After we washed up and had dinner, I prepared for bed but found I couldn't sleep. Without my BlackBerry, without even a book to read, I found it hard to relax. I never went to bed without reading something.

It was late—I was sure Hara and Aleena were asleep— when I heard a knock on my bedroom window. At first I assumed it was the wind pushing a branch against the glass. But the knock returned, more insistent, and I finally lit a candle and stepped to the window.

"Hello?" I said.

There was another bump. Yes, I thought, a bump, not a knock. It bumped twice more while I stood there with my heart pounding in my chest. After all I had been through, I was terrified to pull away the curtain. There was something about a mysterious noise late at night that rattled the deepest part of my brain.

I gathered my courage and pulled aside the curtain, but couldn't see outside. Finally—what could I do?—I opened the window. What was outside did not wait to be invited inside. It almost gave me a heart attack at first, but then I squealed with pleasure.

It was the Carpet of Ka.

It flew inside and landed on my bed and lay there as though it was resting after a long flight. Smiling, I knelt beside it and studied the stars in the center field. They were still bright, still moving, and I thought, even though we were not outside, the carpet might still answer my questions. The night stars were, after all, shining through the open window.

"Hi," I said.

The stars moved quickly. "Hi," it replied.

"Did you take Amesh and his djinn to Istanbul?"

"They were taken there."

"Why did it take you so long to return?"

"The carpet returned quickly."

My questions were off. I was forgetting what it had told me the other night. I was not actually speaking to the carpet, but to someone else.

"Was the carpet detained in Istanbul?" I asked.

"No."

"Then why didn't it fly right back?"

"Time is not a constant."

"What does that mean?"

"You will see."

"Is Amesh all right?"

"He is in grave danger."

"Has he made another wish yet?"

"He will."

"Can you tell me what happens when a mortal makes three wishes to the same djinn?"

"Seek, and you will find the answer."

"But you were about to tell me that first night we spoke."

"I was about to tell you that I could not tell you."

"It doesn't matter. I know if he makes another wish, he's screwed."

The carpet did not respond. Not even one comforting word.

"Why did you obey his djinn and fly them to Istanbul?" I asked.

"I obey no djinn."

I kept forgetting how to phrase the questions.

"How was the djinn able to fly the carpet to Istanbul?"

"Djinn know how to fly carpets."

"But that night, I begged the carpet not to leave."

"The djinn's will was more powerful."

"I thought you said I was a Kala."

"I said no such thing."

"You said I was descended from a royal line."

"That does not make you a Kala. That title must be earned."

"Can you take me back to Istanbul?"

"Yes."

"Can you take me now?"

"Yes."

"Great! Should I go tell Aleena and Hara I'm leaving?"

"No."

"Why not?"

"Why do you want to leave?"

"To stop Amesh from making any more wishes."

"Can you stop him? Can you stop his djinn?"

The two questions, put together, seemed to ask many questions at once.

"Are you saying I lack the power to save Amesh?"

"Yes."

"Are you saying if I stay here I can gain the power to save him?"

"What is the best way to remove a thorn?"

I was familiar with the old adage. "With another thorn."

"Then you know what you must do."

"No. Wait. I don't know."

It did not respond. Of course, I had not asked a question, so it was not required to respond. But I knew what it was trying to tell me; I just didn't want to face the truth.

"To save Amesh from his djinn, do I need to invoke my own djinn?"

"A djinn of greater power."

"But you keep saying how dangerous they are. I saw how dangerous they are!"

"They are dangerous in the wrong hands."

"But I don't have time to learn how to invoke a djinn. I have to stop Amesh before he makes another wish. Isn't it as simple as that?"

"It would be that simple if time were a constant."

"But my dad will be frantic. He'll report me missing to the police, and they'll end up talking to the woman at the hotel counter who was working the day Amesh came in with the package. They'll question Rini, too. That will lead them to Amesh, but he won't talk to them. How can he? If he starts talking about magic carpets, they'll throw him in jail."

The carpet did not answer. I had not asked a question.

"How's my father doing?" I asked.

"He is not frantic."

"I find that hard to believe." I paused. "So am I supposed to spend my time here learning to control a djinn?"

"If you do not learn to control the djinn, you cannot solve the mysteries of the Carpet of Ka. Without such knowledge, you will not be able to fulfill your destiny."

"I have a destiny?"

"All who are born have a destiny. All who die without fulfilling it live and die in vain."

Whew. That was pretty heavy.

"Can I trust Aleena and Hara?" I asked.

"Trust, like titles, must be earned."

"They won't show me the rest of their house. They have secrets."

"You don't want to show them the carpet. You have your own secret."

"True. But would they try to take it from me?"

"There is only one way to find out."

"Do Aleena and Hara know this is the island of the djinn?"

"They live here. They are not fools."

"To invoke a djinn, do I have to return to the valley of the temples?"

"It is not necessary. But they are there. Many are there."

"Is each one connected to one of the temples?"

"Yes and no."

"Is each one connected to one of the artifacts in the temples?"

"There are more djinn than there are artifacts."

"Can I use one of the artifacts, like Amesh did, to invoke a djinn?"

"That would be dangerous."

I felt frustrated. "There you go again, telling me how dangerous they are. At the same time you keep telling me I have to work with them. What's a girl to do?"

"Stop and think and quit complaining."

That shut me up in a hurry. I did stop to think.

"If there are more djinn than there are djinn-bound artifacts, then some of the djinn must be unconnected to an artifact. True?"

"True."

"When a djinn is invoked, does it have to be attached to an object?"

"Yes. The object serves as a link between this world and their world."

"Are the artifacts in the temples impossible to destroy?"

"Only the Carpet of Ka is impossible to destroy."

"Are the artifacts difficult to destroy?"

"Very difficult."

"Is a person's contract with a djinn destroyed when the artifact it's attached to gets destroyed?" I asked, and even before the carpet answered, I was thinking how easy it would be to smash a clay pot.

The stars on the carpet formed a smile.

"The girl is beginning to think," it said.

CHAPTER ELEVEN

THE NEXT MORNING started like the morning before: breakfast followed by chores. I had to milk the goats again, but this time Aleena wanted me to milk as many as she did. I did not think that was fair, but I could not exactly argue with her.

I got kicked again at the beginning and I think it was by the same goat as the day before, but I could not be sure. It kicked me really hard; it broke skin and I bled. Aleena showed not an ounce of sympathy. It took nearly until lunch for me to finish with my goats and she still wanted me to sweep the barn. But she did not take me to the stream. She handed me a fresh pair of pants and a shirt and gestured for me to go on my own.

I found it difficult to relax in the water. I kept thinking of the carpet, which was hidden under my bed. Aleena did not strike me as a snoop, but it was her house. Would she know what the carpet was? If she knew what the djinn were, like the carpet said, then she must know about magic carpets. Perhaps she and Hara would steal it and use it to leave the island without me.

Yet the carpet had returned. That meant a lot to me.

After lunch Aleena resumed her pottery lessons. I paid close attention. After saying good night to the carpet, I had already begun to formulate a plan. I needed to invoke a djinn that could destroy the djinn that was tormenting Amesh. But I needed to attach it to an object I could break. That way I could break my bond with it and circumvent the Three Laws—at least that was my understanding of what the carpet had said.

Aleena was my ticket to the perfect pot. Indeed, it struck me as an incredible coincidence that I needed to make an easy-to-break artifact, and here she was giving me pottery lessons. It couldn't be just a coincidence.

Time was not constant, the carpet kept saying. But I felt that time was my enemy. With each passing hour, I sensed Amesh moving closer to death.

On the fourth day, after supper, I made a bold move. While the other two were resting in the living room beside a roaring fire, I went into my room and got out the Carpet of Ka and talked to it for a while. I asked my usual pointed questions, and it gave its usual disturbing answers. The bottom line of our conversation was that I needed more experience with the djinn before I could hope to control one.

It was telling me to return to the valley of the temples.

I couldn't do that without telling Hara and Aleena. They were not going to sleep for hours, and I wanted to go to the valley while I was still fresh. Yet I doubted they would let me go for a hike in the dark by myself. Just once, in the middle of the night, I had gotten up to go outside to pee, and Hara had immediately awakened to check on me.

I could think of only one way to prepare them for my big surprise. I returned to the living room and took them by the hands and showed them the pieces of Aleena's pottery that reminded me of the carpet's artwork. They both nodded, unsure of what point I was trying to make.

Then I went to my room and returned with the carpet.

I laid it on the living room floor.

Aleena gasped; she made the actual sound, the closest to a word I had heard her make. Hara began to talk in an excited voice. I could not tell if he was happy or upset. He would not stop talking. Not until I encouraged them to touch the carpet.

They reacted shyly, as if it were sacred. But finally they touched it, and began to stroke it, and when their smiles changed to laughter, I knew they could feel the energy the carpet often gave off.

Finally, I stood and hugged the carpet to my chest and pointed to the sky. Again, I was sure they understood. They knew I was about to fly away. They looked worried. I had to struggle to make it clear I was going to return.

Outside I searched for a ley line.

The sky was clear, the stars bright. I did not have to go far to find a line. In minutes I was sitting at the front of the carpet and floating six feet off the ground. It was wonderful to have the power of flight back under my control.

I was ready to blast off, but I was cautious. It was extremely dark. It would be easy to get lost. I had only my compass to guide me. I tried to remember the path that had led me to the house, but I was forgetting a few turns.

Then inspiration struck.

The kind that was either brilliant or foolhardy.

What if I commanded the carpet to fly straight up? To rise up so high that I could see both the house and the valley of temples from one grand vantage point? On the surface it seemed like a simple solution, but it was risky. I might have to take the carpet up a mile to see the valley. That would be higher than I had ever been before. Could it even fly that high?

"There's only one way to find out," I muttered to myself.

I positioned the tassels. But this time I also tried to mentally focus on steering the carpet. Talking to it the last few days, I'd learned that a psychic connection to the carpet was more important than a physical one. In a way, the tassels were like crude instruments for beginners.

I began to rise higher and higher. The air had been calm and warm at ground level, but suddenly I felt a brisk wind in my face. It was so cold it made my nose numb. Yet the wind did not cause the carpet to waver. It remained flat and steady, until it came to a sudden halt without my telling it to halt.

The view was stunning. It took my breath away.

To my left, I saw the valley of temples and its watery pools. Directly below was Hara and Aleena's house—woven so deep into the hill against which it had been built that there were portions of it on the other side. On the far side of the summit were lit rooms I suspected they would never show to me. Perhaps they had more guests than one.

But I did not have time for sightseeing. The air was freezing; I began to shiver. What a fool I had been not to bring my coat!

I didn't dive straight down, but swooped lower in a spiral. I could only assume my ley line had expanded when I'd flown up. After a few minutes of spiraling, I was sitting beside the first temple Amesh and I had entered: the triangular temple with the altar that held the sword hilt. The carpet had already told me that the djinn attached to this artifact was powerful. As I moved to the side of the star field, I asked the carpet just how strong he was.

"The djinn who is tied to this artifact rules this island. Few can stand against him."

"Are you saying he's the king of the djinn?" I asked.

"He is the king of the djinn on this island."

"Do djinn live elsewhere?"

"Of course."

"Can I invoke him without making a wish?" I asked.

"Yes. But he will expect you to make a wish."

"Do the djinn have two sexes like human beings?" I asked.

"Yes."

"Do they marry and have children?"

"Yes. But not all marry, nor have children."

"Is the king of the djinn married?"

"Yes."

"Is the wife powerful?"

"No doubt."

"Can I use the king djinn to reach the queen djinn?"

"It depends on how much information you can extract from the king."

"From what you've told me, it sounds like I need to learn the queen's name."

"Correct. Is that your plan?"

"Part of it. Is the king's mate attached to an artifact?"

"No."

"Excellent! Can I attach it to an artifact?"

"If you're careful, perhaps."

"Why did you add the perhaps?"

"Because the key to your plan lies in tricking the king so you can later ensnare his mate."

"I'll release the queen once Amesh is safe."

"Still, the djinn do not like to be used."

"Is my plan too risky?"

"It is very risky, but also very clever."

I felt encouraged. The carpet seldom handed out praise.

"I know that I need a strong djinn to rescue Amesh from his djinn. I saw what his can do. When you told me a powerful djinn lived in the triangular temple, it got me thinking that perhaps it had an equally powerful mate that was not connected to one of those impossible-to-break artifacts."

"None are impossible to break. But most are difficult to destroy."

"That's why I want to go after the queen instead of the king. If I understand the rules correctly, I can't break my contract with him unless I can break his artifact. But if I can bind his queen to, say, a pot—that I can smash later—then I figure she might make the perfect ally."

"Your reasoning is sound."

I hesitated. "Are there any holes in it?"

"The king of the djinn will know that you want something from him. When you do not ask for a wish, he will get suspicious."

"Maybe I can just ask for one wish."

"One wish often leads to two. Try to avoid that temptation."

"Does it matter that I don't have my pot ready to attach to the queen tonight?" I asked.

"No artifact is necessary if you are not going to invoke her tonight."

"Is there any other warning you can give me about the king djinn?"

"If he tastes your blood, he will realize you are royalty, and he will be anxious to make you indebted to him. Use that desire against him. Also, if you do trick him into revealing his wife's name, but make no wish, he will get angry. He may even seek revenge."

"How is he going to taste my blood?" I asked.

"Be wary of the blade that is not visible."

"Huh?"

"Keep your eyes open."

"But he can't hurt me when there's no contract between us."

"He should not be able to. But he is shrewd. He might find a way."

I swallowed. "Any last piece of advice?"

"Do not tell him your name."

CHAPTER TWELVE

I HAD LEFT THE DOOR propped open. I did not have to fly in through the ceiling. But as I pulled the door wide, I wondered how much these creatures talked. It worried me because the last time Amesh and I had accidentally given out our first names. For all I knew Amesh's djinn was texting his boss right now. *Yo, Your Majesty, it's your lucky night. A wannabe Kala named Sara's going to be stopping by your temple tonight. Just keep her talking and I guarantee she'll end up wishing for the moon.*

The place had an internal alarm. The candles that stood at the corners did not light until I stepped inside. Then once again, they shone brightly. The king djinn was near; I could feel him.

The altar waited, unchanged: shaped like a triangle, made of silver and gold, covered with red cloth, immaculate. I heard no wind or sound. It seemed to be a place time could not touch.

The hilt rested in the center of the altar. Around its top was the long green emerald fashioned in the shape of a serpent. Its mouth hung open; its sharp teeth shone in the candlelight.

The longer I waited, I thought the more my fear would grow. But it gnawed at me that I still did not know the third rule of the djinn. The carpet had hinted that if I searched for the answer, I would find it. What better place to find it than in the boss's temple?

Last time I had barely scanned the stained glass windows. But now I decided to give them a good look.

Hidden in a corner, I found a series of windows with exotic pictures. The first showed a human being bowing to a luminous being, like one of the angels on the carpet. The man had his hands folded in prayer. He was about to make a wish.

In the next scene, the man had a woman standing beside him. It was as though he had asked the djinn for a wife and the djinn had found him one. They were both smiling.

In the third scene the man was alone, probably making a second wish. In the fourth scene, not only did he have a wife, he had a castle at his back and an assortment of servants. Again, everyone was smiling, except for the wife. She looked worried. She also looked very pregnant.

In the fifth scene, the man was handing his infant son to the djinn. I thought of what the carpet had said about the second wish. It looked like he had to hand over the baby to pay for the castle. Bummer.

In the sixth scene, the man was old, sick, and alone again, making what was probably his last wish. For on the seventh window he was young again, healthy. Yet he was not given a chance to enjoy his youth. In the final scene, the djinn had a noose around the man's neck and was leading him away to a fiery hell.

I feared that, after the third wish, the djinn did not merely own a person's body, but his very soul. He did not become just a slave, but a thrall.

I stretched out the carpet near the altar and spoke in a whisper.

"The first wish, the djinn must grant for free. The second wish, you owe the djinn. The third wish, the djinn owns you." I paused. "Are these the Laws of the Djinn?"

The stars spelled out the worst possible answer.

"Yes," it said.

"Oh, God," I whispered.

I had to act quickly. I had to save Amesh. Picking up the hilt of the sword, my fingers curled around and slipped under the fangs. Or else the teeth moved to meet my fingers, it was hard to tell.

Instantly the fangs lengthened and sank into two fingers.

The bite was excruciating. I reacted like anyone else would: I let go of the hilt and swung it wildly. I tried to pull my fingers free. This only made matters worse. The fangs tore my skin. I was no longer the one gripping the artifact. It was gripping me. And it wouldn't let go.

Yet not a drop of my blood spilled from the serpent's mouth. For an instant I thought it had not taken much from me. Then I realized it was able to absorb the blood and not show it. Terror overrode my reason. My fingers were still bleeding, still hurting, but the more I struggled, the worse it got.

Taking slow deep breaths, I willed myself to calm down. A part of me knew that if I did not have a solid grip on the hilt when the djinn appeared, it would be easier for it to control me. It made sense. The artifact was the tool it used to reach into our dimension. It didn't matter if the blasted thing was drinking my blood—I had to hold on to it to show I wasn't afraid.

A shimmering red glow formed above the altar. Quickly it assumed shape. It was twice the height of a man, but it was not human. It had four arms instead of two, an exaggerated torso that ballooned outward. Though it swelled in all directions, the djinn was not fat nor weak. Its four legs were short and strong— elephantine pillars that could support a twenty-foot stone statue. Despite its extra legs, it stood erect. Instead of clothes it was covered in silver and gold feathers.

Its head was large, round, and bald. In place of a nose and

mouth was a beak; its sharpness matched the tips of its six-digit talons. Its eyes were those of a snake. The pupils were fiery red, their gaze infinitely cold.

Given these terrible parts, the djinn should have been hideous.

Yet it wasn't, not to me. Amesh's remark returned to haunt me. "It's magnificent," he had uttered when he had first beheld his djinn. Just staring at it made me dizzy. I had to shake myself to stay alert.

Still, when it wet its yellow beak with a black tongue, it left a red drop, which I knew for certain was my blood. But how my blood was being transferred from the artifact into its mouth was a mystery.

It knew who I was.

I was royalty. And it was pleased to see me.

It spoke. As before, the words did not emanate from the djinn alone, but from the walls as well. I glimpsed its thoughts, sensed it searching for my own. The creature was telepathic to a degree. At first I felt it wanted my friendship, but then I realized that was just a projection, a trick.

I was simply another client to enslave, another chance for it to advance its agenda, whatever that was. I sensed its intelligence, its experience—thick as an ancient book, with endless bloodstained pages of successful conquests.

"You are a welcome sight," it said. "What are you called?"

I almost answered against my will. I had to struggle to stop. I feared to think my name. *Be aggressive,* I thought. *Do not give it a chance to fully enter your mind.*

"Thank you for making me feel so welcome, King . . ." I let the words trail off, before adding, "I'm sorry, I seem to have forgotten your name."

"Have you? I am disappointed. I was confident you would recognize me."

"But I do, Your Majesty. It's only your name that escapes me. Please refresh my memory."

It shifted to my right, a few feet away from the altar. I was not sure why. The candlelight glittered over its feathered body like a lantern over a treasure. I sensed that above all things, it wanted to make me a thrall, like the man with the noose around his neck in the final stained glass window.

I worried it was slowly gaining control. My fingers continued to throb. It was still drinking my blood. How much could it get out of two fingers? I supposed it depended on how long we talked. It licked its beak again, and another red drop appeared at the tip.

Tasty, beautiful girl, I thought I heard it say.

"This is my home and you are my guest. It is proper for a guest to introduce herself," the djinn said.

I forced a smile. "But surely Your Majesty recognizes me?"

It made a disturbing clicking sound with its beak.

"Your taste is familiar. I think I recognize you by one

of your ancient names." It paused. "You are an ancient, are you not?"

I chuckled. "Your Majesty plays with me. You have tasted my blood and know me. But as an old ally, you know I don't possess your great power. Please, let me show you the respect you deserve. Let me bow and address you by your proper name." Then, playing one of my aces, I said, "Besides, how am I to ask Your Majesty for the things I need when you won't share your full name with me?"

Things. I was saying I wanted to make more than one wish.

"Pray tell me what you need. I am sure I can get it for you."

"My Majesty loves to jest. Surely you know I must make a formal wish for each item." I paused. "Tell me how I should phrase my requests."

"Tell me your first wish and I will teach you how to phrase it."

"You would grant my wish without a formal request?"

Again, he moved three more feet to my right. I found my feet locked to the floor. I had to twist my upper body to keep him squarely in view.

"For a female as beautiful as you, I would do this," he said.

"You flatter me! But I'm afraid neither of us will get what we want if we don't follow the rules." I hardened my tone. "I can't make a wish unless I know your name."

He hesitated. "You may call me Trakur."

The name of Amesh's djinn had been Darbar Aloya Ta. Trakur could not be his full djinn name.

"The name Trakur does not tell me much about Your Majesty. Where you are from, your lineage. It does not even tell me the name of your father."

"My father is no more. He perished in the great war."

"A pity. What was his name?"

Again, he moved to the right and leaned close. I smelled the breath from his beak—an odor of fresh blood.

"He's famous among the djinn. You must know his name."

"I'm sure I do. Tell me anyway," I said.

"Why should I?"

I played another ace, sighing loudly. "Your Majesty, with all respect, I tire of this charade. I've come to you for help, but how can I trust you'll get what I need when you won't answer my simplest questions?"

"Tell me what you want and you shall have it."

"Tell me your name and I'll tell you what I need!" I shot back.

The djinn moved almost behind me. Still, my feet remained rooted to the floor. I had to twist far to the right to keep it in view. Finally, however, it seemed to tire of the taunting. It wanted to trap me. It wanted me to start making wishes.

"My father was Trakae Analova Ta," he said.

I smiled. "Of course, a great djinn. Then you must be . . ." To sort out the pattern, I had to assume that he had given me his first name first. I figured *Analova* stayed in the middle, especially since Amesh's djinn's name had also ended in *Ta*. "Why, you're the great Trakur Analova Ta!"

The djinn nodded. "I am well known in these parts."

"I apologize, Your Majesty. Never again will I forget such a worthy title."

He showed impatience. "Tell me your name and your first wish."

I continued to smile, although I was getting more and more worried about how I was going to free my fingers from the hilt. "But King Analova, now that I know who you are, we have so much else to discuss. Why, I have not even asked about your wife. How is she?"

Trakur drew himself up high. I had to bend my head back to follow. Again, he made that sickening sound with his beak, but this time a clot of blood spilled out and stained the altar. If his eyes had been cold before, they were now ice. Crystal shards from an arctic cave, they looked like they could slice me open.

"You lie," he said. "You are the one who plays the charades. You have been interested in my wife from the start. It is she you want, not I." He added in a deadly tone, "You must know the penalty of lying to a djinn such as me."

"But Your Majesty! When did I lie? I was merely trying to . . . AHH!"

A burning pain erupted in my right side. It was so intense that I feared to lower my eyes and see what was causing it. But then I saw the invisible blade was no longer invisible. The carpet's warning had come back to me too late.

A silver sword had punched out of the hilt like a switch blade loaded on a spring. It had pierced my side, and I was bleeding badly. Yet the blood was not going to waste. The blade's shiny surface somehow absorbed it by the mouthful.

With the amount of blood I was losing, the knife had probably pierced an organ. If I tried to pull it out, my wound would change into a red geyser, and I would die in seconds.

"I want to make my first wish now, Trakur Analova Ta!" I cried.

He stood in front of me and clapped his talons in anticipation. I saw then how he had tricked me. He had kept pulling my attention farther to the side to force my torso closer to the tip of his hidden blade.

"Tell me what it is and I will grant it for you," he said.

"Remove this blade from my side and stop . . ." I stopped. I did not complete the wish because I realized I was making two at once.

"You wish me to remove the blade and stop the bleeding?"

"That's not my wish," I gasped. "You did not hear me say that."

"Your wish then. Speak it aloud!"

"Trakur Analova Ta, I wish for you to heal this wound."

He shook his head. "Impossible. The blade has impaled your side. You will continue to bleed until it is removed."

"I'll handle that. You just fulfill my wish."

"It is a deep wound. It may take time to heal."

"You're to heal it as fast as you can!"

Trakur considered. "What is your name?"

"None of your damn business."

"Without your name, I cannot grant your wish."

I dropped to my knees on the hard marble floor, sweat dripping into my eyes. Still, I kept my gaze focused on him. "You lie. You lie because you think I lied to you—and that you are free to do what you wish. But that is not true because you have failed to catch me in a lie. You are a djinn, and you must obey the Laws of the Djinn, Trakur Analova Ta. Fulfill my wish immediately!"

With that, I yanked the blade from my side.

Blood gushed from my side. The pain was so great that I almost blacked out.

Amazingly, the hilt released my fingers.

Trakur went very still. He closed his wicked eyes. I noticed the blood that only seconds ago had been swelling inside his beak had stopped. His mouth went dry. When I looked down,

I saw that my blood was no longer pouring out. The pain in my side lessened but did not stop altogether.

Trakur opened his eyes. "Your first wish has been granted. What is your second wish?"

I set the artifact back on the altar.

The blade had disappeared.

"There will be no second wish. Carpet, come to me, please."

The carpet flew to where I knelt. It took all of my strength to turn so that when I let go and fell, I landed on my back on the carpet.

I couldn't reach for the tassels. It was okay; the carpet was an old friend. It would obey my commands and ask for nothing in return. Trakur appeared surprised by how quickly it responded to my orders.

"Take me out of here," I gasped, and felt myself rising upward. We moved fast, toward the ceiling. The carpet was in a hurry, and so was I. The djinn screamed beneath me, and I felt a wave of air as Trakur tried with all of his talons to knock me down. But either he was too far below or else he was not deep enough in our dimension to harm me.

As we cleared the roof and the stars became visible, I blacked out.

When I came to I was in my room, lying on the bed. The house was asleep. The majority of my pain was gone but I still would have appreciated a modern hospital with doctors and nurses and an IV drip loaded with morphine.

At least I had the carpet, my dear Carpet of Ka. It lay near me, on the floor. The window was open and the stars shone on its starry center.

"I thought I was so clever," I mumbled. "But he tricked me."

"You tricked him as well," the carpet replied.

"For all the good it did."

"You learned his name."

"I had to ask him for a wish! If I ask for another, I'll be in his debt."

"Perhaps one day you will be forced to ask. He is a very powerful djinn. Life is in the blood, and he feeds his power with blood. That is why he is the ruler of the djinn on this island."

I sighed. "I went there hoping to get his wife's name so I could invoke her into the pot I'm making. Now that hope's gone."

"Is it?"

I tried to sit up. "Isn't it?"

"The *Ta* at the end of the name is the same as your *mister*. Otherwise, when a female djinn marries, she takes on the name of the husband."

I had to laugh, although it hurt my side.

"What is the word for Mrs.?" I asked.

"La."

"So his wife's name is Trakur Analova La?"

"Yes."

"Why didn't you tell me that in the first place?"

"I wanted to surprise you."

I fell back on the bed, exhausted. "Cool," I said.

CHAPTER THIRTEEN

THE CARPET HAD ESSENTIALLY ordered me to remain on the island and complete an introductory course on the djinn and the dangerous rules that surrounded them.

But that brought up a disquieting question: Had the carpet purposely put Amesh in danger so I would have to save him? In other words, were the two of us mere puppets? I challenged the carpet on this point, and it replied that I had to have faith, that I had been led to the island and the carpet for a reason. Later, I asked the carpet about other people who had invoked djinn. Its answer was chilling.

"Most of those humans are now thralls of those djinn."

"Where are they now?" I asked.

"You don't want to know."

Frustrated with how slow I was learning to throw pots, I asked the carpet if Aleena could make one for me. But it said if I wished to attach a djinn to the pot, then it had to be an extension of who I was or I wouldn't be able to control the creature.

What was the secret of throwing the perfect pot? It was fearlessness and confidence. Aleena taught me to approach the clay with a quiet mind, but with a firmly fixed vision of what I wanted to create. Then I would be able to mold the lump of clay into a thing of beauty.

I cannot recall how many days it was after I faced the bloodthirsty djinn that I threw my first perfect pot. It could have been three or four days, it could have been a week. But when I did it, the result was exactly what I needed.

I was no longer simply an apprentice. I was a real live potter.

Yet the pot needed a lid; it needed handles. Those took another day to fashion. In the meantime the pot dried and I primed it with a white liquid and set about painting it according to the carpet's instructions. I had to create a specific star pattern, which the carpet said mirrored the djinn's character. In other words, I was recreating the djinn's astrological chart on the pot.

And here I had always thought astrology was for the birds.

I asked why the other artifacts did not have stars painted on them.

The carpet's answer surprised me. "They do. You just can't see them."

The carpet also had me paint and carve the name of the djinn into the pot. It explained that such a technique made it almost impossible for the djinn to disconnect itself from the artifact. Once I returned to Istanbul, it assured me, I would need such control.

The carpet made it sound as if I was going to war.

So be it, I thought. Bring them on; I felt ready.

Or maybe I was just sick of the goats. Their smell, their brutal kicks and constant baying. I tried to convince Hara we should eat more goat meat and less lamb. I'm afraid to say that I never formed a warm and fuzzy relationship with the beasts.

The day after I finished painting my pot, Aleena immersed it in the intense heat of the kiln. The process was fascinating to watch. The clay and paint fused to form a shiny surface that, color-wise, reminded me of the carpet as much as Aleena's finest work. When it was done, she set it out in the cool evening air.

Then we shared a meal that we understood would be our last.

They tried their best to get me to stay longer. I refused. Yet if I was honest with myself, I was pretty sure Amesh had already made his third wish. If that was the case, and he was a thrall, I was not sure how I could use my djinn to free him. The carpet did not answer when I asked such things. It never gave me much hope that he could be saved.

"Act. Do the best you can do. But don't worry about the fruit of your actions. That is beyond your control."

When I was ready to leave, Hara offered to help me carry my pot to the valley of the temples. I politely declined. I planned to fly there. But then the carpet said it wanted Hara to come. He was to fly on the carpet with me. I should have known something odd was up right then.

Hara held my two-foot-tall pot. I carried a torch and the lid of the pot. Aleena stayed behind, but gave me a long lingering hug goodbye. She had tears in her eyes when she let go. We had become close, but I did not know we were that close. Perhaps I had misread her feelings from the start.

We rode the carpet to the valley, but got a late start. The red star had already risen in the east and its sober light shone over the cold pools of water that separated the temples. I tried asking Hara about the star but he shook his head as if to say it was not something to talk about in the dark.

We landed outside the triangular temple and entered through the front door. Approaching the altar, I feared that Trakur Analova Ta would put in an appearance, but the building felt oddly calm. I asked the carpet if Hara should be present while I invoked the djinn and it said no. It added:

"But be grateful for his help. He will watch over the pot."

"Watch over it?" I asked, shocked. "I'm taking it with me."

"You cannot."

"Amesh took his lamp with him when he left with his djinn."

"His artifact is hard to destroy. Yours is easy. It must be guarded."

"But doesn't my djinn go back inside my pot when I'm not using it?"

"Your mind is stuck on cartoons about genies and their lamps. The djinn gets attached to your pot. It is through your pot that it gets attached to this world. But it does not have to stay inside the pot, not once you have bound it to you and to this world."

"Won't the distance the djinn is from the pot affect the control I have over the djinn?"

"No. Especially if she believes you're going to make three wishes."

"That's my point!" I complained. "If I do make wishes, I'll need to destroy the pot to cancel out my contract with the djinn."

"I'm aware of your plan and it is sound."

"But if the pot's here and I'm in Istanbul, I won't be able to destroy it when I want to."

"Do not worry about that."

I shook my head. "This is insane. This is not what I planned."

"You must learn that things do not always go according to your plans. To keep your djinn attached to your pot, and the pot safe, it must stay here."

Hara saw that I was distraught, arguing with the carpet. I'm sure he felt helpless that he could not do more for me. He gave me a hug the same way Aleena had. He shed a few tears, too. Then he took the torch and left the temple. Yet he made sure the door remained propped open. He really was going to check on my pot.

The carpet instructed me to set the pot in front of the altar, and to sit with the pot between me and the altar. I laid the carpet out nearby; I still had some last-minute questions.

"Is Trakur Analova Ta's mate in the temple?" I asked.

"She is near. Remember, she is free, unattached to an artifact. But she will be anxious to attach to your pot, especially after you defeated her mate."

"Why?"

"She seeks revenge."

I shivered. "Her husband got at least four pints of blood out of me. I didn't even scratch him. He has nothing to complain about. Besides, my side's not totally healed. I still have pain there."

"You may always have such pain. It's part of the price you pay to walk the path you have chosen."

"I haven't chosen to walk any path. I'm just trying to save Amesh."

"You have a great destiny set before you. You can try to achieve it, at great cost and sacrifice, or you can run from it and sink into mediocrity. The choice is yours."

"Did I ever tell you that you need to lighten up?" I said.

"Greatness requires commitment."

"Each time I've faced a djinn, I've felt intuitively that I have to try to remain in charge. But it makes me wonder how to act with a djinn that's going to be following me around. Say I tell it to go away so I can sleep. The djinn can always say to me, 'Is that a wish?' You see what I'm getting at?"

"The djinn will try to do that every chance it gets. You have to stop it from taking liberties. Make it clear that you're the master and your orders are not the same as your wishes."

There was a rustle in the air.

"Trakur Analova La comes. Quietly repeat her name. Guide her into the pot. When she is inside, put the top on. Then she will be bound to it."

"Won't I have to let her back out when we head for Istanbul?"

"A part of her will remain connected to this pot. Most of her will go with you to the city. But once she enters the pot, leave her inside."

"I'm finally beginning to see how this works," I said.

"Good. You fly the carpet, not the djinn. They have a tendency to abuse magic carpets and treat them as slaves."

"Okay." Suddenly I could sense an invisible being in the

area. She didn't feel as large as her husband, yet she felt more focused. Her energy was more concentrated.

I began to recite her name. "Trakur Analova La. Trakur Analova La. Trakur Analova La." It wasn't long before a mist formed between me and the altar. Unlike the previous invocations I had been involved with, this djinn didn't quickly assume a form.

I thought I understood why. Unlike the other djinn—who were attached to artifacts and accustomed to ensnaring unwary humans—this one had not put its foot into our realm in ages, if it had ever done so. I continued to chant its name for half an hour before it settled on a shape. I didn't get impatient. I could see it was making progress. Also, the form it chose was pleasant.

She looked like a human queen, with long, black shiny hair, a veritable shawl made out of darkness. She wore a crown, a small gold one, and not much else. Her dress was mostly sheer and black. She was dark-skinned. If not for a wide silver belt around her waist and a similar necklace atop her breasts, she would have been exposed. The necklace and belt were draped in hair-like material and inlaid with precious stones, mostly rubies, which matched the creature's eyes. They were black and had fiery red pupils. The color reminded me of the blood her husband had stolen from my veins.

I wondered if they shared the same appetites.

She stood. "Trakur Analova La," I said in a firm voice. "Come closer."

She came near, glancing at the pot with distaste. To my surprise she gave off a faint camphor smell, which was rather pleasant.

"I am here to grant you three wishes," she said in a husky voice. "Tell me your name and what you desire."

"I've fashioned a beautiful pot for you. It contains the stars of your birth. Your name, both carved and painted on the sides. Signs of the fire element, dear to your kind. In all respects it is perfect for you. Would you like to step inside?"

"I am more interested in what you want."

"You know that you can grant me nothing in this world unless you are tied to an object in this world. Trakur Analova La, I order you to step inside the pot. Now."

She hesitated, moved close to the pot, suddenly shrank in size, and stepped inside. Still, her head and crown stuck out the top.

"Trakur Analova La," I said. "Please sit, relax; I mean you no harm."

The djinn sat, and I quickly placed the lid on top of the pot. The fit was firm but not too tight. So far, so good. Now came the dangerous part—the binding of the djinn to the earthly object. I had to wait until Trakur Analova La tired of being inside the pot and begged for me to let her out.

I was what the carpet called her *Nagual*—her Primal or First. For all of time I would be the one who had connected her to this realm, even if others begged wishes from her in the future.

Yet if I did *not* wait for Trakur Analova La to beg, if I grew impatient and left, then she might break free and chase after me and try to attach me to an object from her world. Then I would be stuck with one foot in her realm. The carpet had emphasized this point. Always, it said, the djinn schemed. I had to stay alert.

I lay down on the carpet, prepared to wait days if need be. But Trakur Analova La did not seem to fear me. She was confident she would be able to get me to commit to three wishes. She waited only half an hour when she asked to be let loose. I said no, beg.

In the end she did beg, but I never took the top off the pot. I ordered her to exit it whatever way she could and gave her permission to do so. As her master, I needed her to know my permission was key. She stepped out and swelled to her previous height—a head taller than myself. She stared down at me with burning red eyes.

"You thought to take from my husband without paying," she said. "You thought wrong."

"Be silent," I said.

I checked the pot lid. It was on tight.

I pointed to the carpet. "I'm flying to Istanbul tonight. You're coming with me. Sit on the back. I'll sit up front and control it from there."

"You? A mortal? What do you know about magic carpets?"

I felt the urge to brag. It might have been a mistake.

"This is the Carpet of Ka, the greatest magic carpet in the world. It is I who command it."

The red in her eyes flashed at the mention of the name, and she stared at the carpet with unexpected reverence. "How did it come to you?" she asked.

"None of your business." I climbed aboard, not worried about finding a ley line in the temple. And when we reached the beach, I was confident that I'd be able to pick up the spot where Amesh and I had landed on the island. I was going to take the same magnetic highway back to Istanbul. The djinn climbed on the carpet and settled at the rear.

"What is your name?" she asked.

"My name's unimportant. But I'm already tired of calling you Trakur Analova La. Do you have something simpler you go by?"

The djinn hesitated. "You may call me Lova."

"Lova. I think we'll get along fine. All I require is your obedience."

"You want me to obey you? Is that a wish?"

"When I make a wish, I'll invoke your full name and

carefully label it as such. Otherwise, do what I say and don't get in my way."

Lova smiled faintly. "I cannot get in your way, not when it comes to interacting with others. You are the only mortal who can see me. That won't change unless our relationship should change."

Lova was talking about taking control.

"Don't even think about it," I warned her.

CHAPTER FOURTEEN

ALL NIGHT, over the calm sea, we flew—twenty feet above the water and traveling fast. The air was warm and humid, but I hardly felt any breeze. It seemed as if the carpet had erected an invisible force field without my even asking. Had it felt my desire to be sheltered and simply obeyed?

The longer I spent with the carpet, the more it seemed to anticipate my desires. I felt at home on it. Even with Lova and her glowing red eyes sitting behind me, I was not frightened. With the Carpet of Ka as my ally, I knew I had a power that was as great as any power she possessed.

I had been through a lot since I left Istanbul. I was returning to the city a different person. My confidence in my abilities was high. I was fifteen, but felt twenty-five. If Amesh could be saved, I would save him.

Like before, the stars were bright on the water. Soon I grew sleepy, and I told Lova to shrink in size so I could lie down without bumping her. The instruction might have been unnecessary—I was not even sure if she was touchable. Yet she obeyed without complaint. I was not trying to be a brat; I was just trying to maintain my position of authority, and to sleep.

My sleep was deep, without dreams. I assumed that I would awake in the twilight zone we had passed through on the way to the island but I did not. One moment I was staring up at the stars, and the next there was an orange light in the sky.

I sat up quickly and saw Istanbul in the distance. The sun had yet to rise but I was no longer worried that the carpet would fail if the stars vanished. It had finally explained that it could fly in the daytime, but the stars were like a power source for its batteries. For example, if I left the carpet out all night, under the stars, and did not use it to fly, then I could use it to fly during the next day. But not the entire day; for three or four hours at most.

The sun peeked over the horizon as I landed on the beach. It was the same shore where Amesh and I had started our adventure. It was hard not to recall how excited and happy we had been that night.

The place was deserted, which was fortunate. How could

I explain surfing in on a carpet? I immediately rolled it up and hid it in my backpack. Lova stood behind me, watching.

"Why do you stand behind me?" I asked.

"It is customary for a djinn to walk behind its master."

"Do you consider me your master?"

She hesitated. "Yes."

"Have you served a human master before?"

"No."

"But your mate has?"

"Yes."

"How many human masters has he served?"

"Sixteen, before you."

"Do all of them serve him now?"

She grinned; it was more of a gloat. "Yes."

"That will not happen with us. I know the Laws of the Djinn."

"All humans say that."

"How long will you wait for me to make my third wish?"

"Until you draw your final breath."

"If I have a friend who has become the thrall of another djinn, can you set him free?"

"No."

The sharpness of her answer surprised and depressed me.

"What if he is close to becoming a thrall, but he's not one yet?"

Lova hesitated. "Djinn do not interfere with other djinn."

"The Carpet of Ka told me differently. You can interfere if you're more powerful than the other djinn, and if I demand that you do so."

"Is that your first wish?"

"I'll tell you when I'm ready to make a wish. Don't lie to me again."

Lova lowered her head and did not respond.

As I walked toward my hotel, I tried to count the days I had been gone. Twelve? Fourteen? Would my father still have a room at the Hilton? Had my mother flown over from the States to help find me? I had not bothered to work out a story to explain my absence. The only practical excuse was that I had been kidnapped. But if I brought up kidnapping, my father would bring in the police and I would have to answer endless questions. Being experts, they would probably figure out that I was lying. Where would that get me?

It was not until I entered the hotel lobby that I glanced back to make sure Lova was following me. She held back twenty feet. To me she looked mostly solid, 90 percent, but the rays of the sun passed straight through her. The image was spooky. She cast no shadow.

Her expression was passive. I wondered if djinn experienced emotions the same way we did. True, they possessed a desire to manipulate, to control, but I wondered if they could feel love.

I hurried through the lobby to the elevator and pushed the tenth-floor button. My card key was still in my day pack, along with my binoculars and compass. Lova hurried into the elevator before the doors closed. We were alone for a few seconds.

The elevator had a mirror. Lova did not show in it, but I sure did. I had put back on the same jeans and shirt I had worn the night I left, which were clean but wrinkled. My hair was the real problem. It was tied up in a ponytail—I never wear ponytails. I quickly took it down. It didn't help.

"Do you need to take the elevator? Can't you just float up to the tenth floor?" I asked.

She hesitated. "This is an . . . elevator?"

"Yes. Do you come from a mechanical civilization?"

"We have tools. But not like these."

"Do you know what electricity is?"

"No."

"Can you walk through our walls?"

"I suppose. I'm not used to this world."

"Are you angry at me for forcing you into this world?"

Lova considered. "What I do now, it is my duty."

"What does that mean?"

"You're human. You would not understand."

"Try me."

Lova did not answer, merely shook her head.

There was a copy of USA Today outside my father's door.

There were copies outside all the rooms. I picked up ours and checked the date.

The paper was dated the day after I had left.

Only twelve hours had passed since I had left.

But I had been gone at least two intense weeks! I had been sunburned, dehydrated, kicked by goats, betrayed by a friend, stabbed by a djinn. My mind overloaded as it tried to squeeze all those events into one normal night. It seemed impossible. So this is what the carpet had meant when it said time was not a constant.

I could not accept it. But I had to; I could not deny the date on the paper. It meant, as far as my father knew, I had only been gone overnight.

I opened the door and walked in. My father was having breakfast in the living room. Eggs, bacon, toast, and coffee. He smiled when he saw me.

"You're back early. How was the slumber party?" he asked.

He had not said my name. I did not want him to use it, not with Lova standing nearby. Eventually he would say it, but the carpet had assured me that knowing only Sara would not give the djinn true power over me. Yet it would give her a little, and I didn't want her to have even that.

I forced a smile. "It was fine."

"How was your new friend?"

"Well, you remember Rini? I introduced you to her."

"I know. Does she live nearby?"

"I was able to walk to her house."

"You met her here, right?"

"Yeah. She works in this hotel as a maid." Which was true, but I was going to have to find Rini fast and have her back up the details of my story.

"Great. I'm glad you have someone to hang out with."

"I like her. She's nice." I paused, glanced behind me, saw Lova studying my father. "Hey, Dad, do you mind if I take a quick shower?"

"No problem. Want me to order breakfast?"

"Please. I'll have what you're having."

Inside my room, I was careful to stow my backpack in my chest of drawers. My father was not nosy by nature, but he was a dad and I was his little girl—it was better to be safe than sorry. I asked Lova if she was tired, and she surprised me when she said yes.

"But you don't have a physical body," I whispered.

"It is a drain to exist in this dimension."

"Are you suffering?"

"Yes and no. It is what you would call . . . stressful."

"Do you wish to rest?"

The red fire flickered in the depths of her eyes. "Djinn do not ask humans for wishes."

"That's not what I meant. Do you want to lie down and take a nap?"

"Yes."

"Lie on the floor, not on my bed. Remain there until I call for you."

She started to stretch out.

"Do you require food?" I asked.

"Nourishment."

"What type?"

"Human blood is preferable."

I spoke firmly, a little louder. "You won't be drinking any human blood as long as you're attached to me. Understood?"

She nodded, although she did not look convinced.

"Are you all right in there?" It was my father.

"Yeah!"

"Who are you talking to?" my father asked.

"I'm just talking on my cell."

"Hurry up with your shower. Your breakfast is coming."

"Okay!" I stared at Lova stretched on the floor and lowered my voice again. "Comfortable?"

"Why do you ask?"

"Because I care. It's a normal human emotion. Do you know what it means to care for someone?"

Lova paused. "Not for a human being."

I turned away. "I won't ask if you want a pillow."

The hotel shower felt delicious. Hara and Aleena's primitive culture had its charm, but there was nothing like a hot shower and white fluffy towels. I exited the shower wearing a soft bathrobe. Lova appeared to be asleep on my bedroom floor. I shut the bedroom door. In the living room, my father was just finishing his coffee.

"What are your plans for the day?" he asked.

I shrugged. "Order more room service. Watch dirty movies on the pay-per-view channel."

"In this country you can only get PG-13 films."

"In that case I'll flirt with the guy who brings the room service."

My father laughed—he was in a good mood. "Mrs. Steward and Mr. Toval were glad to see you again. They told me how witty and charming you were."

"Thank them for trying to get me into that cave." I didn't remember cracking any jokes.

"Maybe you can get in another time."

He made it sound as likely as an asteroid hitting the earth.

Sipping his coffee, he studied me. "I'm amazed at the color you've gotten since yesterday. I've never seen you so dark."

"I went for a long swim yesterday," I said.

"After you returned from the job site?"

It was an odd question. "Of course. I didn't go before."

My father cleared his throat, shifted uncomfortably in his seat.

"I heard you didn't leave the site immediately."

"Who told you that?" I asked.

"Security. They have you down in their logs as having left two hours after I saw you."

"That's crazy. I didn't hang out that long," I lied.

"Did you hang out with a boy named Amesh Demir?"

My heart beat inside my head. My father had greeted me more friendly than usual. Now he was grilling me.

"I think that was his name," I said, trying to sound casual.

"Where did you meet him?"

"What do you mean, where did I meet him? At the job site."

"He just walked up and introduced himself."

"No, Dad. He walked by, and I winked and smiled and asked if he was single."

"Don't get fresh, young lady. I ask because Amesh left early yesterday without explaining to his supervisor why." He paused. "Did he leave with you?"

"Nope."

"So the black hairs in the shower don't belong to him?"

"Nope."

"Sara . . ."

I felt blood in my face. "They belong to Rini. I went swimming with her. Then I let her use our shower. Is that a crime?"

There was a knock at the door. Room service. My father stood and signed the bill and ushered the waiter out. Maybe he didn't want the guy to come in because I had on only the robe. He wheeled over enough food to last me two days. He leaned down and kissed my cheek.

"Sara, please don't feel like you're being interrogated. Amesh has a questionable history with Becktar. He's almost lost his job on a number of occasions. He's not the most trustworthy boy in the world."

It was a mistake to defend him, but I could not just sit there and allow Amesh to be trashed. "That's a shame. He spoke so highly of you," I said.

"What did he say?"

"He said you were his favorite boss: fair, kind, hard worker, smart. He looks up to you." I picked up the toast and began to butter it. "You better get going. You'll be late for work."

I had never hurried him out of the suite before, but I wanted him to know that he was dealing with a new and improved daughter. One who did not like to be pushed around.

He kissed me again, on the other cheek, and left. I ate slowly and without enthusiasm. The day was going to be a killer, I could feel it already.

Amesh Demir. I needed to find out where he lived, speak to his Papi and sister if necessary. I checked the hotel phone book but found no Demirs. They were poor, so it was possible they didn't have a land line. Yet Amesh had a cell and he had spoken of his neighborhood—Kumkapi. Too bad he hadn't mentioned the name of his street.

I tried Amesh's cell. No answer.

Neither he nor his djinn was taking calls.

I called housekeeping and asked for Rini. When I explained to her boss that I was a friend, he connected me to a phone in a ninth-floor room, where she was cleaning. Rini said she would be happy to back up my story as long as I did visit her house some day. I promised.

I also asked Rini about Kumkapi. She had never heard of it.

I dressed—how wonderful it was to put on fresh clothes!—and rushed downstairs to catch a taxi. I brought the carpet and Lova. She sat in the back of the cab with me.

"Did you get enough rest?" I asked.

Lova stared out the window. "This realm is chaotic. Deep rest is not possible here."

"Do you prefer natural settings to human cities?"

"I dislike all things human."

"Do you dislike me?"

She hesitated. "You are the master."

"That's right, and don't forget it." I paused. "The friend I'm going to see invoked a djinn from the round temple. It came out of a lamp. Are you familiar with the djinn I'm speaking of?"

"Yes."

"I know its name. Do you know its name?" I asked.

"Not his complete name, no."

"In your society, names are important."

"It is the same in your world."

"Are you more powerful than the djinn who came out of the lamp?"

"Yes." There was pride in her tone.

"Can you destroy him if I order you to?"

Lova hesitated. "Djinn do not prey on other djinn."

"Answer the question."

"Yes. But to do so will automatically cause you to be in my debt."

"No way. I owe you nothing if it's my first wish."

"Wishing for the murder of another djinn always causes debt."

She was being honest; I sensed the truth in her answer. What surprised me was that she had gone out of her way to warn me. It was possible that killing a djinn was as hard for her as it would have been for me to kill another human.

The taxi driver knew about Kumkapi. It turned out to be an extremely poor neighborhood—no surprise. Yet the depth of its poverty overwhelmed me. I wasn't able to just "ask around" for Amesh. There was the language barrier, and the people were naturally suspicious of an American looking for one of their own.

But I paid my taxi driver extra to be my spokesman. He had grown up in the area and seemed happy to help. We eventually found where Amesh, Mira, and their Papi lived. It broke my heart. Their "house" was a ragtag collection of sheet metal and cardboard.

I asked the taxi driver to please wait and ordered Lova to remain in the cab. I noticed that the driver turned off the meter. He was not greedy. I felt shy knocking on the Demir door. Amesh had said Mira and his Papi both spoke English. While I waited for a response, I prayed it would be Amesh.

No such luck.

An elderly man with thin white hair and a gray mustache answered. Or I should say, he peered at me through a cracked door. The chain was still in place.

"Hi. Is Amesh home?" I asked.

"Who are you?"

"My name's Sara. I'm his friend. Did he tell you about me?"

"No." The man was on the verge of shutting the door. "Now if you can excuse, please . . ."

"You're wondering where Amesh got the money!" I blurted out.

The man froze. Even through the crack, I saw him frown. Glancing up and down the street, he undid the chain and opened the door.

"You come alone?" he asked in broken English.

"Yes. Mr. Demir, right? I really am a friend of your son. We only met yesterday but we spent a lot of time together. He probably didn't mention me because I know how he got his money. But I'm not here to take it away from him."

"Why you here?" he asked in a gentler voice.

"I'm worried about him, just like you are. May I come in?"

Mr. Demir nodded and stepped aside. Although the exterior looked like a box that had been erected in a dump, the interior was neat and clean. A ten-year-old girl, a head shorter than me—and with perhaps the darkest hair and eyes I had ever seen in my life—stood beside a heating pad, making porridge.

"Hi," she said. She was beautiful.

"Hello, Mira," I replied, offering my hand. "Amesh told me a lot about you." She shook my hand, then I shook hands with Mr. Demir. He offered me a seat on a sagging sofa and waited for me to start the conversation.

I was surprised, amidst their poverty, that they had a TV. But then I recalled all the shows Amesh had talked about, and how superb his English was. Mr. Demir must not have watched as much TV. He struggled with a lot of words.

I spoke. "I know Amesh didn't come home from work yesterday. And I know he was out all last night. But if you know about his money, then you must have seen him this morning."

Mr. Demir nodded. "He come by for short time to say he okay. We up all night, worried. We call police. I try to scold him, but he laugh and push lira in my face. He say he find treasure and we are rich."

I wasn't surprised that Amesh had bartered one or more of the jewels for cash so quickly. But I suspected he had made a foolish trade. From what I had seen of the djinn's treasure, there hadn't been a gem in the chest worth less than several million.

"How long ago was he here?" I asked.

Mr. Demir hesitated. I did not have his trust yet. "Some time."

"Besides the money, was he acting strange?" I asked.

"He laugh and throw lira in the air. That not my grandson. I teach him treat money with respect."

"He did something similar to me," I muttered, thinking of the jewel he had pressed on me in the temple.

"What did you do?" Mr. Demir asked.

"I told him the truth. That I didn't care about the jewels. That I was just worried about him."

Mr. Demir sucked in a breath. "He find jewels?"

"We found them together, a whole chest of them."

"Where?" he asked.

Time for a little white lie. I couldn't tell him about the island; it was too unbelievable. "In the desert. My father works for the same company as Amesh. Yesterday afternoon, I found them at the job site. But Amesh was the one who sneaked them past the security guards."

Mr. Demir paled. "Government will say jewels belong to them. Amesh will go to jail."

"That's why I have to find him. The worst thing he can do is run around selling the jewels. The police will hear about it and come looking for him."

"Why you not tell him about police last night?"

"I tried, but when he saw the jewels, he started acting like a madman."

"You say you find treasure in the day?" Mr. Demir asked.

Darn, a mistake in my story. That was what happened when you lied.

"We found the chest during the day," I said carefully. "But we weren't able to open it until after dark."

"Where you do this?"

"At the Hilton, my father's hotel. But my dad wasn't there. He was working late."

"Amesh stay all night?"

"No. He left as soon as he got the jewels."

"Who is your father?"

"Charles Wilcox. Do you know him?"

Mr. Demir nodded, impressed. "Mr. Wilcox good man."

Mira sat at my feet with her bowl of porridge. "Can you help Amesh?" she asked, worried.

I smiled for her benefit. "If I can find him, I'm sure I can help him."

"You here because you want half?" Mr. Demir asked bluntly.

Looking him straight in the eye, I told him, "Like I said, I don't care about the jewels. I just want to make sure he's safe."

Mr. Demir appeared to believe me. "I tell Amesh you want to talk to him when he comes home." He stood as if he was preparing for me to leave.

"He might not come home!" I exploded. I had to struggle to control myself. "Please, listen, the longer Amesh is out there without my help, the greater the chance he'll be arrested. I need to find him now."

"We don't know where he went," Mira said.

My face must have fallen. Mr. Demir spoke quickly.

"He not say where he is going," he said.

"Damn," I whispered.

From their shocked expressions, one would have thought I had just spray-painted obscenities on their walls.

"I not understand why Amesh not give you half the jewels," he said.

"My family has money. Jewels are the last thing I need." I stood. "Is there a neighborhood in Istanbul where there are lots of jewelry stores?"

"Kapali Carsi District. Many blocks of stores. Lots of security. You not from here. You foreigner. You walk around, ask questions, people get suspicious. No good to go there without man." Mr. Demir glanced at his granddaughter. "I take Mira to friend and I go with you."

"That's kind of you, but it's better if I go alone," I said.

"I not understand."

The truth was, Mr. Demir could help me find Amesh. But he would get in the way once we had him. Amesh would clam up. He wouldn't talk about the island any more than I would. But he might speak against me. Chances were excellent that his djinn already had him under its control.

If I didn't take Mr. Demir with me, the instant I left, he was going to leave Mira at his friend's house anyway and look for Amesh on his own. He could only complicate matters, but there was nothing I could do to stop him from trying to find his grandson.

I asked my next question as gently as possible.

"This morning, how was Amesh's arm?"

Mr. Demir stiffened. "What you mean?"

"I don't mean to pry. But last night I thought he hurt his . . . stump."

Mira spoke. "It was bothering him. Papi, I told you, he kept rubbing it."

"Did you ever find out who attacked him?" I asked.

Mr. Demir sighed. "He tell you about that night?"

"First he told me he lost the hand in an accident at work. Later he admitted he was attacked." Besides lying, I was making a calculated guess.

Mr. Demir shook his head. Bitterness entered his voice. "Four boys, we have their names. But we not know who pay them to do it."

"You mean, these guys were not his enemies?" I asked.

"They are boys he work with," Mr. Demir said.

"Did they go to jail?"

"They get expensive lawyers, we don't know how. There was trial but judge say they are innocent."

"Even when Amesh identified them?" I asked, stunned.

Mr. Demir was grim. "I pray to Allah to forgive this feeling. But one day I hope they burn for what they did to Amesh."

I understood. Sadly, I understood much better than he could imagine. It was possible the four guys might be burning before the day was finished.

The Demirs did have a regular phone. He gave me the number, and I said goodbye to Mira. I promised I'd do everything I could to protect her brother.

Mr. Demir sensed another meaning in my remark.

"Others know about treasure?" he asked.

"It's possible," I said.

I did not explain that they might not all be human.

CHAPTER FIFTEEN

LOVA WAS WAITING in the back seat of the taxi, her eyes closed. The driver asked for directions. "Downtown, the Kapali Carsi District," I told him, before turning to Lova. "Do you know when another djinn's nearby?"

She considered. "You want me to help you find Darbar."

"Yes."

"Make a wish and I'll find him for you."

"Gimme a break. You find him and I might make a wish."

Lova hesitated. "I can sense if he's near."

I pointed to a building down the block. "Can you sense if he's that far away?" I asked.

"Yes. Farther."

"Good. Keep your antenna turned on. I'll need it soon."

"Don't you want to keep me hidden from him?" she asked.

I saw her point. She thought I wanted her to kill Darbar. If that was the case, naturally, I would not want to advertise her presence. It annoyed me that my djinn had thought of something I should have.

"Can you sense him without his sensing you?" I asked.

She nodded. "My lineage is older, more powerful. But you cannot bring me near your friend if Darbar is with him."

"Darbar will sense you through my friend?"

"It is possible."

"All right. If we find my friend, you can hang out in a music store." I paused. "Do djinn listen to music?"

"Our music was old when humans were still living in trees."

Again, with one remark, Lova had given me an insight into djinn culture. It was a pity the situation with Amesh was so pressing. I would have loved to sit and question her at length about the djinn.

While we circled the Kapali Carsi District and searched for Amesh, Lova sat with her eyes shut. She was not resting, she assured me. She was trying to sense Darbar.

Mr. Demir had not exaggerated. The Kapali Carsi District was an endless array of shops that sold jewelry but also rugs and other hand-crafted goods, which I liked the most. Of course, many of the shops were not proper stores, but more like displays at a swap meet. They were temporary affairs, erected fresh each morning.

I didn't have a photograph of Amesh. I couldn't go from store to store and ask if anyone had seen him. It was probably just as well—that would have been reckless.

I hoped that Mr. Demir was smart enough not to do the same thing. He was obviously frantic. He knew there was something wrong with his Amesh besides the treasure. Mira had sensed it, too—that was why she had been so scared.

After hours of circling, Lova told me she did not sense Darbar in the area. By then it was two in the afternoon, and I was hungry. The thought of food reminded me of how much Amesh had loved the steak in my hotel room. It occurred to me that if he was hungry—and rich—he would probably buy the same steak again. He would want to go to a Hilton! But not my Hilton because he would be afraid of running into me.

"Do you know of a Hilton that's not at the beach?" I asked our driver.

"There's one at airport."

"How far away is that?"

"Twenty kilometers."

That would be twelve and a half miles. "Is there one closer?"

"No."

"Take me to it," I said.

"May I ask the young lady a question?"

"Yes?"

"You're American, yes?"

"Yeah."

"Is it a custom in your country to talk to people who are not there?"

I had not gone out of my way to disguise my conversations with Lova because I had assumed that the driver wouldn't notice what I was doing. I would have to be more careful.

"I'm a famous actress," I said. "I'm rehearsing lines for a movie."

That got the guy excited, and he talked my head off all the way to the hotel. When we were parked outside, I turned to Lova.

"Is Darbar in the area?" I whispered.

She closed her eyes for a moment, then nodded toward the hotel.

"He's in that building," she said.

I spoke softly. "Good. Stay out of sight in that shoe store over there. How far can you be from me and still hear my call?"

"Far."

"Okay. Wait for my call. I won't be long."

I paid the driver—I owed him a small fortune—and entered the hotel. This Hilton was larger and older than the one at the beach, more conservative. I asked at the desk where lunch was being served and was pointed toward two different restaurants.

"Which one has the best steak?" I asked.

I was directed to the restaurant on the second floor, over-looking the pool and the harbor. It was almost deserted; apparently the other restaurant had the great lunch menu. A man with a white turban wanted to seat me but I told him I was looking for a friend. Before Amesh saw me, I saw him on the balcony eating his lunch.

He had two hands! He was using both of them to eat!

It should not have been a shock. I had heard him ask for the hand. But I had been so upset that night, I did not get a clear look at him after he made his wish. Now, to actually see it attached to his arm—it was like a miracle!

Yet there was something wrong with his right hand. The skin color was ghastly. It was not dark like his normal beautiful skin, but a sick yellow. And the longer I watched, the more I saw him struggling.

He was using it to hold the fork, to keep the meat in place, when he should have been using it to cut the meat with his knife. Amesh had told me that he was naturally right-handed. Yet here he was using his left hand to do the more difficult task.

It broke my heart to see why. His new hand was hurting him. He tried to hide it, but every time the fork slipped from his control, he winced.

I ran over and sat beside Amesh. He took one look at me and tried to escape. He had on new clothes. Expensive tailored clothes. Gray slacks, a white silk shirt, and a gaudy silver jacket. I grabbed him by his sleeve as he went to leave.

"We have to talk," I said.

He shook free. "I don't have to talk to you!"

His words stung. For two weeks I had done nothing but worry about him, and now he did not want to speak to me. The only thing that kept me from bursting into tears was the pain on his face. He did not look like the Amesh I knew. He kept twitching.

"Where's Darbar?" If the djinn was nearby, I did not sense it.

He shook at the mention of the creature. "Don't say his name!"

"Why not?"

"Because I hate him, and it might make him come."

"Fine. Talk to me, and I won't mention him again."

It chilled me to the bone to speak of Amesh's djinn as a "him" instead of an "it." Yet I realized that I usually thought of Lova as a "her" or a "she." Was it because I felt Darbar more evil? Less human? Mentally and emotionally, there could be a danger in getting too comfortable with Lova.

Amesh sat back down. "Is that why you're here? To threaten me?"

"I'm here because I'm sick worrying about you. Did you happen to notice that it didn't matter how long we were on the island? When you returned, it was the next day."

"Of course I noticed."

"Well, I've been gone two weeks."

He was stunned. "You're kidding."

"It's been a very long two weeks, Amesh."

"I'm sorry."

"That's it? You leave me stranded on a spooky island and all you can say is you're sorry?"

He looked ashamed. "The djinn ordered me to leave you. It was like it got inside my mind, and I lost all control. But then I thought of you and I fought it. I sent the carpet back. But I had no idea it would take so long to rescue you."

"It came the next night." The carpet had never told me Amesh had sent it back for me. I wondered why. The information meant a lot to me.

"But you just said—"

"I stayed on the island on purpose to try to help you," I interrupted. "To learn how to undo the deals you've made with your djinn."

He shook his head. "He's not my djinn. I want nothing to do with him."

"But you can't get rid of it, can you? Do you know why? It's because of the Laws of the Djinn that I told you about before you decided you knew everything." I paused. "How many wishes have you made so far?"

"Two."

"Liar."

He went to snap at me but then stopped. "What do three wishes have to do with Darbar taking control?" he asked.

"It's the third law of the djinn. Make three wishes and the djinn owns you. It's like you become its thrall."

His eyes blinked rapidly. "What does *thrall* mean?"

I described to him the series of pictures in the djinn temple. When I got to the part about the man being led into a fiery region with his neck in a noose, Amesh turned white.

"I swear on Allah's name, I've only made two wishes!"

"Then why are you twitching like a drug addict in need of a fix? And why do you jump when I say his name?"

He pointed to his right hand. "It's because of this! Look at it. Do you know what it is?"

"A poor copy of your right hand?"

"No! I asked for my hand back. And you know what? It gave it to me! It gave me back my old hand!"

I gulped. "That's impossible."

"Listen, I'm sorry, but the story I told you about how I lost my hand was a lie. The truth is, I was attacked by four guys and they cut it off. The police caught them and there was a trial but it was a joke. The judge let them go."

"Why?"

"I don't know. Hire the best lawyer in town and you can get away with anything. Anyway, during the trial, my hand was Exhibit A. The doctors couldn't sew it back on, but the prosecutor brought it into the courtroom. To keep it fresh, they put it in a glass jar filled with some kind of weird liquid."

"Formaldehyde," I said.

"Huh?"

"It's called formaldehyde." I could smell it on him.

"Whatever. The chemical didn't keep it fresh enough. When I asked the djinn for my hand back, it went and got my original hand." There were tears in his eyes. "I didn't know it was going to do that. I thought it would give me a new hand, not this old rotten thing."

"God," I said. Be careful what you wish for, you just might get it. It was the oldest saying in the world, and it was the truest when it came to the oldest beings on earth. Darbar had set Amesh up perfectly. Even if Amesh had not made the third wish yet—which I sensed was somehow partially true—it already had him under its thumb.

Amesh lowered his head and sobbed. Moving my chair close, I hugged him and stroked his hair. It felt good to be able to comfort him. At least, I thought I was comforting him. Suddenly he stood as if he was about to leave.

"I'm sorry, I have to go," he said.

Again, I grabbed his coat and forced him back in his chair. "Would you sit and listen? I'm here to help." I paused. "I brought back another djinn."

"The last thing I want in my life is another djinn."

"What if I order this djinn to help you?"

Finally, he showed interest. "What are you going to wish for?"

"I don't know. I need to get a handle on what's going on with you. You swear you've only made two wishes, but you act like Darbar controls you. I don't get it."

Amesh was silent a long time before he answered.

"Darbar can't find them," he said.

"Find who?"

"The people who ordered the attack on me."

"But you know who they are."

"I know who attacked me. But I don't know who paid them."

"Is that your third wish? The one you say you haven't made yet?"

"I'm not a fool, Sara. I learned from my mistake. I said my second wish wrong and look what happened. I didn't make the same mistake with my third wish."

"Did you make a third wish or not?" I asked.

"I made a deal with Darbar. I didn't want just the guys who attacked me to suffer. I wanted the people who hired them to suffer, too. But Darbar can't find them." He added, "So, like I told you, there's been no third wish because the djinn can't find them."

I shook my head. "This deal you've made with Darbar sounds like a third wish to me. The only thing that's keeping him from making you a thrall is that he hasn't been able to fulfill it."

He stared at the ocean. "I hate them."

"Amesh, maybe that's the way out of this. Drop your need for revenge, and maybe Darbar won't be able to collect on the third wish."

"You don't understand; I want revenge. It's all I've thought about for the last year."

"I don't believe that. The time we spent together, we had a great time. You weren't thinking about revenge then."

"How do you know what I was thinking about?" he asked.

"Because I know you, I care about you. I know that you care about me. You told me as much in that temple, just before Darbar came between us. Amesh, I came back from the island to save you. It's the reason I'm here."

"If that's true then call your djinn and order it to fix my hand. And order it to find those monsters who were responsible for what happened to me last summer. The monsters Darbar can't find. That's only two wishes. If you care so much about me, you can do that. Right?"

"More deals with these devils might not be the best way out of this."

"You're afraid, aren't you? You're afraid you'll say the wishes wrong and end up like poor Amesh. Well, at least on my first wish, I got it right. Do you know how much my jewels are worth?"

"Probably a hundred times more than you've been told."

He pounded the table with his good hand, upsetting his drink. A waiter came and tried to clean it up, but Amesh sent him away. It was fortunate we were outside on a balcony and basically alone, or half of Istanbul would have known our business.

"There's the Sara I'm used to! Always ready with the sarcasm. Sure, you cared about me as long as everything was fine. But now that I'm in trouble, do you really want to order your djinn to help me?" He stood and glared at me. "Don't answer. We both know what the answer will be."

"The answer is yes. I'll do anything to ease your pain. But taking revenge on the people who hurt you isn't going to help."

He held up his yellow hand. "Then fix my hand. Fix it so it works the way it used to and doesn't hurt. The pain is killing me. If I can't stop it, I'm going to do something crazy. You know what I'm saying?"

I stood and gently tried to take his hand.

He winced and jumped back. "Ouch!" he cried.

"I'm sorry," I said.

"Don't say you're sorry. Just call your djinn. Help me."

"I will, I promise. Give me a few minutes."

"What for?"

"To find out certain facts. I have to know how far you've gone with Darbar. I have to try to talk to him and find out if you really have made a valid third wish."

Amesh laughed and I swear his laughter was ten times worse than his tears. It was so spooky, so twisted, it sounded as if it came from someone already damned. It was that fear, more than any other, that made me hesitate. What if I was about to sacrifice so much for nothing?

Amesh, of course, knew exactly what I was thinking.

"You want to talk to Darbar to see if I'm worth saving," he said.

"I've learned a lot about djinn in the last two weeks. I might be able to reason with him, or I might be able to scare him. My djinn is more powerful than he is."

"Says who?" he demanded.

"Trust me, I know."

"You only know what that damn carpet tells you."

"Why curse the carpet? It did nothing to you."

"Nothing? It kidnapped us and flew to an island filled with demons who promised us anything we wanted, when what they were really trying to do was steal our souls. I'm a thrall, Sara, I'm already damned. I'm going to spend the rest of eternity in hell, and all because of your carpet!"

"That's not true! Allah's merciful! He wouldn't damn anyone to eternal suffering. Especially a guy like you who has a Papi and a sister who love him. And yes, a friend who loves him so much that she's willing to make however many wishes she has to in order to save him." I paused. "All I'm asking is for you to give me time to figure out the best way to fix this mess. Please, Amesh, I'm not asking a lot."

He stared at me for a long time. His eyes had calmed and I was sure I had reached him. We could return to the hotel together, I thought. To the island if need be, and work together to set everything right.

"I have missed you," he said softly.

"Me too."

But then his right hand spasmed. It flapped without warning against the table like an impaled fish dying aboard the deck of a ship. I only had to hear his frantic breathing to know how awful his pain must be. He cried out in horror.

"I can't stop it! Nothing can stop it!"

I tried to hug him. "Amesh!"

He pushed me away with his left hand. "Stay away, Sara. What you say—I almost believe you. But if you are telling me the truth, then I'm the last person you should help. I'm the last person who deserves it. And if it isn't true . . . well, then it doesn't matter anyway. I'm going to die cursed, but not before I take those others with me."

With that, he ran from the restaurant.

CHAPTER SIXTEEN

LEAVING THE HOTEL, I wandered aimlessly. I did not call for Lova; I did not call for a taxi. *Shock* was too gentle a word to describe my condition. I felt shattered. Even when Amesh had made his two wishes on the island and fled, I had not felt so devastated.

I had returned from the island to save Amesh. I had invoked a strong djinn and brought it back with me for that purpose. Yet I had never stopped to construct a plan on how I was going to free him. I was like a soldier who prepares for battle by buying himself an AK-47. Hey, guys, look at my cool gun. I don't need any training.

In my ignorance, I had assumed that I could frighten Darbar into canceling out the wishes he had granted Amesh. If that failed, I figured I would order Lova to kill Darbar and set Amesh free. But I had never stopped to think that asking a djinn to murder a fellow djinn might cost extra. To be blunt, my whole approach had been barbaric. Terrify Darbar, kill Darbar. In the end Lova was more likely to kill me. Or worse.

I was starting to worry about that *worse*. It had been easy to fantasize about rescuing Amesh from a distance. Sleeping under Hara and Aleena's roof, I had felt safe. I would swoop back to Istanbul like an avenging angel and vanquish the evil djinn. But now, seeing Amesh up close and the agony he was going through, I had to stop and think:

What if that were me?

Plus, I was making all these sacrifices for a guy I had known a few days. I had to ask myself a serious question. Did I owe Amesh my very soul?

Sure, I was the one who had encouraged the carpet to take us where it wanted to go. But it had been his choice to invoke Darbar, not mine. I had begged him to leave the djinn alone and he had ignored me.

What did I owe Amesh? Could such a thing be measured?

Did I love him? Could love ever be measured?

I did have a huge crush on him, but that did not mean I cared for him like his Papi and Mira did. In a way, I realized, they should be the ones to save him. His grandfather would do anything for him.

Was it possible to turn Lova over to Mr. Demir? Give the man a crash course on the djinn? I wished there were a book on the subject: *How to Bargain with Your Local Djinn.*

I had walked far, giving no thought to what time it was or where I was, when I realized that a black van was following me. I was near the airport on a service road that ran between the big hotels. It was little more than an alley. Although the sun was still bright, the road was deserted and I saw that there was no one around to call to for help.

A second black van turned onto the alley in front of me.

I was boxed in. Opening my cell, I dialed 911. No one answered. Of course, I was in Turkey. 911 was not a universal number for help. What was the Istanbul number? I had never thought to look it up. The vans were closing in; they slowed as they came near. Side doors were opening.

The carpet! The carpet could fly for over an hour during the day. As men wearing black ski masks leaped from the vans, I pulled it out and tried to feel for a ley line.

But my heart was pounding too hard to feel anything but fear. Except for their dark masks, the men were dressed in white. Two pulled out knives. But it was a man without a knife who took the lead. He stepped forward.

"We don't want to hurt you," he said. "We just want the carpet."

"Go to hell!" I swore, hugging it to my chest. The power built into the carpet flowed through me. My arms and legs felt energized. I felt strong.

The leader's partner waved his knife and spoke in a deadly tone. "What if we poke out your eyes? You can wear glass eyes the rest of your life. I'm sure your boyfriends will love the poor blind girl."

I thought of Lova. I could call for the djinn; she would hear my call. I could order her to slay the men and, because they were only human, she would charge me just one wish. But I hated to waste a wish on this slime.

Plus, I continued to feel a buildup of power in my limbs. It was odd but the feeling was familiar. Were Kalas stronger than normal people?

"You underestimate the power of what I hold," I said. "It's given me amazing strength. I don't want to hurt you, but I will if you don't back off."

The man who had threatened me lunged forward with his knife. My right foot instinctively shot out. I kicked the knife out of his hand—it went flying. He raised an arm to strike. I kicked again, at his left kneecap. It did not merely bend; it cracked. The man screamed and fell to the ground.

The others glanced at each other. Even with their ski masks, I could see the fear in their eyes. This skinny white chick was behaving more like Spidergirl than a spoiled American babe.

The second man with a knife lunged. I kicked him in the groin, and he fell to the ground, moaning.

I spoke firmly. "Leave me alone and I'll leave you alone. Okay?"

The leader turned toward a van. He signaled.

A sparkling green light filled the interior of the van. Then it expanded outward, in my direction, and a wave of dizziness swept over me. My arms and legs were suddenly heavy, and I felt sick to my stomach.

The green light condensed into a narrow beam and struck my chest. It was like being hit by lightning. I lost the carpet. I lost the ability to stand. Hitting the asphalt, lying on my side, I was gripped by a brief seizure.

I must have blacked out for a moment.

When I came to, the leader was peering down at me with the carpet in his hands. "Where are Bora and Hasad?" he demanded. "Where did he take them?"

"Beats me," I whispered.

The man I had kneed in the groin kicked me in the side. I heard a rib crack. He had knocked the wind out of me. Gasping to fill my lungs, I saw the leader try to hold his partner back.

"We know you know Amesh," he said. "Tell us where he took them."

He was probably referring to two of the guys who had attacked Amesh. Chances were Darbar had them. It was a wicked thought to imagine anyone in the clutches of an angry djinn.

"The thing that took them isn't human," I mumbled.

The leader spoke with his partners in Turkish. Then the guy who had kicked my side wound up his black boot and smashed my head. Everything went dark.

When I came to I was in pain. My whole body ached, even places that had not been struck. It was curious how heavily armed the gang had been, when you considered it was just there to steal a carpet from a girl. They obviously knew the value and power of the carpet.

But who were they? And what was that green light?

One thing was for sure. Amesh and I had not discovered the carpet without at least one other person noticing. But was that an absolute fact? I had come under attack only after returning from the island. When we had first found the carpet, we had been given plenty of time to learn how to use it. Certainly, no one had followed us to the island.

Amesh had to be the cause of my new popularity. The guys in the masks had been anxious to find him. That meant either he or Darbar had kidnapped their partners. Yet the way Amesh was running all over Istanbul and selling gems, I was surprised they hadn't been able to find him on their own.

Maybe the gang's first priority had been to get the carpet. But how did they even know about it?

I forced myself to sit up and take stock of my damage. The kick to my right side had definitely broken a rib. It hurt to move, even to take a breath. My hair was sticky with dried blood, and I felt a lump the size of an egg forming at the base of my skull. The sun was still up but the sky was darkening. I estimated I had been unconscious an hour.

I sat cross-legged and closed my eyes, let my mind calm down the way the carpet had taught me on the island. I took ten slow breaths—gently, with my sore ribs. Then I imagined a pillar of white light pouring into my head from above. Don't ask me how this worked; I don't know. It was a form of meditation the carpet had taught me. Within minutes a healing sensation began to seep through my body.

It also cleared my mind, and when I was calm, I mentally reached for the carpet. But I felt something was off. The carpet heard me, I was sure, but it was blocked. Its captors had probably figured that I was capable of calling to it and had locked it in a vault or a chest. I could call for hours and get nowhere.

I saw no choice. I had to summon Lova and make a wish. Damn.

"Lova, come to me," I said aloud.

She appeared instantly, standing above like a shadow in the failing light. "You are hurt," she said.

"I was attacked. They took the carpet." I paused. "Do you know who they are?"

"I cannot retrieve the carpet for you unless you wish for its retrieval."

"That would be my first wish with you."

"Yes."

"I have already made a wish with your mate."

"I know."

"But wishes with different djinn do not overlap. If you retrieve the carpet for me, I still owe you nothing."

"That is correct." Lova paused. "But are you sure you don't desire something other than the carpet?"

"I don't know what you're talking about."

"Your friend, who is with Darbar. It is a boy, is it not? You want his love back. You want him to love you like he did before he met Darbar."

I felt a flash of anger. "You're not to bring him up unless I mention him first. Do you understand?"

Lova smiled faintly. "Yes."

"Sit, Lova." She sat. "I also want to know who attacked me."

"I would have to question them to get their names. Since they cannot see or hear me, that would be difficult. I have told you, I'm not familiar with your realm. I would probably have to kidnap them and torture them to get them to talk. That would require a second wish."

I pulled out my cell and set it to take pictures.

"Can you hold physical objects?" I asked.

"If I focus on them."

"Well, focus hard and take this cell phone. Point it at each person in the house or the warehouse or wherever it is that the carpet's being kept. Then push this green button. It'll automatically make a record of their faces."

"That should cost you a second wish," Lova replied.

I hardened my tone. "Don't think that because I just got beat up, you can take advantage of me. Push me and I push back. If you don't agree to get the carpet now and take the pictures, then you won't get a single wish out of me. Understand?"

"Yes." Lova paused. "What's your name?"

"You don't need my name."

"To get a wish from me, you must order it using your name."

Amesh had not told Darbar his first name before making his first wish. Nor had Lova's mate needed my first name to stop my bleeding. I pointed those facts out to her. She nodded as if she had expected the argument.

"Darbar and my mate have experience fulfilling human wishes. I do not. I require your name to sharpen my focus, so that your wish, and only your wish, enters my mind and is fulfilled."

"Are you saying that you might pick up a stray wish from someone in the area and accidentally fulfill it?"

"Yes. There are many humans in this city. Every few seconds they desire something. As a djinn, I feel their desires. I am constantly having to block them."

It was weird, but I heard the truth in her words.

"I'll tell you my first name, that's all."

"I need your complete name."

"Then I guess you're out of luck."

Lova considered. "Your first name will be sufficient."

"Sara," I said.

"And the meaning of the name?"

"I don't know the meaning."

"I must know the meaning."

"Most human names have no meaning. They're just names." I added, "Besides, I think you're trying to manipulate me. I suggest you stop."

Lova hesitated. "You are the master."

"I suspect the carpet is being held in a vault or some kind of box. If it's made of steel, do you have the power to break through it?"

"Yes."

"What if you accidentally damage the carpet?"

"The Carpet of Ka cannot be physically damaged."

It had been a trick question to see how much the djinn knew.

She knew a lot about my carpet.

"All right. Let's begin. Get as many pictures as you can of

the people in the immediate area—before you bust into where the carpet is being held."

"Understood." Lova tucked the cell phone in her silver belt.

"Trakur Analova La," I said in a firm voice. "It's my wish, the wish of your master, Sara, that you retrieve my magic carpet, which is known as the Carpet of Ka. Locate it, free it, and bring it back to me. This is my wish, Trakur Analova La." I paused. "Agreed?"

"Yes."

"Go. Do not return without it," I said.

Her fiery eyes flared with red light. Lova stood and walked north, down the alley. She had only gone a few steps when she vanished.

Naturally, I had forgotten to tell her something. I did not feel like hanging out in an alley. Sure, she might be back in a few minutes, but she might be gone for hours. I needed to find a more comfortable place to recover.

The men had not stolen my pack. As a result, I still had cash, credit cards, and my passport. I did not want to return to my father's hotel beat-up. The blood in my hair had to go. But I did not want to check into a new hotel using a credit card or my real name. My father would be able to track me in minutes. And in Istanbul, hotels wanted to see passports before accepting foreign guests. It was a dilemma, but I wondered if maybe a little smooth talking wouldn't save the day.

Walking proved difficult. My right side was on fire. It was interesting how the jerk had kicked me in exactly the same spot where Lova's mate had stabbed me.

I was dizzy. Sitting in the alley, I had not noticed how bad my head was. But now that I was standing, I feared that final kick had given me a concussion. The lump was massive. The tear in my scalp, below the bump, wouldn't stop bleeding. What if I needed stitches?

A visit to a hospital would definitely cause my dad to be notified. I planned to call him at some point, but I wanted him to think I was staying with Rini again. I had warned her that she might hear from him and have to cover for me for two nights. Man, I was going to owe her when this was all over.

At the first ATM I came to, I managed to withdraw five hundred lira, about three hundred bucks. I flagged down a taxi and told the driver to take me to a nearby hotel. I let the guy choose. He had good taste—he chose a four-star Embassy Suites.

My dried blood and bruises helped me register at the hotel. I started to explain how I had been mugged and didn't have my passport or credit cards.

But I just happened to have cash. I smiled.

The clerk quickly raised his hand. Say no more. Except he wanted me to go to a hospital. I assured him that I had already spoken to a paramedic and I was fine.

Up in my suite, I quickly undressed and headed for the bathroom. I couldn't wait to take another warm shower!

Unfortunately, the running water opened my scalp wound wider, and I started bleeding more heavily. I had to struggle to get it to stop. In the end I used scissors and cut a towel into thin strips and tied them around my skull. That worked.

The Embassy Suites had room service, but less selection than the Hilton. I ordered a hamburger and fries. It was hard to go wrong with the basics. The waiter had just wheeled in the food when Lova materialized in front of him. His eyes rolled back in his head, and he fainted on my bed.

"I thought no one could see you but me," I said.

"He didn't see me, but he sensed me, and it frightened him."

The excuse sounded pretty thin.

"Give me the carpet and my cell," I ordered.

Lova handed over both. She continued to eye the unconscious guy. It struck me then that she was looking at him the same way I was looking at my hamburger.

"You startled him, hoping he would faint," I said. "You want to drink his blood."

Lova took a step toward the man. "I don't need a lot. Two pints will suffice. It won't harm him. He won't even remember I was here."

"Are your kind responsible for our vampire legends?"

"We are responsible for virtually all your legends."

That I could well believe. "What do you do, bite him on the neck?"

"Nothing so crude. Here, let me show you."

"No! Take him in the bathroom and shut the door. Do what you have to do. But he'd better be up and out of here in ten minutes."

"I need longer than that," Lova said, grabbing him by the shoulders.

"No. And you're only taking a pint. That's all that's safe. Plus we have to talk."

Lova left with the man and turned on the water in the bathroom. I didn't know why. My hamburger and fries were delicious. I wanted to order another round, but was afraid they would ask me where their server was.

Well, you see, he didn't just deliver dinner. He is dinner.

Lova reappeared in ten minutes and escorted the dazed room-service guy out the door. Then she came and sat on my bed. She seemed in a better mood. We talked as I finished my fries.

"Tell me what happened," I ordered.

She explained that the Carpet of Ka emitted a powerful beacon of light and that it had not been difficult to locate. But the thugs had known exactly how to protect it. They had it locked in a bank vault.

"Are you sure it was at a bank?" I asked.

"Yes."

"Do you even know what a bank is?"

"I know your language, for the most part. The building had the word *bank* on the side. But it was a deserted bank."

"What did you do when you first arrived?" I asked.

"As you instructed, I took pictures of everyone present. There were six young men."

"Did you happen to hear what they were talking about?"

"Money. They were excited at the reward they would receive for the carpet."

"Did they say who was going to pay this reward?"

"No. But I had the impression they were waiting for the person to appear." Lova paused. "But someone else came first and I had to hide."

"Who was this someone else?"

A note of fear entered her voice. "Someone who could see me."

"How do you know he could see you?"

"It was a woman. She stared right at me, and she immediately pressed her palms together and started to invoke a spell."

"A djinn spell?" I asked.

Lova hesitated. "Perhaps."

"But she was human. She wasn't a djinn."

Lova was doubtful. "She might have been a djinn in a human body. She built up a ball of light between her hands— what we call a *pashupa*. It's a subtle weapon. It can destroy a djinn."

"What if it were to hit a human?"

"It would kill them instantly."

"Tell me, is a pashupa usually bright green?"

"How did you know that?"

"I was hit by one today."

Lova's mouth dropped open. She was stunned. "No human being could survive being struck by a pashupa."

I acted casual. "I'm tougher than I look. What happened next?"

"I hid inside the vault. The woman knew where I was. She ordered the others to unlock it. But the moment the door swung open, I was prepared. The woman tried to hit me with the pashupa as I ran out of the vault but I was able to use the carpet as a shield. Then I flew out the window."

"Did anyone try to follow you?"

"No human could follow me. But that woman is skilled in the magical arts. She tried to attach an eye to my field."

"An eye to your field?"

"She wanted to track me. But I knew what she was up to. I was able to expel the eye."

Eye and *field.* Two new words I had to add to my djinn dictionary. Never mind *pashupa.* No wonder I had felt so weak when that light had struck me.

"You did well." I studied the snapshots she had taken. The men were strangers to me, but I suspected Amesh would be able to identify a few. They had asked about him enough. I continued, "Before the woman arrived, did you hear the guys talk about . . . Amesh?" I hated to give out his name.

"No. Who is Amesh?"

"Never mind."

Mr. Demir and Mira might know some of the guys. I owed them a call anyway. I wanted to see Mr. Demir before I slept, if I was going to sleep. I had a feeling it was going to be a long night.

Because Lova seemed in a talkative mood, I teased her again about scaring the room-service guy into fainting. But she returned my remark with a cold stare. She spoke as if I were the child and she were the parent.

"Do not presume to know the mind of a djinn. We walked this world before you. We were the masters of this realm."

"What happened?" I asked.

"You command the Carpet of Ka and you don't know?"

"Just answer the question."

"There was a war."

"Between humans and djinn?"

"Humans cannot harm djinn. Not then and not now."

"So you warred with another race? Who were they?"

"You mean, who *are* they. They were not destroyed."

"Did they win the war?"

Lova hesitated. "Yes."

I tried to get her to speak more about this third race but she clammed up. She pleaded exhaustion. Escaping the woman with the pashupa had drained her, she said. She asked if she could rest. I said fine, but that she should be prepared to respond in case I called.

"I might need you to destroy Darbar," I said carefully.

Lova lay on the floor beside the bed. "That is one wish you should avoid," she said.

"I might have no choice."

"I've warned you of the consequences, Sara."

"Why did you warn me, Lova?"

She shut her eyes. "The Carpet of Ka would not serve a fool. You must be worthy of respect."

"Why, thank you," I replied.

Her compliment was the last thing I had expected.

To leave my suite, I had to remove my makeshift bandages. Unfortunately, there was still blood in my hair. But I could not risk reopening the wound by washing it out. I arranged it as best I could and hobbled downstairs to buy some fresh clothes in the hotel store: black pants and a black shirt—the ultimate stealth uniform. With the carpet in my pack, I headed out into the Turkish night and grabbed a taxi.

Going straight to Amesh's home was not an option. The same men who had tried to steal the carpet could have it staked out. Better that Mr. Demir and I meet in a public place, I thought, although I did not want our meeting observed.

Using my cell, I called Mr. Demir. Mira answered.

"Did you find Amesh?" she asked.

"I met him for lunch."

"Thanks be to Allah!" She sounded so relieved. "Is he all right?"

"He's okay but things are complicated. Is your grandfather there?"

"He's coming right now. Please tell Amesh to come home."

"I will, when it's safe," I promised.

Mr. Demir came on the line. "You saw Amesh?"

"Yes."

"I search everywhere, I could not find him. Where was he?"

"I'd rather talk in person, but I can't come to your house. Others know about the treasure. I was attacked this afternoon and badly beaten."

"Are you okay?"

"I'll live."

"We should go to police."

"The police can't help. This situation has gone way beyond them. Please, meet me in an hour in the lobby at the Sheraton by the airport. Make sure you're not followed. This is very important. I'll be waiting for you."

"I leave now," Mr. Demir said.

"Bring any paperwork you have on Amesh's trial. Any photographs of the defendants. If you have a transcript of the trial, bring that."

"Why?"

I hesitated. "The people who beat me up today asked if Amesh had kidnapped some of their friends."

"My grandson is cripple, one hand. He could not kidnap goat."

"Trust me, there's a connection between what's happening now and what happened last summer. Please, I need to know about the trial."

Mr. Demir was silent a long time. "I bring papers."

"Thank you."

We exchanged goodbyes. I had my taxi drop me at the beach, not far from the hotel, and told him not to wait for me. I wanted Mr. Demir to approach the Sheraton carefully, but I planned to arrive in a manner nobody had ever used before.

The beach was silent, the stars bright, which was what I was hoping for. I needed time to talk to the carpet and consider everything that had happened. It did not take me long to find a powerful ley line to rest the carpet on in case we had to leave in a hurry. It floated a few inches off the ground in front of me.

While the stars glowed in the center, I asked my first question.

"Did I waste a wish by having Lova rescue you from the men?"

"What do you think?"

"I feared that the carpet didn't have the strength to break out of the vault."

"It was never a question of the carpet's strength. It was a question of yours. Had you been able to focus your will on nothing else, you could have forced the carpet to break down any door. A Kala could accomplish such a task. But you are just a beginner."

"So this time I probably did need Lova's help."

"The greatest help comes from inside. The djinn offer the opposite with their wishes. That is the trap in using them too often. They offer quick solutions—when you need to learn how to create your own miracles."

"But there's only so much a person can do," I protested.

"A person is limited by his conception of himself, nothing more. If you really knew who you were, you could stop the sun from rising tomorrow."

"That's hard to believe."

"That's why the sun usually comes up each morning."

"Today, after I saw Amesh, I went through a period of doubt where I was scared to help him. I was ready to abandon him to his djinn."

"A person can only demonstrate their courage by overcoming their fears. Someone who is never afraid is either a Kala or a fool."

"These Kalas sound superhuman. Can I really become one?"

"It is the path you have chosen for yourself."

"When did I choose it?"

"Before you were born."

"Is there a connection between what happened to Amesh's hand last summer and my finding the carpet this summer?"

"Several players in this drama overlap. There must be a connection."

"Did Amesh almost stumble on the carpet before?"

"He stumbled onto something. But it was your destiny to find the carpet."

"What did he stumble onto?"

"Mr. Demir will know."

"I'm going to see him soon." I paused. "Amesh was in so much pain today. I worry I won't be able to save him. It was a struggle to get the truth out of him. Do you know if he has made three wishes or two?"

"A djinn cannot control a human unless he has delivered on the three wishes the human has made. So far, Darbar has been unable to deliver. Yet he keeps trying, and he is close to success."

"So Amesh still has free will?" I asked.

"He is driven by a desire for revenge. He is far from free."

"But Darbar tricked Amesh by giving him that useless hand."

"Amesh asked for his hand back. Darbar was required to give him that hand. Had the hand been destroyed, Darbar would have given him a new hand. But such was not the case."

"Sometimes I feel like you're on the side of the djinn."

"Not true. But I understand them."

"Is Lova an ordinary djinn?"

"She was born into a powerful lineage, but is inexperienced when it comes to humans."

"Somehow I can't see her making me into a thrall."

"That's a dangerous conceit. For all you know, she acts kind toward you so you will drop your guard."

The carpet's words chilled me—I had given myself the same warning earlier in the day. Yet it was important to hear it from another source. I had begun to act too carelessly around Lova. I should never have let her feed on the room-service guy.

"Today, when I was attacked, someone in a van hit me with a bolt of green light. It drained my strength. I think the same person attacked Lova when she went to get the carpet. Do you know who it was?"

"What did Lova say?"

"Lova thought she might be a djinn inhabiting a woman's body."

"Wouldn't Lova know if it was a djinn?"

The answer was such an obvious yes that I was annoyed I hadn't realized it before. "Why would she try to mislead me about this being?"

"That's a good question to ask yourself."

I tried to get the carpet to say more on the topic, but it refused.

"I'm afraid I'm not using the full potential of the carpet. When we were flying home from the island, I felt as if it had erected a shield to deflect the wind."

"Yes."

"Why?"

"You wanted it so."

"I want to fly over this city unseen. Can the carpet become invisible?"

"That's an advanced skill."

"But it can be done?"

"Yes."

"Can you teach me how to do it?"

"Keep experimenting. You will learn."

I had more questions—I was never done asking my questions—but I sensed it was done with me. I felt the presence behind the carpet withdraw.

CHAPTER SEVENTEEN

I T TOOK ME A WHILE to find a ley line that flew directly over the Sheraton. But in the end I was able to land the carpet on the roof. The view from the twenty-story building was beautiful—brightly lit city on one side, dark ocean on the other. I almost left the carpet on the roof to give it extra time to charge beneath the stars, but I was too paranoid to part from it.

I arrived at the hotel lounge before Mr. Demir and ordered a Coke. While waiting for my drink, I called my dad and told him I would be staying with Rini again. He didn't mind. He seemed tired, anxious to go to bed.

It might have been the danger I had faced—and had yet to face—but I felt the sudden urge to call my mom. I owed her a call. When my Coke came, I took a sip and then dialed my home number.

"Sara!" my mother squealed with delight. "I was just telling Sally and Alice you've been avoiding me. How are you?"

"I've been busy, Mom. I met a new friend, Rini. You'd love her. So what's new with you?"

My question may have appeared harmless, but directed at my mother, it was dangerous. She could rattle on for hours about what she'd done—or failed to do—in the last week. It didn't matter how inconsequential the act might have been. She told me about picking up milk at the 7-Eleven late at night because she had forgotten to get it during the day. She remarked on how much more the milk cost there than at a regular supermarket. She complained how the guy at the cash register spoke poor English and did not deserve the job. She swore that he was an illegal alien. My mother disliked anything illegal or alien, and somehow, when she combined the two words, they ended up sounding atrocious, like something better not talked about. Except that it was okay for her to do so because she talked about everything.

When I spoke to my mother, I did not need to respond. I just had to grunt occasionally. Twice since I had arrived in Istanbul, she had called and I had managed to go to the bathroom and return without her noticing.

I let my mother ramble for ten minutes when I suddenly thought to myself, *This is ridiculous.* There was an excellent chance I might die tonight, and here I was wasting time having another fake conversation with my own mother, the person who had given birth to me, who had brought me into the world. Sitting up abruptly, I told her to stop. To just stop talking.

She wanted to know what was wrong.

"It would take too long to explain," I said. "Just believe me when I say my world is falling apart. I don't want to chitchat about nothing. If we're going to talk, I want to have a real conversation, and if you can't do that, I'm going to hang up."

"Oh, Sara, don't be so dramatic. I'm sure whatever the problem is, it's not that serious. Tell me the truth. It's a boy you've met, right, not a girl."

"You're right. I have met a boy," I said.

"See, I knew it. And you just had your first fight and you think your whole world is falling apart."

"No. You're way off-base."

"Then what happened with him?"

"He's not important, not this second. I just don't want to talk about errands or what Alice said about Sally or why she's a fool to listen to Alice."

"Sara! This isn't like you. You're being awfully rude."

"I should've been rude long ago if being rude is what it takes to get you to act real. For once, let's talk about something important. Okay?"

"I asked if you wanted to talk about the boy." She added, "You're not spending the night with him, are you?"

I sighed. "No. And I don't want to talk about him."

"At least tell me his name."

"Amesh."

"So he's a Turk?"

"Yeah. I'm in Turkey, remember? The place is full of them."

"Oh dear," she muttered.

"Why did you marry Dad?" I asked.

"What kind of question is that?"

"An honest one. I mean, really, you two have nothing in common." I paused. I thought I heard her pouring herself a drink. She drank when she was nervous. What the hell, she drank every night. I continued. "Last week I asked him why he married you, and he said it was because he loved you."

"Good for him. That's why I married him."

"I don't believe either of you. Like I said, it's hard to imagine two more different people. Dad's a loner; he hardly speaks. You have to be surrounded by friends 24/7. You even talk in your sleep."

"Sara . . ."

"You can talk in a minute, Mom. I have another question. Have you ever been in love?"

"I told you, I loved your father."

"Then why did you two divorce?"

"He asked for one. I didn't want it. You know that."

"I didn't know that, but thank you for finally telling me. You didn't seem all that broken up when he left, though. It was like, after you went to the lawyer and Dad promised to take care of us financially, you didn't care if he left or not."

"That's not true!"

"Have you ever loved someone besides Dad?"

She hesitated. "Are you asking because you love this boy?"

"He's part of the reason, but he's not the main reason. I know this is going to sound cliché, but it's the truth. I want to know who you are so I can better understand who I am. Please answer my question."

"Yes." A very soft yes.

"Who was it?"

"I'd rather not say."

"You mean you're too embarrassed to say."

My mother was a long time answering.

"It was complicated, Sara. You see, I met Harry first."

"Before or after you met Dad?" I had never heard of a Harry.

"Before. We dated a few times, but that was all it took from my side. I fell madly in love. And I knew he cared for me as well. Then I introduced him to my sister."

"Aunt Tracy?"

"Yes. The four of us went away for a weekend, to go skiing. Tracy had another boyfriend at the time. I can't remember his name. But right from the start, I noticed something between her and Harry. He laughed at all her jokes. I felt sort of left out. He didn't laugh at any of mine."

It would have been cruel to interrupt and point out that she had never cracked a decent joke in her life.

"What happened?" I said.

"Harry and I dated another month before he came to me with the news. He said that he was in love with my sister. I was shocked, hurt, angry. I asked if he had been seeing her behind my back and he said no. He told me he had no idea if she liked him. But he wanted my permission to find out."

"Wow." I was stunned. "What did you say?"

"What could I say? I had seen the chemistry they had. But when I told her Harry wanted to date her, she refused. She said the usual things people say. She was my sister. She couldn't stab me in the back. She would feel too awkward. But all the time I could tell she wanted to go out with him. When I insisted that she have coffee with him, she said okay, coffee couldn't hurt." My mother sighed. "That was the end of that."

"Did they get married?"

"They got engaged, but they never married. The whole thing shook me up pretty badly. I was a mess."

"When did you meet Dad?"

"Two years later, and no, I didn't marry him on the rebound."

"But you were still in love with Harry?"

Silence. My mother didn't answer.

"I'm sorry," I whispered.

She spoke in a soft voice. "I'm surprised you don't remember. Tracy and Harry were together a long time after you were born."

That caught me off-guard. I had visited Tracy often.

"How long after I was born?" I asked.

"He was with her up until the accident. That's when he left."

I almost fell out of my seat. Her remark made no sense.

"Hold on a second. That's impossible. I spent summers with Aunt Tracy. Every time I was able to get free, you let me go to her house. And I never once met a Harry."

"He was real. What can I say? But they were never married. He was like your father. He traveled a lot with his work."

"But when Tracy had her accident and went into that coma, he was never at the hospital. I would know; I was there all the time."

"That was a painful time," my mother said, as if that explained it.

"So he vanished as soon as she got hurt? That doesn't make sense. You don't leave someone you love."

"You don't know, Sara. Harry did love her. When she got hurt, he couldn't bear it. He said it was like a part of him died. He just left and we never heard from him again. To this day I have no idea where he is."

"Why can't I remember him?"

"You were awfully young."

"I was nine. No, I was ten. And I was eleven when you guys suddenly pulled the plug."

"We did not suddenly pull the plug. Her condition was deteriorating. There was no hope she would wake up again. Her doctors told us they had done all they could. Also, we were worried about you. She was lying in a hospital bed two hundred miles away and she was all you could think about. You don't remember, but you started having trouble at school. Half the time I couldn't get you to go. She was my sister and I loved her dearly, but the nightmare had to stop. We had to let her go so we could all start to heal."

My eyes burned. "You never told me you were going to kill her."

"We didn't kill her. The drunk driver who hit her killed her."

"But you could have warned me. Did you know I had bought a bus ticket to visit her? I bought it with the money I earned babysitting. I was about to leave when you suddenly showed me this urn of ashes and said, 'Hey, guess what, this is Aunt Tracy. Sorry to shock you like this but the hospital bills keep coming and she wasn't getting any better and . . .'"

"No one said a word to you about the hospital bills."

"I heard you and Dad fight about them at night. Look, I understand about Aunt Tracy. I think you could have handled her death better, but I believe you when you say the doctors felt it was hopeless. What I have trouble believing in is this Harry guy."

My mother sounded far off, lost in her own memories. "I understand. He was like a dream to me."

"Sounds more like a ghost. What was his last name?"

"O'Malley. Harold O'Malley. I'm not making him up. You can ask your father about him. Only . . ."

"I won't tell him you loved him, Mom. I'm not that dumb."

"Thank you, Sara." I could hear her crying, "Please, tell me about Amesh. I'm sure he's a wonderful person. I would love to hear about him."

"I'll tell you about him tomorrow," I promised.

For once my mother had nothing to say, except goodbye. Goodbye, Sara, take care. It was painful to break the connection this time, since it had taken fifteen years to establish.

CHAPTER EIGHTEEN

WHEN MR. DEMIR APPEARED, I could tell he was uncomfortable being in such fancy surroundings. He reminded me of his grandson that first afternoon at the Hilton. But I coaxed him into ordering a drink—he had mango juice—and we sat in overstuffed chairs in the corner, where we could talk.

"Your bump on head looks bad," he said, concerned.

I smiled. "You should see the rest of me."

"Why men attack you?"

He was a good man and I was tired of lying to him. So I told him an abbreviated version of what had really happened to

Amesh and me, leaving out the island, of course, and now we had been gone for days. That part of our tale was too far out. He would never accept it.

Unfortunately, pretty much all of our story was bizarre. It was like choosing between daydreams, trying to figure out what to say. In the end I had to lie a little. I told him about the magic carpet, but I said it had led us to a treasure chest in the desert. I even let him peek at the carpet in my bag.

"I understand it's hard to believe," I said. "You won't really believe me until you see me fly away on it."

He thought to humor me. "You can show flying?"

"When I leave here from the roof of this hotel, you can watch if you want. Then you'll know for sure this carpet can fly."

He saw I was serious. His face filled with doubt.

"Why not talk of carpet before?" he asked.

"I thought it would be too much to absorb. Look at you now. You want to believe me but you can't."

He sighed. "It is strange story. And you keep changing."

"I'm sorry. The carpet really did lead us to the treasure."

"Talk about people who attacked you," he said.

"I have pictures of them on my cell." I called up the best set of photos and handed it over. Mr. Demir got a shock. He recognized two of them.

"I know them!" he said. "Jemal Lomal and Omer Sahim. Two of the boys who hurt Amesh."

Finally! Proof that what had happened last summer was

connected to what was going on right now. Like the carpet had said, some of the players overlapped.

"There were four total, right?" I asked.

"Yes."

"Are the names Bora and Hasad familiar to you?"

He got another shock. "Bora Lomal and Hasad Sahim. The other two who hurt Amesh. Amesh told you their names?"

"No. The leader of the gang told me. He acted like your son had kidnapped Bora and Hasad. That's why they beat me. I wouldn't tell him where they were, or where Amesh was."

Mr. Demir was looking at me with fresh confidence. He saw I had been beat up and he saw I had pictures of the guys who had beat up Amesh. Even if he didn't believe in flying carpets, he had to believe that his grandson was out there with money and bad people were after him.

Mr. Demir also helped by supplying me with photos of the two faces that had been behind the ski masks—those of Bora Lomal and Hasad Sahim. How did I know it was them? They shared last names with the others. Indeed, I was confident I was looking at two sets of brothers.

Unfortunately, Mr. Demir remained stubborn. He refused to believe that Amesh had kidnapped anyone.

"He cripple. He has one hand," he said.

"Amesh has lots of money." I tried again. "He can hire help. When I saw him this afternoon, he spoke about finally getting revenge on these guys."

Mr. Demir kept shaking his head. "Amesh gentle soul."

"You're a gentle soul and this morning you said you wished these guys would burn. You never seriously thought of taking revenge on them because you didn't have the resources. Well, now Amesh does. I'm almost positive he's taken Bora and Hasad captive. I'm just not sure where he's put them."

"No. It is not true."

I saw I was not going to convince him. I asked if I could see the transcript of the trial. Mr. Demir handed over a cardboard box.

"Do you mind waiting while I study it?" I asked.

"Take time." He added sadly, "Nowhere to go with Amesh gone."

I was grateful the transcript was in two formats, Turkish and English. Since Becktar was an American company, and was in a sense liable for what happened to Amesh, I was not surprised there was an English version.

Like in America, the transcript contained every word spoken during the trial. There were only a few people involved. Amesh. The four young men accused of cutting off his hand. The defendants' lawyers. Amesh's lawyer. The judge. Spielo. And Mrs. Steward and Mr. Toval.

I was relieved to see that my father was not listed.

The trial had been brief and to the point. The four young men swore they had been working at Mr. Toval's house the night Amesh was attacked—forty miles away from the job site, where

Amesh was injured. They had witnesses who testified to this fact. Their main witness was Mr. Toval himself. Under oath, he supported their story.

It was Mr. Toval's testimony that swayed the court against Amesh. He was the president of the Middle Eastern division of Becktar. He was a rich and powerful employer. Why should he lie to hide such a ruthless act? The guys' lawyer asked this question repeatedly.

The irony was that in America, being called a rich and powerful employer would have made a jury suspicious of the man or woman. But in Turkey, wealth equaled credibility. By the time Amesh reached the stand, he had already been thoroughly discredited.

Mrs. Steward also spoke against Amesh. She sabotaged his character. She said he was not a hard worker. That he had lied about his age to get the job. And that he had snuck into the Shar Cave on the job site, a place that was off-limits to all but high-level executives.

I had to stop reading. Mr. Toval and Mrs. Steward were family friends. They were my father's friends. How could they tell such lies? Were they pressured by the company? That was the only excuse that made sense. Had Amesh won the criminal part of the trial, his lawyer could have sued Becktar for millions.

I spoke to Mr. Demir. "The Shar Cave. My father took me to that spot when he was giving me a tour."

"Did father take you inside cave?" Mr. Demir asked.

"No. A team of archaeologists was studying it. Their leader wouldn't let me inside. I know my father's been inside. He's an archaeological buff."

"Buff?"

"It's a hobby of his."

"Did he say there was temple inside?" Mr. Demir asked.

My heart began to pound. Now there was an amazing coincidence. "He said nothing about a temple. Is that why Amesh kept going to see it?"

"Amesh saw temple only once, with Spielo," Mr. Demir said.

"Spielo fell in the cement the other day. Do you think someone was trying to kill him?"

Mr. Demir shrugged. "Amesh and Spielo saw temple inside cave. My grandson lost hand. Spielo almost lost life."

"Amesh said that he's still in the hospital?"

"Yes."

"What's the name of the hospital?" I asked.

Mr. Demir told me and I wrote it down, as well as the address.

"I'm confused," I said. "I know Mrs. Steward and Mr. Toval. They're friends of my father, and they're nice people. But they testified against Amesh in court."

Mr. Demir nodded. "It make no sense. Mrs. Steward say Amesh bad worker. But Amesh hard worker. And Mr. Toval lie. Those boys not at his house that night. They were at job site."

I flipped through the transcript. I wanted to get this next fact right.

"Is that where Amesh was attacked?" I asked.

"He attacked in Shar Cave. Near temple."

"I can't believe he never told me this."

Mr. Demir raised his hand. "Many strange things. The four boys lost jobs after trial. But Amesh got job back."

"They gave him his job back instead of millions of lira."

"I not understand," Mr. Demir said.

"Amesh should have sued them."

"Amesh cannot sue. He lost trial." Mr. Demir added, "Your father help Amesh keep job. Others want to fire him."

I hesitated. "You speak of my father like a friend."

"When Amesh in hospital, he visit every day. He get best doctors. Pay all the bills." Mr. Demir paused. "But sometimes I feel his guilt. Like he know bosses lied. Like trying to help Amesh to make things right."

"My father was not called to testify?"

"No."

"I can't believe he'd bury something like this."

"You want me believe carpet is magic."

"That's different. My father has honor. If he knew a crime had been committed, he wouldn't let it get swept under the rug."

"He work with bad people many years. Who know pressure they put on him?"

There was not much more I could learn from Mr. Demir. It was time to say goodbye. He surprised me when I went to leave. He did not want to accompany me to the roof.

"You not really flying away," he said.

I took his hand. "Some things have to be seen to be believed."

But he shook free. "Part of me believe you."

I studied him. He seemed almost scared. "You're worried about what I said earlier. That the treasure we found was cursed."

He hesitated. "I do believe in such things."

"So do I. But this carpet is the opposite of curses. It's sacred."

"Where in scripture does it say magic carpet sacred?"

"I don't know the scriptures that well, but I know what I feel. There's an energy surrounding this carpet that's as holy as any shrine or temple. I wouldn't be surprised if you felt it." I paused. "I'm going to give you a ride home."

"What?"

"On the carpet. I'll drop you off a couple of blocks from your house so no one sees us."

Mr. Demir shook his head. "Not possible."

"Let's just say your vision of possibilities is about to expand."

I led him up onto the roof and we stared out over the city. It took me a minute to find the ley line I had flown in on. As I unfolded the carpet and set it floating, I heard Mr. Demir gasp.

"It's true!" he cried.

I chuckled. "Do you want to sit on the front or the back?"

"No! I not get on that thing."

I led him to the carpet and put his hand on the material and let him feel how soothing it was.

"Do you feel the energy?" I asked.

He went to reply, then frowned. "Feel something."

"Does it feel evil?"

"Sara . . ."

"Seriously, in this business, the only thing you can go by is your gut feeling. That's why I keep trying to help Amesh. I feel he's worth saving."

Mr. Demir placed both his palms on the swirling stars and briefly closed his eyes. When he opened them, he wore a faint smile. "You wise, Sara," he said. "Wise beyond years."

I hopped on the front. "Tell me if you feel the same way after you've seen me fly."

As promised, I set him down on a street a few blocks from his own. There were no streetlights; the area was black as the beach at night.

"Will you call if you find Amesh?" he asked.

"Of course. And I'm going to find him."

Mr. Demir hugged me. "I know most of your story I not understand. It does not matter. I trust you, Sara. Allah blesses you. With His help I pray you bring Amesh home safe."

"Thank you for your blessing. Don't worry if I call late. I have a lot of ground to cover." The carpet began to rise, almost of its own volition. "Take care, Mr. Demir."

"Goodbye, Sara!"

It was possible someone was watching us. The carpet kept rising without any instruction from me—perhaps it sensed danger. Soon I was higher than any skyscraper and had a splendid view of the city. Yet I was concerned about the time. It was already after midnight.

There was so much to do before dawn. I had to use the carpet to its fullest capacity to find Amesh. That meant I needed the stars to keep it charged.

"Lova, this is Sara. Come to me now," I ordered.

There was a long pause—perhaps she had been asleep—before she materialized on the opposite end of the carpet. We sat cross-legged, facing each other.

"You want to make a wish?" she asked.

"I want you to adjust your radar for Darbar. We're going to crisscross this city from this height. I want you to focus on what's below us."

"What are you going to do?" she asked.

"None of your business. Just do as you're told."

I increased our speed to as fast as cars generally drove on

the freeway. I couldn't have withstood the wind had I not been able to raise a force field around us.

How did I accomplish this latest miracle?

I focused on the carpet and willed the shield to appear. I was learning fast!

It was eerie, flying along in such a silent cocoon, and at such a speed, swooping back and forth across Istanbul. If Darbar was in the city, I knew we would find him.

But then we got interrupted. Big time.

Lova suddenly opened her eyes. "I feel something," she said.

"Is it Darbar?"

"No. A flying object, with two humans inside. It's big, made of metal, has wings, and is armed with an assortment of weapons. It's coming toward us at high speed."

That sounded like an extremely accurate description of a fighter jet.

"Which direction is it coming from?" I asked.

Lova nodded toward the desert. "It will be here in a few seconds."

By increasing our altitude and speed, I must have made us visible to the local radar. Turkey has a modern air force. It was no surprise they had dispatched a jet to check us out.

I spoke to the carpet. I was frantic—I assumed that meant I was mentally focused.

"Carpet! Increase our speed to four hundred miles an hour!

Dive down to, I don't know, five hundred feet. Turn toward the sea."

The carpet obeyed my command, although I wasn't sure if it responded to my verbal or mental instruction. We went into an extreme dive, so steep I slid forward and bumped into our invisible shield. For the moment, at least, there appeared to be no danger of falling over the side. Nevertheless, I said, "Keep the shield in place so we cannot be knocked off the carpet!"

A large, partially lit building swung by on our left.

"We almost hit that!" I gasped.

Lova pointed in front of us. "We're about to hit that one."

She was right; another building loomed before us. We were rushing toward it at an incredible speed. My problem was, frankly, I was no pilot. I didn't know how to give specific instructions that involved speed and distances, especially above a busy city like this.

"Carpet! Veer to the left! Go back up to a thousand feet!"

We missed the skyscraper by inches. The jet was still on our tail. I wished I could just order the carpet to fly us to safety. Indeed, I mentally made that order but the carpet ignored it. I assumed that meant it wanted me to think for myself. That was hard to do when I was hyperventilating. I had to struggle to take long deep breaths and calm down.

I spoke to Lova. "Are there skyscrapers taller than a thousand feet?"

"I don't know, this is your world."

"A big help you are," I snapped.

"I can help. If you are willing to make a wish," Lova said.

"What kind of wish would that be?"

"I can cause their armaments to explode."

"The pilots will die if we do that."

"You'll probably die if you don't do something soon."

"Why do you say that?"

Suddenly, there was a high-pitched ringing sound.

"They've locked their weapons on us," Lova said calmly.

"I'm not killing innocent people to save myself," I replied, although the idea was tempting. I was scared—no, terrified. Using the carpet to get rid of them crossed my mind.

But my gut told me the carpet was not to be used for killing, though I had no time to discover if it even possessed weapons. Plus, it would be reckless to assume that the carpet's shield would stop the missile. Maybe it could, maybe not. I had to stop relying on the carpet to save us.

On the left side of the fighter jet, I saw a red light begin to blaze. It was seconds away from firing a missile.

I did my best to speak in a calm voice. "Carpet," I said. "Reduce our speed and drop our height so that we move beneath the jet. Do it now and do it quickly."

The jet gained on us and seconds later we were floating beneath it. The ringing stopped, but the turbulence caused by the plane seemed to disturb the carpet's trajectory. The carpet was thrown back and forth. So were we.

"Carpet," I said. "Raise us up high enough to where I can touch the jet if I stand."

The turbulence decreased quickly; then it all but vanished. Soon we were sitting five feet beneath the jet, the smell of diesel thick in the air. A magical combination of speed and stillness gripped me. The jet's landing wheels were close enough to touch. I knew the men inside the plane must be wondering where the heck we had gone. They might guess.

"Carpet, this instruction is important. I want us to move exactly as the jet moves. If it banks to the right, we go to the right. Keep us directly under the jet."

The red fire around the missile on the left side seemed to have gone out. I was pretty sure we had vanished from the jet's radar. I was pleased with myself. I had been hoping to turn the carpet invisible but now I had done the next best thing by using my head instead of magic.

The pilots must have suspected that I had slipped beneath them because a minute later they suddenly banked left, then right. Fortunately the carpet was able to match their reflexes and we continued to remain out of sight.

Now I just needed patience. The jet could only carry so much fuel. Even quicker, I hoped, the pilots might get restless and want to return to base, especially with nothing to chase.

That was what happened after forty minutes of circling the city. The jet suddenly turned toward home and the desert. But I was ready with one last smart move. I could not allow the carpet to reappear on their radar. To do that I had to drop away from the jet as we passed a . . .

"Carpet!" I shouted. "A skyscraper's approaching on our right side. As we near it, I want to break away from our position beneath the jet and fly around the building. Circle it as many times as you need to lose our speed, but stay close to it." I paused. "Ready! Break toward the building!"

I doubted that we reappeared on the jet's radar. The carpet required only one circle of the building to lose its vast speed.

I quickly brought the carpet down to a low level where we flew between homes, factories, and warehouses. Even if someone spotted us, I figured they wouldn't have the nerve to call and report us. I mean, it was the Middle East, the home of tales of magic carpets and powerful djinn, but who really believed in such things?

CHAPTER NINETEEN

AN HOUR LATER, with my nerves significantly more fried than when I had started the day, I flew the carpet to the hospital where Spielo was recovering.

Spielo's hospital was more of a clinic. It had only two stories and it was T-shaped. The rooms for the patients were all on the second floor. I circled the building twice before I found Spielo's room. I was able to land on the roof and still get a clear view into his window. With my dark clothes and the moonless night, I was not worried about being seen. Still, I hid behind an air vent.

It was late. He was one of the few people who still had his light on. He was in bed, hooked up to a bottle of oxygen. I was not surprised to see that he had a visitor.

Amesh was inside, sitting on a chair beside his friend. Every now and then Spielo would explode in a fit of coughing. It was likely Spielo still had some cement in his lungs.

I probably could have used the carpet to translate what they were saying, but Lova was faster. I listened as Amesh tried to convince a confused and sick Spielo that tonight was the night they had to take revenge on those who had wronged them.

Amesh kept rubbing at the hand hidden beneath his long-sleeve shirt.

"I showed you the jewels I found," Amesh was saying, and I could hear for myself the agitation in his voice. "I have hundreds of thousands of lira. I can get more if we need it. I've hired private investigators and mercenaries. They captured Bora Lomal and Hasad Sahim earlier today and took them to a secret place where they're being tortured. And now they have Jemal and Omer, too."

"Why torture them?" Spielo did not appear to like the idea any more than I did. The question angered Amesh.

"They deserve to suffer the way I've suffered! The way you're suffering!"

That was Amesh's theme. He kept repeating it like a broken record. But I knew it was really Darbar who kept repeating the line in his head, to keep Amesh focused on his need for revenge. Darbar was too close to closing the deal on this human. Whatever it took, the djinn was going to fulfill that third wish and make Amesh his thrall.

"But I'm not even sure those were the guys who pushed me into the cement," Spielo said.

"It doesn't matter. That's what I'm trying to tell you. I've discovered who's been behind this plot."

"What plot? You were attacked last year. I got hurt two days ago. Or was it yesterday? Anyway, you knew you were taking a risk when you kept sneaking into that cave. You were warned to stay away from it."

"So they warned me to stay away! So what! Did that give them the right to chop off my hand? You were there. You saw what they did to me. If you hadn't heard my screams and rescued me, they would have killed me."

Spielo shook his head. "I don't know."

"What don't you know? They tried to kill you two days ago. These people are evil. And there's evil inside the Shar Temple."

The Shar Temple, I thought. There had to be a connection between that temple and the ones on the island.

"Amesh. You're talking like a crazy person," Spielo said.

Amesh stood and began to pace. "You don't know where I've been the last few days. I was taken to a secret island on that magic carpet I found, where there were many temples. The island was shown to me because I had the courage to challenge the evildoers who control the Shar Temple. That's where I mastered my djinn. That's where I got the jewels from!"

"Lower your voice. You're going to wake the other patients."

"You think I'm crazy, huh? Even after I showed you the jewels. Well, I have something even more crazy to show you."

I leaned closer to see what Amesh would do. He stepped back from the bed and tore off the knot that kept his transplanted hand hidden. With a wild look on his face, he held it up for Spielo to see.

"Look! This is the hand those animals took from me. But the djinn I command was able to retrieve it and put it back on my arm, when the best doctors in the world said it was impossible."

Spielo sat up, impressed. Until he touched Amesh's new hand. "Does it work like it used to? It looks . . . funny."

Amesh withdrew the hand. "It works. Allah has blessed me. The djinn I control can work miracles for you, too. But you have to show him that you're strong. You know what it says in the Koran. It's our right and duty to strike back at those who have struck us. And this is not just about us. I keep telling you, the Shar Temple has power. It's like the place Allah took me to."

Spielo was confused, and I couldn't say I blamed him. I kind of liked the guy. He had a comical face, with big ears and a huge nose, but there was an innocence in his eyes. He was taller than Amesh, but skinnier.

"But you just said the Shar Temple is evil," Spielo said.

"No! It's controlled by evil people! It's a place of great power!"

"You flew to this island on a magic carpet?"

"Yes. I flew there, across the sea."

"But you told me that girl found the carpet and forced you to go to the island. You told me her name. What was it?"

"Forget her. You misunderstood. The carpet is mine. The djinn is mine. They're all under my control now."

"Show me the carpet. I need to see it with my own eyes."

Amesh shook his transplanted hand in front of Spielo's face. "I have shown you enough miracles! If you don't believe me, I'll get someone else to go with me and help me do Allah's work!"

I was disappointed to see Spielo respond to the childish threat. I got the impression he was used to following Amesh. I watched as he unhooked himself from the oxygen tank and got his clothes from the closet. Now that Spielo was joining him, Amesh's mood suddenly improved. He began to boast again.

"Do you remember the first night we snuck into the cave and saw the Shar Temple? There was a row of holes in the ground. We stopped to peer in them. They were ten feet deep, wide enough to put a person in." Amesh paused and grinned. "Guess what? My djinn put Bora and the others into their very own holes."

"I thought you commanded the djinn. Was it your idea or his?"

"The djinn does what I say. You'll see when you meet it."

Spielo did not look anxious to meet it. "You said the djinn was torturing them. How?"

Amesh giggled. "Each hole is deep but narrow. All they can do is stand. They can't sit down and rest. They've been in the holes since nightfall and already they've given up their bosses' names."

"Why would they crack from just standing a long time?"

"It's an American invention. It's called passive torture. It works better than pulling out a person's nails or even burning them with fire. Stand long enough in one place and your whole body cramps!"

I had never heard of passive torture before, but it sounded awful. It was no wonder Bora and his partners had talked. But now Darbar would be able to gather all those who had hurt Amesh.

Amesh's third wish would be fulfilled!

He would become Darbar's thrall!

But wait . . . not so fast.

Amesh was no fool, and he knew the rules of the djinn. And he was desperate.

Was Amesh going to try to have Spielo take his place?

The idea was not as far-fetched as it sounded. It would be easy to get Spielo, who knew nothing about the Laws of the Djinn, to make wishes, maybe even three. If so, Darbar would still end up with a thrall, and he might let Amesh off the hook.

But I did not believe Amesh could escape so easily. Already, he was almost Darbar's thrall. He *had* made three wishes. According to the rules, as soon as Darbar fulfilled the last wish, it would be all over for Amesh. The carpet had never said another person could become a thrall in your place. Still, I feared Spielo might end up a thrall as well, that Darbar would harvest two tonight.

I felt sick to my stomach thinking about it.

Amesh patted Spielo on the back. "Don't worry, my friend. When we reach the Shar Temple, you'll be happy. All those who hurt us will be there. And my djinn will be waiting to punish them."

"How are we going to get through the gate?" Spielo asked.

Amesh brought out a wad of lira. "The men who work security are as poor as the rest of us. They'll be happy to take our money and let us through. Just as long as we're not carrying a bomb. I have a limousine outside. It's beautiful! It has food and drink in it. We'll travel in style!"

"Why not fly there on the magic carpet?" Spielo asked.

Amesh got angry. "Why do you keep bringing up the carpet?"

"You're the one who told me about it. Why won't you show it to me?"

Amesh went to snap at him again but paused. A weird look came over him, a look I had seen before on the island when Darbar had spoken in his head. He closed his eyes; he could have been falling into a trance. Spielo reached out and shook him.

"Amesh?" he said.

Amesh opened his eyes. "You'll see the carpet tonight."

Spielo was excited. "Can you take me for a ride?" he asked.

Amesh glanced in our direction. He could not see me, I knew, but maybe he sensed me.

"Is Darbar looking through Amesh's eyes right now?" I hissed at Lova.

"Yes," she said.

"Does Darbar sense you here?" I asked

"Yes," Lova said.

When Amesh spoke next, even though Darbar was talking to Spielo, I felt as if what he said was for my benefit.

"I'll take you places you never dreamed of," he said.

They left the room. Lova and I hopped back on the carpet and flew above the parking lot. I had to stay low to hear them. But I felt safe in the black sky, with black clothes and the black bottom on the carpet. I was also pretty sure I was below any citywide radar.

A long white limousine waited for the boys. Amesh had not been exaggerating when he said he had hired guards. Two armed men jumped out to welcome them.

Then Amesh bent over in pain and started yelling at the men. Lova translated. She said that Amesh wanted them to break into the hospital pharmacy. But they shook their heads and said that would alert the police. Amesh pulled a wad of lira out of his pocket. He gave it to the bigger guard.

"Bribe whoever you have to. But get me medicine that stops pain."

Spielo was no dummy. "Your hand's hurting you. There's something wrong with it."

"My hand's fine! I just need the medicine!" Amesh yelled.

Spielo spoke to the guards in whispers we could not hear. One of them went inside. The spasm in Amesh's hand kept up. He *was* in terrible pain. But oddly enough he kept looking up at the sky. I knew Darbar was telling him I was near.

Spielo watched him. "What are you looking at?" he asked.

"She's up there," Amesh said.

"Who?"

"Sara. She's spying on us."

Spielo looked around. "I don't see her. Where is she?"

Amesh pointed to the sky, but in the wrong direction. "Up there!"

Spielo sucked in a breath. "Does she have the carpet?"

Amesh got annoyed. "She stole it from me. I'm going to get it back."

The big guard returned in a few minutes with a bag full of medicines. Amesh studied them while Spielo tried to talk him into letting a doctor look at his hand. Amesh refused.

"Doctors can't help me," he said.

"Can your djinn?" Spielo asked quietly, so the guards could not hear.

Amesh paused before answering. "Sara promised me she would. But she lied. American girls are like that—you can't trust them."

"Yesterday you told me that she was the greatest girl in the world."

I had no idea when he had told Spielo this, but it warmed my heart to hear it. Maybe I was grasping at straws, but I knew deep inside this was not the real Amesh I was seeing. The pain in his body and the agony of the djinn in his mind had turned him into someone he would ordinarily have hated.

His last words, before they left, confirmed my belief.

"Yesterday was a long time ago," Amesh said.

CHAPTER TWENTY

THEIR LONG WHITE LIMOUSINE rode
through the dark streets of Istanbul—and out into the desert,
where it was even darker—toward the hydroelectric plant. I
commanded the carpet to follow the limo no matter where it
went. It occasionally skipped its position above the road, probably to stay on a ley line, but it remained near the vehicle. Still,
I kept my altitude low, barely above the building tops. There was
no way I wanted to face another jet.

To make myself more comfortable, I told Lova to shrink
in size so I had room to stretch out on the carpet and stare up
at the stars. A half moon rose in the east, but its soft white light

worried me. I was pretty hard to see, up here in the night sky, but I was not invisible.

With the moon up, I instructed the carpet to let the limo have a half-mile lead. I was no longer eager to hear what Amesh had to say, and I had another reason for backing off.

Spielo was obviously fascinated with all the limo's gadgets, including the skylight. He had opened the roof, and I worried that he might spot us. It was cute, his fascination with magic carpets, but his curiosity could cause problems.

After listening to Amesh and Spielo talk in the hospital room, I realized that Amesh had lied to his grandfather when it came to the Shar Temple. Amesh had told his Papi he had seen it once, when it was clear he was obsessed with the place. But why obsess over it unless it had something he wanted?

Then it struck me.

Was the Shar Temple a djinn temple?

Boy, it was obvious! I should have realized it earlier! It explained so much. For one thing, it explained the mystery of why Amesh had changed into a wild man on the island when he heard we were surrounded by djinn temples. He already had an obsession with them long before we met.

He was not alone. Whatever Amesh knew about the Shar Temple—Mr. Toval, Mrs. Steward, and my father knew ten times more. They were the bosses in charge of the job site. They could go into the temple whenever they wanted. I was confident that I had not been allowed in to see it because they didn't want it seen. The whole idea of asking the archaeologist's permission had been a charade.

Had they found the cave by chance? Or had they chosen this location for the hydroelectric plant because it gave them an excuse to dig up the area with modern equipment?

It was doubtful Mr. Toval and Mrs. Steward had ordered the four boys to attack Amesh. The act was brutal. By its very nature it would call attention to the temple. But the two bosses had probably arranged for the four young men to guard the cave. And the security measure had gotten out of hand.

Way out of hand. No pun intended.

Mr. Demir had talked about how the four guys had shown up in court with lawyers they should not have been able to afford. That meant there was money behind them, which was another way of saying that Mr. Toval and Mrs. Steward were protecting the guys—and the temple. It was a fact that the bosses had lied.

It was also a fact that my father knew they were lying.

It made my heart ache to admit my father was involved, but it was the only explanation that made sense. My father was honorable. Yet when push came to shove, he'd kept his mouth shut to protect his superiors. The guilt . . . it must have torn him apart.

Mr. Demir had praised my father for his selfless acts. How he had visited Amesh every day at the hospital. How he had arranged for the best doctors for Amesh. But all the while my father had been acting out of guilt.

That was why my dad was worried I was seeing Amesh. He feared I was going to learn the truth. It probably terrified him that I would see him as a criminal.

Yet there were bigger issues when it came to the Shar Temple. Once again, it dealt with the possibility that Mr. Toval, Mrs. Steward, and my father were deliberately searching for such sites. Since I was a kid, my dad had read books on archaeology. He had a whole library of them at his house.

Was his interest in the djinn in his blood?

It was possible. We shared the same blood.

But who had hired the guys who had almost killed me that afternoon? My dad would never have done anything to harm me, which meant he couldn't know about the carpet.

Looking back, it might have been a mistake not to tell him about it. With all his research in this part of the world, he might even know of its existence. I couldn't wait to see his face when I showed it to him.

The pictures on the carpet caught my eye. Now that I had been to the island, discovered my destiny as a Kala, and fought with the djinn, I felt as if I saw the images anew. I certainly saw things I had not noticed before.

Once more, I assumed the carpet's story began in the upper right-hand corner. There was the equivalent of the Garden of

Eden scene, filled with two types of beings—humans and angels, which I now suspected were djinn.

I had only seen two djinn with my eyes and one had been a monster. Yet I think the carpet portrayed them the way they saw themselves.

As the story flowed around the star field, there was the fuzzy red image of the dragon. It could have been any kind of monster, actually. Its red light poured down on the soft green of the garden and stripped it bare, transforming the garden into desert.

The dragon reminded me of the red star I had seen above the island. Indeed, the star had been fuzzy because of the gaseous nebula that surrounded it.

A third type of creature entered the picture, one that interested me more than before. They were taller than humans and djinn, and darker than both, with brownish gray skin, and strangely shaped faces. The bottom half of the carpet showed these creatures fighting the djinn and the humans.

I assumed that this was the third race Lova had mentioned at the hotel.

As the story swept up the other side of the carpet, the dragon reappeared, but the djinn and the third race disappeared. And as the dragon receded, all that was left were humans. Only now they wore robes instead of skins, and they were not as tall or as beautiful as their ancestors.

I ordered Lova to resume her normal size. I had questions.

"Tell me more about the beings the djinn warred with long ago."

Lova's red eyes glowed. "Why do they matter to you?"

"Because I don't believe I was attacked by a djinn today. Nor do I think that woman who wanted the carpet was possessed by a djinn. You're clever, Lova—you would have known if she was. It surprised you that the woman had a pashupa. That means it can't be a djinn weapon. It must be part of the arsenal of weapons of the race that defeated you before."

"You're guessing."

"You were scared when you returned with the carpet. I saw it in your face. What scared you, Lova?"

Lova slapped the carpet with her palm. "You could not have been struck with a pashupa! It would have killed you!"

I had never seen her show such emotion.

"But I *was* hit with one and I'm still here. Does that scare you?"

Lova looked away, at the desert. "No human scares me."

"What was the name of the creatures that defeated the djinn?"

Lova hesitated. "The Anulakai. But we do not speak of them."

I pointed to the angels on the carpet. "Are these djinn?"

"Yes."

I pointed to the third race. "I assume these are Anulakai?"

"Yes."

"You act like the djinn were the only ones who fought the Anulakai," I said. "It's clear from the carpet that humans fought them as well."

"Humans were created by the Anulakai. They were their slaves. They only rose up to fight them when . . ." Lova stopped.

"When they got tired of being slaves?" I asked.

Lova shrugged. "By then it was too late. The war was lost."

"Do the djinn resent humans because they didn't help earlier?"

"What is there to resent? Humans are inferior. We did not expect their help and we were not disappointed when we did not get it."

Lova was an elitist. One minute she was complaining humans had not risen up in time to help her race. The next minute she was saying it wouldn't have mattered.

"Where did the Anulakai come from?" I asked.

"Out of the darkness."

Swell, I thought. That could mean just about anything.

"Did they come from Mars?" I asked.

"No."

"Another solar system?"

"No. They came out of the darkness."

"Are they here now on Earth?" I demanded, frustrated.

Lova hesitated. "The djinn do not believe they totally left."

"Are they going to return here? In force?"

"Who can say? They might be already on their way."

"Why do you say they made us?" I asked.

"They genetically enhanced your race. Not to help you, but to make you better slaves. You mean nothing to them."

That threw Darwin and creationism out the window at the same time—not an easy thing to do. I sensed Lova was giving me only part of the story.

"At most, there are only a few Anulakai here now," I said.

"How do you know?"

"Well, I've never run into one. That means we must have beat them the last time."

Lova was annoyed. "You did not defeat them. They withdrew."

"But not before they punished the djinn by enslaving them. That's true, right? You lost the war and they hid you away in another dimension."

Lova glared at me. But I could tell my words had hurt her as well. I assumed that meant my insight was correct.

"This is no time to gloat, Sara," she said.

I disliked her using my name.

"How come the Anulakai didn't punish humanity?" I asked.

Lova lowered her head. "They come in cycles. Perhaps this

time we'll defeat them. Perhaps this time you'll fight alongside them and we'll destroy you both."

"Do you want humanity destroyed?" I asked. When she didn't answer, I said, "Why don't we fight together like last time and defeat the Anulakai?"

Lova stared me in the eye. "We don't trust humans. We never will. They were bred to be slaves. Anulakai slaves or djinn slaves—it makes no difference. Humans were not meant to roam free."

I held my anger in check. "What does the word *Shar* mean in djinn?"

"It is an Anulakai word."

"What does it mean?"

"Center."

"Center of what?" I asked.

"I don't know."

I let the interrogation end. Lova was giving me a headache.

The limousine continued to roll through the desert and into the night. The moon rose farther in the sky.

As we neared the job site, the carpet began to make a ringing noise. It reminded me of when the jet had locked on its radar. It made sense—the six-billion-dollar hydroelectric plant would have a radar system that would notify its security people if a low-flying object was approaching.

What to do? I could go up or I could go down.

Whatever I did, I had to do it fast.

I could not repeat the game I had played with the jet. But I spotted a large truck following the limo, not far behind us. Since there was nothing else out here, I assumed it was headed for the job site. I flew over it to take a closer look.

It was a garbage truck. Empty, but nevertheless smelly. The ringing noise grew. I immediately ordered the carpet to land inside the truck and was relieved when the ringing stopped. Lova complained about the odor, but I told her to hush.

"We won't be here long," I said.

We stayed inside the truck only as long as it took to pass security. I doubted the job site swept itself with radar. Its antennas must all be pointed outward, away from the plant. Once we were away from the gate, I flew out of the truck.

Unfortunately, now I had lost track of Amesh and his limo. I assumed that he was heading for the cave and Shar Temple, on the far side of the pit, but I had to raise the carpet pretty high to get my bearings. The place looked different at night. I reached for my binoculars, searching.

Eventually I saw the limo and Amesh. He was holding my father captive, and he had a sword in his hand. He was shouting for me to come down from the sky.

"Last warning, Sara!" he yelled. "Surrender or he dies!"

My father tried to tell Amesh something but Amesh struck him on the side of the head with the blunt side of the sword.

My dad was bleeding from his nose and ears. I sat back and stared at Lova, my heart pounding.

"If I order you to destroy Darbar, will you do it?" I asked.

"If you will agree to be my thrall."

"I'm only your thrall if I make three wishes."

Lova chuckled but said nothing.

I sighed. "Carpet. Take us down to ground level."

CHAPTER TWENTY-ONE

WE LANDED NEAR THE CAVE, not far in front of Amesh and my father. There was no sign of Spielo. I couldn't see Darbar but felt he was near. Hell, he was practically on top of us, and it was the djinn who was holding my father in place, not Amesh, not even with the threat of the sword. The instant we landed, before I could roll the carpet up and put it away in my backpack, Amesh pushed my father forward.

"You're late," Amesh said. "I didn't think you'd come."

"You knew I'd be here," I told him, before turning to my father. "How are you doing, Dad?"

I hardly recognized the man. Not because he was hurt, although he had been roughed up. It was the two emotions I saw on his face—confusion and fear. I had never seen him show weakness before. To me, growing up, my father had always been so sure of himself. And of course I had never seen him frightened of anything.

Yet for my sake, I think, he tried to project steadiness.

"I'm doing okay. It's been an interesting night." He stopped and peered at me more closely. "What's that bruise on your face?"

"It's nothing important. Do you feel like you're in the grip of a large invisible hand?"

He nodded. "How did you know? What is it?"

"It's a djinn. For the moment, it's under Amesh's control."

"For the moment!" Amesh repeated. "I command Darbar! He obeys me!"

"For how long?" I said, keeping my voice calm. "You know he's about to fulfill your third wish."

Amesh grinned. "Poor Sara. You think I'm a fool, don't you?"

"I think you're in pain and I think you'll do anything to stop that pain. But hurting the people you've trapped inside that cave isn't going to ease your suffering one bit."

Amesh poked my father with the sword, hard enough that my father winced. "It isn't just those inside who hurt me. Your father was one of them. Imagine that, Sara—all this time, I thought he was trying to help me. When he was the one who ordered the attack on me."

"Who told you this lie?" I demanded.

"You know who. And he doesn't lie, not to me, not to his master."

I turned to my father. "Dad. Did you order an attack on Amesh?"

My father sighed. There was so much guilt in the sound, it broke my heart. "Sara. There are things I never told you about last summer. Things I'm responsible for. Amesh has a right to hate me. I lied to him."

I hesitated. "Are you lying now?"

"No."

"Did you give the order to have his hand chopped off?"

"Of course not." My father looked to Amesh. "I knew the boys were guarding the cave. I hired them to guard it. I knew you and Spielo and some of the other young men were curious about the underground temple. But what happened that night—when you lost your hand—none of that was planned."

"Liar!" Amesh said. "Darbar says he lies! He was behind it all!"

"Amesh, think of how much pain you were in last summer," I pleaded. "Who came to the hospital to see you every day? Who found the best doctors for you?"

"He did it to cover up what he had done to me!"

"He did it because he cared about you!"

There followed a silence as our words echoed into the vast pit behind us. Once again, I noticed the area looked as if it had been struck by a meteor. The image was uncanny.

"I did it for both reasons," my father said. He saw the shock on my face and tried to explain. "Sara, I've been living something of a double life here in the Middle East."

I shrugged. "I know about your interest in the djinn."

He was amazed. "You do? Then you must know—I've been standing here with my head spinning. I saw you fly in on that carpet. It's a real flying carpet! Where did you get it? I've been searching for one all my life."

"I found it near here. It's amazing. It's called the Carpet of Ka."

My father forgot all about the sword in his back. All about the djinn that held him in place. He tried to take a step forward. "The Carpet of Ka!" he gasped in wonder. "So the stories are true!" But then he was suddenly thrown to his knees and let out a cry of pain. "Ahh!"

Amesh chuckled softly. "It's not like we can let Daddy go for a ride on the carpet, now can we, Sara?"

"What will it take for you to release him?" I asked.

Amesh was amused. "Have you come to bargain? That's so unlike you. When you bargain you have to give up something, then you get something in return. But from what I've seen, you like to talk about giving but in the end that's all it is—talk."

"Amesh—"

"I'm not finished!" He shook with pain as he tried to hold his right hand down. He was having another spasm. "I've learned a lot in the last year, more in the last week. Nothing in this world's free. But a girl like you—who has the nerve to say she loves me—would never sacrifice a lira to help me."

"How does your hand feel?" I asked.

"Don't ask about my hand!" he yelled.

"It's hurting pretty bad right now. Darbar won't do anything to fix it. He gave you that hand knowing full well it would hurt you. Don't tell me he's your ally. He's your enemy. Not me or my father. Yes, I know my dad got involved with some bad people. And I know he tried to protect these people by hiding certain facts." I paused. "You have Mr. Toval and Mrs. Steward inside that cave, don't you?"

Amesh shrugged. "They testified against me at the trial. They lied so the others could go free."

"I know. I read the transcript from the trial."

"You did?" Amesh asked, surprised.

"Your grandfather shared it with me. It was filled with lies. But if you think about it, Amesh, my father was the only one who showed any guilt. It's because he's the only one with a conscience. The only one who cared about what you were going through."

"Sara, you don't understand. I am guilty," my father said.

"Not the way the djinn says you are," I replied. "You have to listen closely and trust that I know more about this situation than you do. If not, Amesh's djinn will take your head with that sword, and Amesh will end up a thrall for all of eternity."

Amesh snorted. "Talk, talk, talk. That's our darling Sara. Do you have anything else to say before Dear Dad does lose his head?"

"Why is Spielo here? Is he here to be a thrall in your place?"

My remark caught Amesh off-guard, but his surprise quickly changed to anger. "I'm not a traitor like you. Spielo's here to witness the revenge that's his due. That's all."

He spoke with conviction. I realized then he might have been telling Spielo the truth, or at least as much truth as a possessed person could. I saw the loneliness Amesh's pain had brought him. Still, it was hard to trust a guy with a sword in his hands.

"I hope so. I hope you're not about to put him through the same pain you're going through."

"No one knows what I'm going through!" he shouted, and his damn hand wouldn't stop flapping. He was right, in a way. I had to shut up and deliver. Fixing his hand wouldn't save him in the long run, but at least he would know a moment of peace.

Also, even more pressing, if I healed Amesh's hand, my father would probably get to keep his head. It was possible

Amesh might try to return the favor and stop Darbar from harming my father. But I doubted anything would keep the djinn from collecting his ultimate prize.

I just wished I could order Lova to kill Darbar and end it. But if she killed him, it would be equal to two wishes. Then I would end up the thrall!

I stepped forward and took Amesh's wounded hand.

He tried to shake free but I wouldn't let him.

"I can stop your pain," I said. "I've brought my own djinn with me. Darbar knows she's here and he knows she's more powerful than he is. That's why Darbar's afraid to kill my dad. He knows I'll take revenge." I paused. "I told you, I'm willing to bargain."

Amesh finally showed interest. "What are you offering?"

"My djinn will heal your hand. Make it like it was before you were attacked. When it was strong and you were whole."

Amesh stared at me a long time, the moon bright in his black eyes. He was not aware but the sword in his hand began to lower.

"Will that be your first wish?" he asked.

I shook my head. "My second."

"It will cost you."

"I don't care."

"Why?" he asked.

"Because you're in pain."

"Why?" he repeated.

"Because you're right, there's no love without sacrifice." I paused. "I'm going to prove to you that I do love you."

His voice trembled. "You don't know what the price will be."

I turned to Lova. "What will it cost?"

She spoke quickly. "The Carpet of Ka. I fix his hand, you give it to me. Agreed?"

I turned back to Amesh and my father and repeated what they had been unable to hear. "She'll fix your hand in exchange for the carpet," I said.

"But you love that carpet," Amesh said.

"Not as much as a certain Turkish boy."

My father was worried. "Sara, I know you're trying to do the right thing. But I've researched flying carpets, and if this is in fact the Carpet of Ka, then you mustn't hand it over to the djinn."

"Why not?" I asked.

"They could use it to destroy mankind."

Lova came forward so she stood by my side. "We would only use it to defeat the Anulakai," she said.

I knew what a skilled liar Lova was, but I sensed that she was telling the truth. The djinn wouldn't waste its power turning against mankind.

"I'm sorry, I can't let Amesh suffer any more," I told my father. "I have to surrender the carpet."

"Sara, no. It's too important," my father pleaded.

"I'm sorry, my mind's made up." I sat down across from Lova, who seemed more than pleased to sit near me. For a while I meditated, letting my mind settle. Then, when I was ready, I started my wish.

"Trakur Analova La," I said firmly. "It is the wish of your master, Sara, that you fix Amesh's right hand in exchange for the Carpet of Ka. You are to use all the powers you possess to make his right hand whole, free of pain, strong, like it was before it was severed from his body. In exchange, Trakur Analova La, I'll turn over the Carpet of Ka to you. This is my second wish with you, Trakur Analova La, and it is binding in so far as all wishes between humans and djinn are binding—as specified in the ancient laws governing such contracts." I opened my eyes. "Agreed?"

Lova hesitated. "You put extra conditions on this wish."

"Only the conditions that have existed since humans and djinn began to exchange services. You know the laws as well as I do." I paused. "Do you agree to fulfill my second wish?"

"Yes. Give me the carpet."

"Fulfill my wish and I'll give you the carpet," I said.

Lova did not argue. Standing, she walked toward Amesh, but he raised the sword and stepped back. Naturally, he couldn't see her. I wasn't sure what his problem was. Then I realized that Darbar was doing everything he could to interfere.

"Relax, Amesh, listen to me," I said. "Stand still; let her heal you."

Amesh seemed to hear me. He relaxed somewhat and put down his sword.

Lova was near Amesh when she suddenly raised her hand and struck out to the right. I saw blue sparks and smoke in the air. "Darbar is trying to hinder me," she said calmly.

"Can he stop you?" I asked.

"He lacks the power. And he is spread thin."

I could only assume her last remark related to Darbar's control over the others inside the cave. Lova acted unconcerned about the interference. But she raised a hand and shot out more sparks.

I heard a faint telepathic message pass between the two djinn.

"This is the Carpet of Ka. We must obtain it at all costs."

It was Lova lecturing Darbar. He heard her and backed off.

The message was chilling. The djinn must want it a great deal.

Was my father right? Was I making a mistake?

I glanced over at my father and he was focused on Amesh. I could see that Lova had lifted his transplanted hand into her hands. Now she was gently stroking it, all the while humming a hypnotic melody, a song that needed no words. Even though Amesh could not consciously hear it, I suspected that her song and her touch were having a profound effect upon him.

Lova signaled for me to approach.

I stood and walked over. "What do you want?" I asked.

"Sara?" Amesh whispered, confused, his eyes closed.

"Shhh, relax, everything's okay. I'm talking to the djinn," I said.

"Your hand," Lova said.

"My hand?" I asked.

"Your touch transmits your energy, and Kalas are powerful. It will help with the healing."

Lova was flattering me. It made me wary.

"You're changing the deal," I said. "You're supposed to heal him on your own."

"It requires tremendous energy to offset the wish of another djinn."

At least she wasn't asking for blood. I offered my hand, and Lova gripped it tightly. I immediately felt slightly dizzy.

I spoke to Amesh. "You didn't hear what was said, but I'm giving my djinn some energy to help fix your hand."

"The pain's going away," Amesh whispered, his eyes still closed. I stroked his hair with my other hand. He had laid down the sword.

"That's good, that's all that matters," I said.

"Sara," he gasped.

"Shhh. Don't say anything. Let the healing continue."

"I'm so grateful."

"You never deserved this pain in the first place," I said.

The healing took another ten minutes, with me giving

energy the whole time and Lova sucking it up. My dizziness increased, and I staggered. My father stood silent and did not interfere.

Lova suddenly stopped humming and I opened my eyes, which I did not recall closing. I was pleasantly surprised to see that Amesh's right hand had lost its sickly yellow color. Indeed, it was impossible to tell his right hand from his left.

Amesh flexed his fingers, causing my heart to shake with joy. Relief filled his face and he leaned over and kissed me on the lips. Yes, right on the lips, and if a first kiss like that was not worth one magic carpet, then it was pretty close. It was the greatest kiss of my life.

"It's perfect," he kept saying. "Just perfect. There's no pain." He hugged me, with both hands. He was able to hug me hard. And I hugged him back. "I cannot believe you did this for me."

"I only wish I could do more," I said, feeling weak.

Our eyes met and he nodded. Because he knew what I meant. We were not out of the woods yet.

Lova had her hands out. "The carpet," she said.

I reached for it in my pack. "You have promised never to use it to hurt mankind."

"So I have," Lova said, taking the carpet and tucking it under her arm. To the others it appeared to float in midair without support. Lova turned to her invisible partner, then spoke to me. "Darbar says he has business to complete inside."

"My father's no longer a part of this business," I said, then to Amesh, "Tell Darbar to release him."

Amesh turned and tried to do as I said but met with resistance. Once again, I couldn't hear everything Darbar said but it sounded like he was trying to imply that my father was the ultimate authority when it came to the attack.

"How does he know that?" I demanded.

Amesh relayed the question. Darbar replied that if my father was not killed, then the third wish would be left unfulfilled. Amesh took a step back at that suggestion.

"Then we'll leave it unfulfilled," he said.

Darbar screamed at him. I did not hear words—I heard a screech in the ether. Darbar was not going to let Amesh get away on a technicality. Shaken, Amesh looked to me for help. The pain had left his eyes but his fear had not. He put his head near mine.

"Do you have a plan?" he whispered.

"Sort of."

Darbar ordered Amesh to pick up the sword and the shiny black djinn lamp, which I had not seen since the island. With Darbar leading the way, keeping a firm hold on my father, and Lova bringing up the rear, we entered the cave.

I whispered to Amesh. "Where did you get that sword?"

"In the Shar Temple." He paused. "But that's not what you really want to know."

He was right, of course. There was another question that had haunted me for a long time.

"When you made the second wish on the island," I said. "And Darbar gave you your hand. What did he ask for in return?"

Amesh looked miserable. "Your full name."

"I was afraid you were going to say that."

CHAPTER TWENTY-TWO

WE WALKED DOWNHILL at a steep angle for fifteen minutes before we reached the cavern that housed the Shar Temple. It was different from the ones we'd seen on the island. It had marble columns supporting a pretty golden roof. And it was much larger and not enclosed.

The size of the cavern that sheltered the temple was stunning. Modern lights had been brought down to provide a steady source of illumination, but even a dozen high-powered search-lights were not enough to brighten the chamber. I was looking at an excavation job—if Becktar had in fact done the work—that had taken years to accomplish.

Inside the temple I saw a large pool of water that circled an altar. The rear of the pool appeared separate from the rest and it was not a mere hot spring—that sucker was boiling, pouring off layers of steam. The backside of the temple was choked with red-colored fog.

Yet there was an even more intriguing sight.

Along the edge of the cavern were other structures that looked like vaults of some kind. They appeared to be made of a mixture of metal and plastic. It was hard to be sure in the weird light. They were dark blue and had doors that riffled open and shut like those on an elevator. A few of the doors were open and led to dark hallways.

I did not see any lit buttons or control panels per se. However, there were clusters of crystals near the doors. I suspected these were the controls. Frankly, the vaults and the temple looked as if they had been built by two different races.

The exterior of the temple was ringed with torture holes, from which I could hear unceasing groaning sounds.

I turned to Amesh. He was still carrying the lamp, but had put down the sword. "Tell Darbar to stop torturing those guys," I said. "And to lay off my dad. He's not going anywhere."

Showing shame, Amesh turned to his invisible djinn and ordered it to remove the captors from the holes. He assured Darbar he had control of the situation. It was nice to see the dramatic change in Amesh. Now that he was pain free, he was almost normal again.

Yet I was getting my hopes up too soon. He was desperate, having made his three wishes, and desperate people did desperate things.

"Darbar says they're to suffer as I have suffered," Amesh told me after conferring with his djinn. I chose not to argue, but turned to Lova instead. I wanted to see how she stacked up against Darbar.

"Lova, release all the prisoners from those holes," I said.

"Is that your third wish?"

"No."

"That's asking too much without making a wish."

"Lova, if you don't do what I say right now, we'll part company and you'll never see me again."

Lova was not ready to let me go. I had only one more wish to make and she had me. In minutes, she managed to lift the four boys—as well as Mr. Toval and Mrs. Steward—out of their pits. My dad went over to help his partners to their feet, while the guys collapsed on the floor. They had been in the longest and their legs were shot. Yet the good thing about this kind of torture—good in a relative sense—was that their relief was immediate. A minute after they lay down, their cramps began to ease up.

As they squirmed on the ground, I recognized two from the photos Lova had taken, Jemal and Omer. I could not help myself; I strode over and stared at them.

"I warned you jerks not to mess with me," I said in a cold voice.

The younger guy cried. "Please don't put us back in there."

"Behave yourself, and I'll think about it." I did not approve of torture but two of these guys had really hurt me.

Spielo was wandering around, dazed. But he did summon the courage to approach me. "Are you Sara?" he asked timidly.

"Yeah. I'm the evil American chick."

"Amesh didn't mean—"

"I know, I know," I interrupted. "Are you scared?"

"Yeah. Are we going to get out of here alive?"

"I honestly don't know."

"If we do, can you take me for a ride on your magic carpet?"

I had to smile. "Sure. We'll fly down to the beach."

We were in the middle of a crisis, yet my father was not with me. He continued to stay near his bosses, exchanging whispers with Mr. Toval and Mrs. Steward. Surprisingly, none of them looked scared. I assumed Darbar still had a hold on all of them.

But something was going on that I was missing.

I spoke to Amesh. "I need to talk to you alone."

He pointed to a spot near the weird vaults. "Over there."

"Wait. Tell your djinn to leave us alone so we can talk in private."

Amesh tried to tell Darbar this. But every time he spoke, it sounded like he was groveling. As a result, Darbar treated him as if he were already a thrall.

"He says no secret conferences are allowed," Amesh said, his voice tense. "It's time to complete the third wish. Those who attacked me are all here. The same with those who were behind the attack. I'm sorry, we've run out of time."

"We?" I asked.

"Your father and I."

"My father just wanted this place guarded!"

"Darbar doesn't see it that way," Amesh said.

Out of the corner of my eye, I saw my father shoved to the ground.

"Sara!" he called out in fear.

I began to panic and turned on Amesh. "Order Darbar to stop hurting my father!"

Amesh tried but got nowhere. "He says that for my wish to be fulfilled, your father must die."

"What kind of wish did you make, exactly?"

Amesh sighed. "I wished for all my enemies to be destroyed."

Mrs. Steward and Mr. Toval backed away from my father. For once, the bigwigs appeared free of Darbar's grip. At least they were able to move around in a restricted area. It looked like Darbar was focusing his energy on delivering a final blow to my father.

I hurried to his side, feeling the weight of Darbar's presence.

"Be careful, Darbar," I warned. "My djinn will destroy you if I give the word."

My father shook his head. "Sara, no more deals with these devils. You don't know the cost. You think you do but—it's more horrible than you can imagine."

I knelt by his side. "Are you in pain?"

"I deserve what's happening to me," he gasped.

"Quit saying that. You didn't hurt Amesh on purpose."

"This isn't about Amesh. We wanted to keep this temple and these vaults secret. That was wrong."

"That was natural. I kept the carpet secret as long as I could."

He looked at me with weary eyes. "And now you've lost it."

I glanced at Lova. She looked at me. Waiting.

"Lova, you're to protect my father from Darbar," I said.

"Is that your third wish?"

"It's an order."

Lova smiled at me and my father. "No," she said.

To my left, a marble column suddenly cracked. The weight of the temple roof kicked a chunk of it loose, and it rolled toward us at high speed. I was not given a chance to change my order to a wish. All I could do was pull my father out of the way.

But his body refused to budge.

"Go, Sara!" he shouted, and shoved me aside. I tripped over the steps. My feet went up in the air, my head went down. It was concussion time all over again. The blow to the back of my skull, the second one today, almost knocked me out. It was only my fear for my father that kept me conscious.

I was lying on the ground, on my side, when the massive pillar rolled over his lower half. I heard a sound then that I'll never forget—a hundred human bones snapping. My father was not given a chance to scream, not even when the pillar rolled away and came to rest above one of the torture holes. He had been crushed.

On my knees, I groped my way to his side. His breathing was ragged. Blood leaked from his mouth onto the temple floor. His feet, his calves, his knees, his thighs, and his hips— they were flat. Red mush soaked his pants. He looked down and groaned.

"Oh, God," he whispered.

"Dad," I said, taking his hand. Amesh and Spielo ran up behind me. "Hang on a minute. I can save you."

His hand was drenched with blood and sweat. His words came out as a moist rasp. But I could hear him. I knew what he was trying to tell me.

"Let me be. I don't deserve to be saved." He coughed up red spittle. "The price is too great, Sara. Let me go."

Tears burned my eyes, like the fire that burned inside Lova's red orbs. It was not necessary to call her to my side. She was already near, waiting. In one hand she held the carpet, in the other she would hold my soul. I turned to her.

"Trakur Analova La," I said. "I, Sara, wish you would save the life of my father, Charles. Trakur Analova La, return him to the state of health he enjoyed before this awful injury. Heal him now, before he dies. This is my third wish with you, Trakur Analova La, and it is binding in so far as all wishes between humans and djinn are binding—as specified in the ancient laws governing such contracts." I stopped to catch my breath. "Agreed?"

Lova studied my father. "Agreed. But I will require your help again. This time I need your blood. It will speed up the healing, and we have little time."

"I'm a human being," I said. "My blood is not special."

"You are human, true, but the power of the Kalas flows through your blood," Lova said, as if that explained everything. She took my father's hand, and with a sharp fingernail on her other hand, she impaled my wrist and began to draw my blood in pulsating gulps. She spoke. "Focus on the healing. It will take both of us to save him."

I closed my eyes and let the white light pour down from above. My body was already hot—I felt as if my individual cells vibrated, and I could feel my body's energy entering my father's body. I still felt weak from helping Amesh, and I suspected Lova was drawing off more of my blood than she needed. However, this blood-sharing strengthened our link.

Suddenly Lova's thoughts were clear to me. She was not just worried about healing my father. She was concerned about after, when she would make me a thrall. She had doubts she would be able to control a potential Kala. Very interesting, I thought.

But then a heavy sinking feeling paralyzed both my mind and body. I couldn't move an inch, and my thoughts were not free either. I was being drawn down into a black place where I sensed no normal human could survive. For a time I let myself sink deeper into the abyss because I could tell life was returning to my father. I heard him draw in several deep breaths.

But I was not a true Kala. A wave of very human fear shook me, and I attempted to escape the darkness. I knew if Lova let go of my father and focused on me—in my weakened state—she would have me, and once she had me, it would be forever.

With my eyes still closed, I sensed how she was psychically trying to enter my brain. She was coming in the back of my skull. But she was slow and clumsy. Before she could get inside my head, I willed my hands to rise and pulled her nail from my wrist.

As if from far away, I heard her complain.

"Your father still needs your blood," she said.

"Liar. You're taking it for your own use now," I mumbled. I swayed where I sat. With her nail no longer drinking my blood, my thoughts began to clear. On the surface Lova's plan appeared clever. Make me her thrall in the middle of the healing. Yet in her haste I believe she had made a mistake. She had not yet fulfilled my third wish. Therefore, by the Laws of the Djinn, she had no right to claim me as a thrall.

I finally had the strength to open my eyes.

My father's eyes were open, too. He was staring at me.

"Are you all right?" I asked.

He reached up and touched my hair. "Thanks to you."

I smiled. "I'm glad."

His hand dropped to his side. "You shouldn't have, Sara."

I squeezed his hand. "You would have done the same for me."

He shook his head. "No. I don't think so."

My father drew in a deep invigorating breath and sat up and stared directly at Lova. That surprised me. I did not think he could see her.

"Can you take her or do you need help?" he asked my djinn.

Lova hesitated. "Why would your kind help us?"

"The offer is there. It is up to you to accept it," my father said.

It was then my universe fell apart. Not over time, not piece by piece, but all at once. Everything I knew and trusted shattered. In seconds, I realized that I was not a powerful princess but the queen of fools.

Lova eyed me suspiciously. "She is strong. Her bloodline

is ancient. I tried to take control during the healing but she repelled me. She'll be difficult to possess."

"What's going on here?" I cried.

My father ignored me and stood. He spoke to Mr. Toval and Mrs. Steward. He did not care that we all heard, even Amesh and Spielo, who looked ready to faint.

"As we suspected," my father said. "The first djinn's power over us has been negated by a collision with the more powerful second djinn. Darbar has lost the ability to fulfill Amesh's third wish. Therefore, the contract between them is now void. Amesh can no longer be made a thrall of Darbar."

Mrs. Steward spoke to my father. "Your plan was intelligent but it left too much to chance. If Sara had not used her djinn to negate the first djinn, we would have had to rely on other resources to fix your body and control her."

My father shrugged. "I know the girl. She is driven by a need to do what is right, no matter what the cost to herself. See how she didn't hesitate to save me?"

Amesh was as confused as I was. "Does this mean I'm free?"

"You're free of your contract with Darbar since he's unable to fulfill your third wish," my father said. "He is taking his lamp and leaving the area. But you're not free."

Amesh blinked and in that instant Darbar's lamp vanished from his hands.

"Best we kill them all," Mr. Toval suggested.

Amesh and Spielo paled. They tried to speak, but couldn't.

Mrs. Steward nodded. "Yes. Put them in the holes and leave them. If thirst doesn't kill them, the pain will."

I managed to stand. The cavern swayed—my blood-starved dizziness was like a wound. What they were talking about? They were like goblins in a childhood nightmare casually discussing how they would cook and spice their next human meal. I stared at my father and did not recognize him. His face was the same, but he was not. He was the nightmare.

"All this was a setup?" I asked.

My father studied me with clinical detachment. "Yes. I knew about your bloodline. It's why I moved into your house when you were a child. It's why I took you down here two days ago—to see how you would react."

"But I never left the Jeep," I protested. The words were no sooner out of my mouth than I realized how I had been used on my first visit to the job site.

Either the surroundings or my father's remark jogged my memory.

Mr. Toval and Mrs. Steward had approached the Jeep while we were sitting outside the cave. I remembered now. She had forced me to drink a bottle of freezing water and I had grown dizzy. It must have been drugged. Then there had been a gap—I had felt like my father was taking forever to return from the cave, but in reality he had taken me *into* the cave. Indeed, he had forced me to stand in the exact spot where I now stood and answer a question. He had asked it over and over again.

"Where is the carpet, Sara? The Carpet of Ka."

My answer had been "I don't know." They had asked two hours too soon. I did not find the carpet until after Spielo's accident, until that strange woman had led me to it.

Now, in the present, I had to focus on what my father was saying. He spoke almost mechanically, his voice free of emotion, his tone hypnotic.

"We assumed the carpet was down here but we were wrong. This morning, when you returned to the hotel, I was unaware you had discovered the carpet and been to the island of the djinn, although I saw a djinn follow you into your room. That made me curious. While you were in the shower, I found your pack and saw the carpet. I almost took it then but thought it would be best if I sent a team after it. That way you would waste a wish retrieving it, which would move you a step closer to becoming a thrall."

"Plus it gave us a chance to see how the pashupa worked on you," Mrs. Steward said in the same flat tone.

"You're the one who shot me with that green light," I said.

The old woman nodded. "You should be proud. It contained enough power to kill a dozen humans, and you recovered in less than an hour."

"Dad, how can you do this to your own daughter?" I pleaded.

"You're not my daughter. I'm not your father. But your bloodline was identified at an early age and steps were taken so you would grow up under my watchful eye. Our goal with you has always been twofold. First, we hoped you would retrieve the Carpet of Ka. Life after life it's been attracted to you, and to your bloodline. Second, we hoped to make you a thrall. That is why we're willing to help this djinn enslave you, if she should need our help."

I could not keep up. "Are you all djinn?"

"No. The djinn are actually our enemies. But you may have heard the old saying: 'The enemy of my enemy is my friend.' That is true for now, in this situation. The best way to neutralize your powers as a potential Kala is to make you a thrall."

I spoke sarcastically. "That works better than killing me?"

"Yes," my father said. It was impossible not to think of him as my father.

"What do you mean, the carpet has been attracted to my bloodline?"

"It's served many of your ancestors. For that matter, it served your mother."

"Mom?" I said.

"Your real mother, the one you call Aunt Tracy."

The revelations were coming too fast. I was going into shock. Still, I recognized this particular truth almost before he spoke it. I had never felt close to my parents because they had not been my parents. Tracy was my mother. That meant . . .

"Was Harry my real father?" I asked.

"I suppose he still is. There's no reason to think he's dead."

"Who are you? What are you?" I asked.

"An Anulakai overshadowing a human mind and body."

"You mean, you're possessed by an Anulakai?"

He shook his head. "Possession implies lack of freedom. All we have become, we did so out of free choice. Years ago our research led us to the secrets of the Anulakai. Think of these secrets as a rare form of knowledge that taught us how to contact them and attune our minds to their minds. In return we were given power and insight, and freedom from emotions and other limiting human qualities."

"This process started when you discovered this temple?" I asked.

"No. It began years ago when we found a smaller site that belonged to the Anulakai. From it we gleaned enough information to find other sites. From all of these sites combined we were able to put together enough knowledge to contact our masters."

"So if they're the masters, you must be the slaves."

He shook his head. "It is an honor to serve them."

"What about this Shar Temple? It looks djinn to me."

"You are perceptive. This temple was built by the djinn before the Anulakai conquered this part of the world. We know it is connected to what you call the Island of the Djinn. That is why it became necessary to control it." He pointed to the structures along the side of the walls. For the first time I noticed they were giving off a faint humming sound. "These ancient devices keep the djinn away from here, and trapped where we want them to be."

"Where do the Anulakai live?" I asked.

"In darkness. Yet they crave light. For that reason, they come again and again to this world."

"From where? Another world?"

"You would not understand. Space is not a constant. When the time is right, they come out of the darkness and into the light." He added, "That time is now."

"Charles," Mrs. Steward interrupted. "Enough."

"Now we must get rid of all loose ends," Mr. Toval said.

My father nodded in their direction before turning back to me. "We harbor you no ill will. But you have the potential to be an extraordinary Kala, and we must destroy you before you awaken to your true powers. We tried to do likewise with Tracy, but she caused us tremendous damage before she could be stopped."

"She was not hit by a drunk driver," I said.

"I was perfectly sober when I ran her over."

I slapped his face. "I should have let you die!"

"I told you not to heal me." He turned to Lova. "She's lost a lot of blood and is weak. We'll put her in the water and she'll lose her core heat. Her heart and lungs can be stopped for thirty minutes before you revive her, without any risk of damage to her brain. The best time to enslave her soul is when she's technically dead but still capable of revival."

Lova acted impatient. "It was the djinn who invented cold baths to facilitate the process of possession. Just put her in the water and leave. I'll take care of the rest."

My father shook his head. "We will stay to make sure the possession is complete. This bloodline has caused us too much grief in the past. We need to be a hundred percent certain it has been eliminated."

Something crucial struck me right then.

"You say you're not my father, but my third wish was for my father to be healed. By the Laws of the Djinn, I cannot be made a thrall."

"You wished for *Charles* to be healed. I healed him. You are not going to escape on a false technicality."

The discussion appeared to amuse my father.

"Who am I to argue about how many wishes you made."

I glared at him. "You disgust me."

He ignored me and turned to Lova. "Hand over the carpet."

"I earned this carpet by performing a specific djinn wish. It is mine."

Mrs. Steward raised a green crystal and pointed it at Lova.

"You don't have Sara's resistance to a pashupa," she said. "You would be wise to turn over the carpet."

Lova stared at the crystal and trembled. She did as she was told, giving the carpet to my father.

CHAPTER TWENTY-THREE

THE POOL OF WATER they threw me into was not deep. At first it did not intimidate me. The water reached only to my waist. There was no way I was going to go into hypothermia and lose consciousness with my upper half out of the water.

But I was naive. I did not understand that I was facing a tried and proven method. They had thrown me into a pool where the sides were made of polished marble and were extremely slippery. Wet, this marble was almost impossible to get a grip on. It seemed incredible, but I was trapped in a mere three feet of water. My shoes could not get any traction on the floor of the pool. The others didn't care when I swam away from them, to the other side of the pool, and tried to climb out. I just kept slipping. The more I fell down, the more my upper body got soaked.

They knew it was only a question of time.

I shivered. I was not sure what to do. I decided to explore the pool. It was roughly horseshoe-shaped. I half walked, half swam to the hot spring at the rear of the temple and saw it was separated from the cold water by ten feet of rock. It kicked up plenty of steam but was useless when it came to warming me up. It was just too far away.

There was another problem. At the back of the pool, the water got a lot deeper and I could no longer feel the bottom. I ended up struggling to keep my head above water. Not only that, the steam had a thick sulfur odor. It stunk of rotten eggs and made me gag. In the end, I was forced to retreat to the shallow end at the front of the temple.

There was no way out.

By the time I returned from exploring the pool, the young men were already back in their holes, moaning in pain. I saw Lova sitting at the edge of my pool with her eyes closed. So far she had not attempted another attack on my mind but I knew one was coming. She was waiting until I got weaker. But her inexperience was showing. I knew her mate would have throttled me the instant I had healed my pseudo-dad.

My dad, Mr. Toval, and Mrs. Steward had lost interest in all of us. They'd taken the carpet and locked it inside an Anulakai vault. The structure must have been heavily shielded. No matter how much I called to the carpet, nothing happened. It was a pity I was not yet a true Kala.

"Sara. Are you there?" Amesh called from somewhere below. He was not far away, over the edge of the pool and down a few steps. But I could not see him, so he felt farther away.

"Yeah. Taking a nice cold bath. How about you?" I said.

"I'm in one of these holes. I can't climb out and I can't sit down."

"Just wait until you have to go to the bathroom."

"I was an idiot to make such a big deal about that."

"You were just being shy is all," I said.

"I've been such a jerk. If I had listened to you when you told me how dangerous the djinn were, none of this would have happened."

"I don't know. You heard the Anulakai gang talking. They've been plotting this for a long time. I think we were screwed before we even found the carpet."

"It's hard to believe that man's not your father."

I felt terrible sorrow but tried to keep my voice even. "Tell me about it. And my mother's not my mother. It probably explains why I grew up with an attitude."

"You don't have an attitude. You're smart and you know what you want. That's what makes you strong."

I shivered. I could not stop shivering. "I wish I could come up with a clever idea to get out of here."

Amesh was silent for a moment. But when he spoke next, there was pain in his voice. "I know the djinn is waiting for you to pass out so it can make you its thrall. That's not right. I was the one who made all the selfish wishes and you're the one who has to pay."

"Well, being tortured to death is nothing to look forward to."

"I know, but you don't deserve this. Everything you've done with your djinn has been to help others. I can't believe your compassion and kindness will lead to an eternity of suffering."

"I can't believe it either," I muttered, in no mood to debate the issue.

His voice cracked. "Sara, I swear to you, if I'm allowed into Paradise after I die and I get to speak with Allah, I'll plead for your release. I'll offer my own soul in place of yours."

Knowing Amesh and how frightened he was of a literal hell, I knew it took a lot of guts for him to make such a promise. "I have faith we're both going to be okay," I said.

"It's strange—up until I met you, I thought all non-Muslims were infidels. I didn't dislike Americans or Europeans, but I didn't think they could get into Paradise. But you've made me see that it's not the name of the God you worship that matters, it's who you are."

I smiled, although my jaw was freezing up. "Amesh, the only reason I've been helping you is because you're so darn cute."

"I'm serious, Sara. You're the best person I know. You're so good."

"Good?" I muttered. "I'd rather be hot."

"Sara. You're real . . ."

"Real?"

He stammered, "Really hot."

"Thanks. So are you."

Speaking of hot, it was scary how rapidly the heat was leaving my body. The cold had become the center of my universe. My feet were numb, which made it hard to stand. When I lost the feeling in my legs, I knew I would fall over. After that I would be unconscious in minutes and Lova would try to break into my brain.

I decided to taunt her. I had nothing better to do.

"Hey, Lova," I said. "It's pretty weird of you to accept help from the Anulakai, don't you think?"

She opened her eyes. "Did you say something, thrall?"

"I'm not your thrall yet. You couldn't get your claws around me, could you?"

"I have time. And you have very little."

"Well, you might want to listen up before you return to djinnville. Think about this. You're accepting help from your sworn enemies. How do you think the other djinn are going to feel about that?"

"They won't care if I return with you."

"What's so special about me?"

"You were born to be a Kala. Now you will be my thrall."

"All right. But they'll know you had the Carpet of Ka and gave it up without a fight. Mrs. Steward just had to wave a crystal in front of you and say the word *pashupa* and you couldn't hand it over fast enough. At least they had to beat me to a pulp before I gave it up."

"I am not a coward!"

"You sure acted like one. But hey, I think I know how to fix your rep."

"Rep?"

"The way other djinn see you. Listen, you have to fight to get the carpet back. It's worth a hundred of me. In fact, if you can get me out of here, I can help you get it back."

"Why should I trust you?"

"I handed it over after my second wish. I'll do the same again."

Lova glanced toward the vault where the Anulakai were probably examining the carpet. "They have a pashupa," she said.

"I know it scares you. But think how they'll be able to use the carpet against your people if there's another war. Who knows what kind of power it'll give them? I'm telling you, you've got to get it back."

Lova considered. "What's your plan?"

"Get me out of this place, back to the surface, where I can warm up, and I'll call for the carpet. It'll come to me. From there, we can fly to the island and I'll hand it over there. You'll return home a hero."

"You needed me to get the carpet back this afternoon."

"I didn't know then what I know now. Later, at night, the carpet taught me a secret technique where I can get it to break down any cage."

Lova was interested, but like always, she wanted more.

"You'd still have to be my thrall," she said.

"No way. You can have the carpet or me, but you can't have both. And you'd be a fool not to take the carpet."

"Teach me this secret and I'll help you escape."

"Do I look like I was born yesterday?"

Lova stood. "I was born thousands of years ago. You're just fifteen years old. To me, yes, you look like you were born yesterday."

I shrugged. "Fine. I'm glad I'm going to be there—even as a thrall—to watch you explain to your friends how you lost the Carpet of Ka without even putting up a fight."

Lova glanced at the others. They looked preoccupied.

"If I help you, you'll have to free the carpet immediately."

"Fine."

"How come you can't do it right now?"

"Because, my dear, I'm freezing to death. I can't concentrate in here. Now you make up your mind. Help me or not. But if you're going to help, then it's got to be now."

Lova considered a moment longer. Then she moved, fast. She strode to my side of the pool and stuck out her djinn arm. I tried to grab it with my right hand but my fingers were numb. I had to rely on her to pull me from the water. Then I discovered my feet were numb. I couldn't stand, never mind run out of the cavern.

"Go now or they'll see you!" Lova hissed.

I leaned on a pillar for support. "Help me to the cave entrance. The feeling's beginning to come back to my feet."

"Where did the feeling go?"

"Nowhere. The cold just stopped it."

"You humans are so frail." Lova shook as she helped me up. "They'll see me!"

"Stop whining and do what I said."

Lova supported me as far as the cave entrance. By then I could stand without help. We stumbled past the entrance and started to hike up the long tunnel that led back to the surface. I had feeling in my feet but was unable to run. One more minute, I swore, that's all I needed, and I would sprint to safety.

A green light suddenly crackled behind us and Lova pulled me in front of her, shielding herself. Such a brave djinn. I shoved her away just in time to dodge the oncoming pashupa.

As it was, I was the one who saved us. Like an angry ball of lightning, the pashupa flew past the gap between us and hit the wall farther up the cave. It exploded with the force of a cruise missile. The shock wave and shower of dirt and rock did not scare me. I still wanted to make a run for it. But Lova froze in place and I wasted valuable time trying to get her butt in gear.

I should have left the stupid djinn behind.

Mrs. Steward and my father appeared. Neither seemed angry at me. Of course I was the dead Kala, the sacrifice, the meat on the altar. No one could blame me for wanting to escape.

But Lova had broken their deal.

They were not pleased, nor did they seem like the forgiving type.

My father spoke to Lova. "We have gone out of our way to help you possess this human, and yet you try to help her escape. Explain yourself."

Lova was stunned. She looked to me to defend her. What a joke. I was going back in the freezing water. I wasn't going to waste my breath on her.

"This behavior cannot be tolerated," Mrs. Steward said, her pashupa still sparkling with green light. "This djinn should be terminated."

My father disagreed. "Destroy it and its hold on Sara is terminated."

"That doesn't sound so bad," I muttered.

"Then kill them both," Mrs. Steward said.

My father spoke mechanically. "We want the djinn to enslave her to take her out of our future equations. Kill her and there's a chance her kind will locate another body for her spirit and restart her work against us. You recall I have experience in these matters. Look at how long it took me to negate the one called Tracy."

"You're all cowards," I said. "Put me back in your pool, I don't care. I'll never be anyone's thrall. You may kill my body but none of you will ever touch my soul."

My father stared at me with blank eyes. "Return her to the pool."

An hour had passed since my failed escape, and I was sitting in the shallow end of the pool with my head nodding. I was flat on my butt and the warmth seemed to be flowing out of my body so fast they could have been pumping ice water into my veins.

I had passed the point of shivering. My physical warmth was being washed away, but I felt a deeper warmth begin to glow inside. It was a psychological warmth, maybe even a spiritual one. It was surprisingly pleasant. It kept urging me to close my eyes and relax and let go.

Lova sat nearby. They had put some kind of weird eye above her head. The strange thing was, I could see it only when I closed my eyes. It looked like a snake's eye. It floated in the air, watching and waiting.

"Stay with me!" I heard Amesh yell. "Sara?"

"Tired," I mumbled.

"Fight it. Fight the djinn. You're strong. Remember what the carpet told you. You have powers they don't know about."

"I'll fight them after I die," I muttered.

"I'm not going to let you go!"

I struggled to get out some nice last words.

"Amesh," I whispered.

"Talk louder. I can't hear you."

"Listen, I'm going to black out. I can't stop it. But I want you to know it's not so bad. What I mean is, I'm not scared."

"Stay awake. Keep talking to me."

"Can't. Amesh, I don't mind it ending this way. I feel like we got to be close, and that makes me happy. I'm going to die now, but I want to say I love you. Yeah, I love you. Is that okay?"

"It's better than okay. It's fantastic. I love you, too."

"Really? You're not just saying that because I'm dying?"

"Sara. I loved you the moment I met you."

"Is that why you hit me?"

"I didn't hit you."

It was hard to remember. "How did I end up on the floor?"

"We were fighting over a package."

"Oh, that's right. I'm sorry."

There were tears in his voice. "It doesn't matter. You're great, you're amazing. You were a much better girlfriend than I was a boyfriend."

"It was easier for me. I wasn't possessed."

"I'm sorry I acted so crazy."

"No, Amesh, no. It's not like that. I don't care what you

did. The love I feel for you just loves. So when I say I love you, everything is sweet and wonderful like the day we met."

"We only met two days ago," he said.

I smiled to myself. "That's what's so amazing about us. It feels like we spent a lifetime together."

"Thanks for taking away my pain."

"No problem. It's what good girlfriends do," I said.

Those were the last intelligent words I said. Amesh told me again that he loved me but his voice was far away. It came to me like an echo down a long cave. *Love . . . Sara . . .* They were the best last words to hear in my life.

Even though I could no longer feel my body, I somehow knew I was sitting with my chin on my chest, my blond hair hanging in the water. Since I was about to die, it did not really matter if I slipped under. I was so far gone I doubted I would feel any choking sensation. But I felt there was something dignified about sitting up while I died. I tried to open my eyes one last time to make sure I was upright.

Then I heard my name.

Sara Sashee Wilcox, listen to me. Obey me.

I knew immediately the voice did not belong to a friend, but it took me a moment to recognize its source. Then, for the second time that night, I felt weird tendrils trying to enter the back of my skull. It was fortunate that I had felt them before because they immediately put me on the defensive.

It was Lova, reaching for my soul, trying to make me a thrall.

I did three things in that instant to block her.

I remembered the white light and it was there.

It filled my head as if by magic.

I remembered my father was no longer my father.

That meant Lova did not know my real last name.

My father had forgotten to tell her what it was.

That fact caused her to panic. I felt her scream inside.

What is your last name, Sara?

Then I laughed, at her fear, and I think it was this laughter that saved me the most. Because only someone who feared they could lose their soul could have it taken away. I was never going to become anyone's thrall.

I lost all awareness of where I was. I was just gone.

But I did not black out. If anything, a switch was thrown on the inside and I began to feel another part of me waking up. This part of me had always been there, I realized. I had just not been aware of it because for fifteen years my head had been consumed with trivia. It was sad but true—99.99 percent of my thoughts as Sara had been worthless. For example, I realized I had spent up to two hours a day thinking about my body—whether I was cute or not. That seemed impossible but it was true. Worse, I had spent another two hours a day fantasizing about what I was going to eat. Finally, when it came to guys, forget about it. I thought about guys even when I was looking at myself in the mirror or eating a cheeseburger.

Yet these thoughts didn't bother me because they were not me. I'd had them, of course, but that part of me seemed far away. That part concerned a girl named Sara. The rest of me had just sat back and watched.

That was what I felt like right then. Like I was the Watcher.

The Watcher was huge, and I was her, and I could go where I wanted and do what I wanted. These Sara thoughts—I could worry about them later, or never. They sort of bored me anyway.

Bored me to death. Ha! I think the Watcher had just made a joke. I suspected I was dead, and although it was nothing like I had imagined, it was not bad. Where I was and who I was felt pretty perfect. Still, a sublime restlessness swept over me. The Watcher wanted to communicate with another Watcher.

The Watcher thought of Tracy and just like that I flew to her.

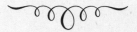

CHAPTER TWENTY-FOUR

THE NEXT THING I KNEW I was sitting in a hospital room beside a patient. The woman was lying on her back in bed with a tube down her throat and another tube attached to her belly. She also had an IV line dripping a clear solution into a shunt in her left arm.

The woman on the bed was Tracy. She had once been beautiful, but years in a coma had eaten away her fat and what was left was the proverbial bag of bones. Still, there was something in the contours of her sunken cheeks, in the color of her hair, and especially in the glow that lit her sleeping face that said her beauty was far from exhausted.

"Do you really think so?" a woman across from me asked. She was sitting on a chair on the other side of the bed. Her shiny blond hair was cut short, her nose was cute, small like my own. She had blue eyes like mine, too, but hers were pure cobalt.

"Tracy!" I said.

"Hi, Sara."

"Are you alive? Did they lie when they said those were your ashes?"

"My sister didn't lie. She thought I had been cremated. Your father lied."

"He's not my father."

Tracy chuckled. "Don't you think I know that?"

I laughed with her. "This is amazing, sitting here, talking to you. It's something I've dreamed about for years." I paused. "It's not a hallucination, is it?"

"Does it feel like a hallucination?"

"It feels real, more real than the life I just came from. You wouldn't believe what I've been through."

"I wouldn't believe it? Sara, I've been watching you."

"How?"

"How do you think? Through the carpet."

"You can see through the Carpet of Ka?"

She nodded solemnly. "I can speak through it as well."

I almost fell off my chair. Honestly, I was the ghost who almost fell.

"Are you saying I've been talking to you this whole time?"

She grinned. "Who else would have taken the time?"

She teased me to keep the mood light. But this new information didn't just fill me with joy. It made me want to explode. The carpet was so dear to me and here we had shared it in such an intimate way. No wonder when I had found it, I had felt like I had found my best friend. I wanted to run around the bed and hug her.

She must have read my mind. She made a gesture for me to remain seated. "I don't know how much time we have. And there are things you must know."

"What sort of things?" I asked.

"The rules have not changed. I can tell you many things but it is still better if you ask the right question. Then I'm free to say more."

"Who gives you permission to answer any of my questions?"

She smiled. "I'm sorry, I can't answer that one."

I considered. "You're acting like I might survive this ordeal."

"You can survive but you must act soon."

"But I'm dying in a pool of freezing water, never mind the fact I'm surrounded on all sides. I've got Lova waiting to change me into a thrall. And I've got the three Anulakai sitting around with their pashupas." I paused. "How am I to escape?"

"What do the temples on the island and the Shar Temple have in common?"

"Cold water?"

"True. What else?"

"They're both djinn temples."

"Excellent. They're connected—the djinn connected them. Your fake father said as much. But what he doesn't know is that at the height of the war with the Anulakai, the djinn created a gateway between the temples."

"But my father said the devices the Anulakai installed in the cavern are there to keep the djinn out."

"This gateway is secret and is not affected by those devices."

"Are you saying I can use the gateway to reach the island?"

"Yes. Lova knows about it, the others don't. But she doesn't imagine for a second that you'll be able to use it to escape."

"How do you know about it?"

"I've used it in the past."

"What do I have to do?"

"Swim."

"Swim where?"

"Down and out. You've seen how the pool deepens as it approaches the rear of the temple. You have to swim to the center and then down. If you swim deep enough, a powerful current will take hold of you and sweep you to the island."

"But the island is a hundred miles out at sea," I protested.

"Time and space are not constants."

"You're saying this gateway is like a dimensional doorway between the Shar Temple and the island?"

"If you like. Humans have yet to invent the right words for these things."

"Hold on. Don't start talking like the carpet again."

"The carpet did not talk to you. I talked through it."

"Why?"

"It's very old, ancient, and it's sacred."

"Sacred? Does that mean it's alive?"

"That's a mystery you must solve for yourself."

"I think I know the answer. It feels ten times more alive than most people I've met." I paused. "Have you owned the carpet before?"

"No one owns the carpet. It chooses a different partner at different times. Right now, it has chosen you. You belong together."

"Who built it? Or made it?"

"That's a great mystery. Many mysteries surround it. Another time, I will tell you stories about it, some so beautiful they'll bring tears to your eyes."

"Can I ask about the djinn island?"

"Of course."

"You wanted me to go there."

"You had to go. You had to begin your education."

"My education to be a Kala?"

"Yes."

"What will I do as a Kala?"

"Right now a war between humans, the djinn, and the Anulakai is about to start. You must help stop it or you must help win it."

"Where do the Anulakai come from?"

"Out of the darkness."

I sighed. "What do they want with Earth?"

"They're a race that seeks to enslave other races. But they're not all evil. There are many among them who question the direction they've chosen. It's my hope that you'll be able to contact such beings in the near future. They could be of immense help to us."

"Who is 'us'? What are we trying to do?"

"'Us' are people like you and me, and others who are human beings descended from powerful bloodlines. We are the Order of the Kala. Our purpose is simple: survival. We are fighting for the survival of mankind."

"Could the Anulakai propel us into another realm the way they have the djinn?"

"It's possible. It's possible they could wipe us out altogether."

"Lova says they made us. Is that true?"

Tracy hesitated. "She mixes truth with lies."

"Did you set up what happened to Amesh on the djinn island?"

Tracy looked puzzled. "I didn't set up anyone."

"But the way things turned out, I was forced to remain on the island and learn about the djinn in order to save Amesh. You admit that's what you wanted."

"Last summer, when Amesh heard of the Shar Temple, he became obsessed. He did everything he could to learn about it."

"Was that bad?" I asked, although I knew the answer.

"His interest wasn't innocent. He heard it was a djinn temple and he wanted the djinn inside it to grant him wishes. Of course, there were no djinn inside it."

"I guessed as much," I said with a sigh, thinking of his poor behavior on the island.

"I'm sorry," Tracy said.

"Why are you sorry? Is he not cut out for this type of work?"

"He's a nice boy—with faults and strengths like anybody else—who might grow into a great man. I know you care about him but I cannot predict his future."

"Are there Anulakai on Earth?" I asked.

"At present, they work through agents like the man who pretended to be your father."

"Didn't you recognize him when he appeared in my mother's life? I mean, in your sister's life?"

"Not at first. I apologize for that. His disguise was subtle. He has a great deal of knowledge, but it's a different kind of knowledge than what we aspire to."

"How so?" I asked.

"The Kala seek to learn the secrets of nature. There's a place deep inside every Kala that knows the creation is alive. We trust in the creation. We have faith in nature and believe it has a plan for each and every one of us. The Anulakai are the opposite—they're more interested in controlling nature, not working with it. They trust more in machines than in life. They seek to control life through the use of technology."

I frowned. "Does that mean technology is evil?"

"Not at all. But it must be used in harmony with nature."

"Can humans and djinn be allies?" I asked.

"They fought together against the Anulakai in the past."

"Lova acts like we contributed little to that war."

"Lova has her prejudices. But she was a perfect djinn to invoke the first time around." Tracy paused. "You know how to negate your contract with her?"

"Yes."

"Good. Do it as soon as you escape."

"How many djinn have you worked with in the past?"

"Too many. That's one of the reasons I'm stuck here."

"Are you joking?" I asked.

"My road has been complicated. I've probably taken too many risks." Tracy smiled. "But that sounds like someone else I know."

"Hey, no guts, no glory. Where is 'here' by the way?" Out of the corner of my eye I saw a window, and beyond it something tall sparkled. It looked like the Chrysler Building! Was I in New York City?

Tracy was amused. "Don't you know? Right now we're stuck between life and death. We're in what the Tibetans call the Bardos Realm. The world between the living and the dead."

"Interesting. Okay, you've told me how to escape this place. Can you escape?"

"Don't worry about me. I ran up too many debts with too many djinn. At the same time, I'm being chased by your father and his gang. It's a wonder I'm in a coma and not dead."

I stood. "I'm not going to leave you in this condition."

Tracy also stood. "Sara, now is the time to worry about yourself. I'm asleep in a hospital. Let me be."

"We'll see," I said.

"Sara!"

"I'm not going to argue with you."

"Same here. You're to make no rescue attempts."

"All right."

"You have to promise me."

"I promise. Now how do I wake up and find the strength to swim through this gateway you've described?"

Tracy grabbed the plastic tube that fed oxygen down her body's throat. "In a moment we'll remove this. We'll have to both focus our energy to get it to move because we're not in the same dimension as the tube. That will set off an alarm but don't worry. A nurse will come along and fix it. But before she arrives, you must breathe in as much air as possible."

Tracy studied the buttons on the computer monitor above the bed and pressed down on one with two fingers. "I'm adjusting the oxygen concentration and the air temperature. I'm making it as hot and full of oxygen as possible."

"Will that be enough to revive my physical body?" I asked.

"Yes. The air is coming fast and hot now. Grip the tube as tight as possible." Tracy paused. "Are you ready?"

"I have more questions to ask."

Like the biggest question of all.

She was my mother. Why had she let me go?

"Ask them later on the carpet," she said.

"The carpet no longer belongs to me."

"Nonsense. The carpet decides who it belongs to." Tracy smiled. "Now pull out the tube and breathe in as much air as possible."

Tracy did not give me a chance to say goodbye. Our hands met over the center of the bed, where the tube hung from a wire, and I was given a jolt of her power just by touching her. It made me realize how advanced she was. Together we pulled the tube free but I'm convinced she did most of the work. The tube hissed loudly. Tracy nodded and I stuck it in my mouth and breathed.

Ah, the feel of that artificial air in my lungs. For some reason it tasted like the fresh air of a jungle. It was wonderfully warm. I did not realize how cold I was until I began to suck on it. It was like a miracle; the hospital air in New York was making my freezing corpse in Turkey come alive. The harder I sucked on the tube, the warmer I felt but the less clear the room became. Soon I could see only the tube and my mother's smiling face. I remembered that look from long ago, and knew she was proud of me.

CHAPTER TWENTY-FIVE

I GASPED AS I SUCKED in a deep breath and raised my head above the shallow end of the pool. A quick glance showed me that Lova was still sitting by the side of the water, her eyes shut. In the background I could hear several of the boys crying in pain. I didn't see my fake father or his cronies but I didn't search for them either.

I was in no condition to go anywhere. My limbs were almost frozen. Yet there was life left in them, in the deep muscles of my legs and arms, even if my toes and fingers were numb. Leaning forward, I pushed off the side of the pool and waded around to the deep end. When I could no longer feel the bottom, I floated on my back and tried to relax. Then I took a series of deep breaths and let myself sink.

It was dark down below. I could not see where I was going. All I could do was trust and swim into that darkness. It took courage; it went against every instinct in my body. I trusted Tracy but I could have sworn I was swimming toward my death.

Then I felt the grip of a current. It was not subtle. It grabbed me and pulled me deeper. The pain from the pressure in my ears was intense. I kept trying to pop them by holding my nose and blowing, but the current was too fast for my feeble efforts.

I was pulled down far when I suddenly noticed warm sky above. It made no sense. The roof of the cavern that held the Shar Temple was dark. Yet the water above me was now a beautiful blue, pierced with rays of yellow sunlight.

I swam upward. As I neared the surface I got my first clear view of my surroundings.

I was back on the island! It worked!

I swam to the edge of the central pool with arms that weighed tons. I had to rest at the side before I finally pulled myself out of the water and lay panting on the walkway that led to the triangular temple. I had no idea if my pot was where I had left it, but there was something wrong with the entire basin.

The walkway was covered in dust. Not the type of dust that gathered overnight, or even the sort that built up with a recent storm. This dust was old—it had caked over the marble floor like a dozen separate coats of paint.

Staggering to my feet, I saw a layer of dirt covered the walkways that separated the six temples. Yet the pools that shone beside them were clean. The only explanation was that the water was being constantly replaced.

Where was Hara? He would never have let the basin get so dirty. Plus he was supposed to have been guarding my pot. I worried something had happened to him and Aleena since I had left. But I didn't know how long ago that had been. The word *since* scared me. I had to keep reminding myself that time was not a constant when one traveled to and from the island.

Walking like a drunk, I headed for the triangular temple.

Thankfully the door was still cracked open with the stones, although they were now worn down to a third of their original size.

Inside was unchanged. It was clean and cool. The candles lit at my entry and I saw Trakur's artifact resting on the altar. The emerald snake and its fangs, the gold hilt, and most of all, the hidden sword—hidden inside the hilt. I was not likely to forget that blade and its hunger for blood.

I saw my pot as well. It looked the same as the night I had left it, although I was beginning to fear that had been centuries ago.

Picking up the pot, I raised it over my head.

There was a reason I had added conditions to my last two wishes.

"It is binding in so far as all wishes between humans and djinn are binding—as specified in the ancient laws governing such contracts."

The carpet had taught me it was only the most ancient laws between humans and the djinn that allowed for contracts to be negated by the destruction of the artifacts. But I had not bothered to add the extra language to my first wish because that wish was not binding.

It was just another tactic I had used to throw Lova off.

"Trakur Analova La!" I shouted. "I, Sara, now negate our contract!"

Goodbye, Lova, I thought. *And good riddance.*

Bringing the pot down hard, I shattered it on the altar. A scream emanated from every wall inside the temple. There was no mistake; the sound was feminine. I had to smile.

I picked up the hilt. Since I wasn't going to be invoking its boss, I did not have to grip the handle and risk the piercing fangs. Still, we were connected, that artifact and I, and its djinn. Bound together in blood. I had already made one wish using Lova's mate. I hoped I would not have to make a second.

I shoved it in my pocket and returned to the pond.

Sitting on my knees beside the water, I drew in several deep breaths and let my body relax. This time, when I focused on the white light flowing into the top of my head, it was much stronger. I knew why. I had died and been reborn. Indeed, I had entered the realm where that white light shone eternally, and from now on I would always be a part of it.

I may not have been a Kala but I was no longer a beginner.

I focused on the carpet and my longing to be with it, and to fly it from one end of the world to the other. I had no idea how far I was from Istanbul. I could not even have said what century it was. But I felt a strong link form between me and the carpet, strong as a rope. If I pulled on my end and it pulled on its end, working together, we could help each other escape.

Minutes after kneeling beside the pond, the carpet flew out of the water and landed beside me. I was not surprised, my faith in it was that strong. But I cried as I held it again. I always felt incomplete when we were not together.

Time, time—I did not know how fast it was flowing back in the Shar Temple. For that reason I did not linger, although I longed to fly over Hara and Aleena's home and see if they were okay. Even the goats would have been a welcome sight. Yet a part of me was afraid of what I would find.

Hanging on to the sides of the carpet, I asked it to erect an air bubble and take me back through the gateway that led to the Shar Temple. The trip was smoother and faster this time around. But I think the carpet wanted to play. It managed to splash me and get me wet.

When I flew out of the temple pool, all the guys were moaning now, including Amesh and Spielo. But there was no sign of my father and his gang.

I had no idea what time it was.

When I flew over Amesh's hole and he saw me on the carpet, and saw I was alive, he burst out crying. I had never seen him weep so openly—he didn't bother to hide it. Of course, being a natural-born sap, I wept with him.

"I knew. I just knew," he whispered.

Rescue time. The four who had hurt Amesh were guilty. But he told me to go ahead and help them. The hole had given him a taste of an agony he wasn't eager to prolong for anyone, friend or foe.

Of course I freed Amesh and Spielo first.

I did so by putting the carpet in reverse—yes, it had such a gear, after all—and slipping backwards into each hole, where the carpet magically curled and scooped out one boy at a time. The four bad guys were so glad to see me they started praying. They kept thanking Allah, instead of me, but that was okay.

It took me only a few minutes to get everyone out of their holes, but I wasn't comfortable leaving anyone on Becktar's property. At the same time, Amesh and Spielo were my priority. In the end I flew my boys out to the desert, to a spot beyond the compound. Then I returned for the four scoundrels. I wanted to only take two at a time but their nerves were shot and I could understand why.

The carpet managed to expand its shield and keep all four aboard while we flew to Istanbul. Along the way I encouraged them to find new jobs. I set them down close to where they lived.

Finally I was able to pick up Amesh and Spielo in the desert.

They were in remarkably good spirits. They said they had only been in the holes two hours after I left, but it had been a long two hours. It seemed that when I had vanished, my father and his partners wondered if I was receiving help from a "higher source." Then the Carpet of Ka disappeared on them— exploding a vault in the process—and they got really worried. They left in a hurry. They did not even take time to kill Lova for letting me escape.

The boys had no idea where they went.

"Your dad could be back at the hotel," Amesh said. "Why don't we grab him and fly a few miles out over the ocean and dump him?"

"Why don't we forget revenge for one night?" I said.

Amesh held up a hand. "It's not personal anymore, I swear. But those three are a danger to all of us. It's smart to strike while they're confused and not sure what we're capable of."

"I don't want to kill my dad," I said.

"He's not your dad," Amesh said.

"I don't want to kill anyone. I've seen enough grief."

"I have an idea," Spielo said. "Let's celebrate." When neither of us responded, he went on. "Hey, things worked out good. Amesh got his hand back and it looks great. He's got gems and lots of lira. Not to mention . . ." Spielo patted the carpet. "We got a magic carpet. Let's fly around town, and buy what we want, and eat wherever we want."

"You're supposed to be in the hospital," I warned him.

Spielo shook his head. "I screamed so much in that hole, my lungs got real clean."

"I wouldn't be opposed to spending a few lira," Amesh said.

"It's the middle of the night. The stores will be closed," I said.

"Show enough money and all the stores will open for us," Spielo said.

"Show enough money and all the police will want to know where it came from," I said.

"Don't be paranoid," Amesh said. "We can spend some."

"A little," I corrected. "But you need to see your Papi and Mira. They're worried sick about you."

Amesh frowned. "There's no way we're going to be able to explain this flying carpet to him."

"He might believe us," I said.

Amesh waved his new hand. "Trust me, he'll never understand."

I smiled. "You know your Papi."

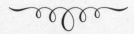

CHAPTER TWENTY-SIX

S PIELO WAS RIGHT, our situation looked posi-
tive. Everyone had been rescued. Amesh had his hand and gems.
I had the Carpet of Ka. And the bad guys had fled.

But from another perspective, my life was in ruins.

I could not go home. I could not go to any place where my
father might find me. Amesh and his family would probably
offer to take me in, but I was an American. I had to return to
the States and somehow try to rebuild a home life.

I knew of only one way to do that. But it was dangerous.
Yet if I did not act immediately, the danger would only increase.

I had to get my mother back, my real mother, and that meant I had to get to New York.

But I did not bother the boys with my problems, at least not at first. I let them relax and have some fun. They took me to an all-night Turkish restaurant—which served lamb and goat!—and then we went shopping. Turns out there were plenty of mom-and-pop stores that would open at the sight of cash.

Amesh and Spielo loaded up on all the electronic equipment they had always wanted but could never afford: iPods, iPhones, a Wii, an Xbox—the works! They also took me shopping for clothes but ended up buying a dozen outfits for themselves. Amesh got some designer jeans and a leather jacket he looked pretty darn cute in. He made me accept a similar outfit so we looked like a couple, and then insisted I put it on.

How could I say no?

Finally, we swung by Amesh's house. He had presents for his Papi and Mira, but the biggest present of all was his hand, although Mr. Demir looked at it with concern. I reassured him that his grandson did not "owe" anyone or anything for this miracle. Mr. Demir wanted to believe me but we both agreed that Amesh would be better off keeping the hand out of sight for the time being.

Mr. Demir deserved a much longer explanation of what was going on, and I promised him that he would have it. But I excused myself by saying I still had to rescue someone close to me. Mr. Demir understood. Again, he and Mira gave me warm hugs and I was reminded of Tracy.

As Amesh walked me away from his home, I explained that I had to take a long journey, and why. He listened closely, he was very sympathetic. But he worried I might be walking into a trap.

"Your father and his people must have agents all over the world."

"I'm sure they do," I said. "But there's no reason for them to think I know the truth about Tracy."

"How long has she been in a coma?" Amesh asked.

"Four years. Maybe five."

He whistled. "What makes you think you can wake her up?"

"I'm going to do what it takes."

"I thought we agreed to keep away from the djinn."

I caught his eye. "Whatever it takes," I repeated.

Amesh sighed. "Then I have to come with you."

"You can't. You don't have a passport and I can't hang around and wait until you get one. They could send someone to the hospital to stick a needle in her vein while we're waiting."

"I'm surprised they haven't killed her already," Amesh said.

"They must have some reason for keeping her alive."

Amesh pointed to the carpet in my pack. There was a faint light in the east. Another hour and the sun would be up.

"How fast did you say you went when you outran that jet?"

"I hid from it. I didn't outrun it."

"But to stick with it you must have flown more than a thousand kilometers an hour."

I translated that to be about six hundred miles an hour.

"So?" I said.

"There's your answer. And I bet it can go twice that speed if need be. Hell, for all we know, it can go a hundred times that speed."

"Amesh!"

"What?"

"You just swore!"

He smiled. "I know. It felt good."

"Are you saying I should fly the carpet to New York?"

"I'm saying *we* should fly it there."

I gestured toward the east. "We're about to lose the stars."

"At high speed, the carpet can easily stay ahead of the sun."

I considered. As fast as a Boeing 747 was—with all the stops along the way, and customs and security checks—it would take at least a day to get us to New York. The carpet could get us there in a few hours.

"Go tell your Papi and Mira you're taking a trip with me," I said. "But don't tell them where you're going. They'll freak."

He reached out and pulled me close.

"I already told them I was going with you," he whispered.

His concern for my well-being touched me. I had to wipe away a tear.

"I want you with me," I whispered back.

Once again I unrolled the carpet and we lifted up into the air and prepared to head west. The fading stars worried me, but Amesh insisted on a quick stop outside of town.

"We need to pick up the jewels. They'll be safer in America."

"Where did you put them?" I asked.

"In the middle of nowhere."

He had buried the chest in a shallow hole in the desert, not far from the job site. It took us only minutes to uncover them, but the sun seemed to be rising faster than ever. As we soared back into the sky, I worried that the weight of the chest might slow us down.

"You just lifted those four jerks to safety," he said.

"You're not still mad at them, are you?"

He paused, then laughed. "Not on a night like tonight!"

As we left Istanbul and flew over the sea, I decided to take another approach to the global problem we faced when it came to advanced radar systems and jetfighters. I explained my idea to Amesh and it was his turn to look worried.

"You don't want to stay close to the surface?" he asked. "If we fly below a hundred meters, we can evade any radar."

"I'm not comfortable flying at two thousand miles an hour that low. God only knows what we might run into."

Amesh glanced over the side. We were up a half mile and still climbing. But with the shield the carpet had erected, we felt neither the wind nor the cold.

"Exactly how high do you plan on going?" he asked nervously.

"Carpet, raise our elevation to fifteen miles." I enjoyed bragging about the carpet. "There isn't a jet on earth that can fly that high."

"There are rockets. And we're going to enter American air space. We could get shot down."

I waved a hand. "This carpet's more advanced than anything the U.S. Air Force has in its arsenal. We'll be fine."

Ten minutes later, we were up so high, there were no clouds, and overhead the stars burned bright. The moment was pure magic. Likewise, the stars on the carpet shone with extraordinary brilliance. It was only then, after so many amazing flights aboard the carpet, that I got an inkling of what it had been truly designed for.

To travel to other stars, to other worlds.

No human being had built the Carpet of Ka.

For the first time since we'd ridden the carpet together, I lay beside Amesh, our heads inches apart. He had brought some of the new clothes—Spielo had taken the rest for now—and he molded a warm down jacket into a pillow. At our extraordinary speed, we were outracing the moon, and soon it was straight overhead.

I found myself almost hypnotized gazing into his eyes—such dark round wells, lit by soft moonlight. I fell into them, I suppose, into him, and I do not remember who made the first move.

We kissed.

His mouth was warm, his lips were sweet. He could have kissed me once or a hundred times. For me it was like one long ache that kept being soothed. I was more than happy; I was joyful, and even when we paused to rest I felt a contentment inside I had never known before. I felt complete.

Afterward, it was nice just to relax in his arms and talk nonsense. I didn't even discuss my plan to rescue Tracy. It was enough just to be with him.

I told myself it did not matter that he was not a Kala.

We could be together. We could have a future.

He was not going to lose it again. I trusted him.

Yet why did I have to keep telling myself these things?

I had instructed the carpet to head for New York, but I had not given it a precise plot to follow. With the help of the moon shining on the Atlantic, and my binoculars, we saw numerous icebergs. Tiny white points on a black field. I realized that the carpet was following the path of intercontinental jets, going over the pole, or at least near Iceland and Greenland. Amesh got a kick out of the icebergs.

"I saw *Titanic* a dozen times," he confided. "I loved when the ship hit the iceberg and began to sink. It was so realistic."

I poked him with my foot. "Yeah, right. You loved it when Leonardo DiCaprio painted Kate Winslet without her clothes on."

His eyes widened. "She really took off her clothes?"

"You saw the movie."

"That scene was taken out in my country."

I patted his leg. "We'll get you an unedited version while we're in New York," I said.

We were flying over what appeared to be Nova Scotia when the radar alarm came on. It scared Amesh but I did not panic. We scanned the area below us. Sure enough, there were two fiery dots approaching from our right.

"Carpet. Increase our elevation by ten miles. Double our speed."

Amesh whistled. "Wow! Six thousand kilometers an hour?"

"I wouldn't be surprised if it can fly faster than the speed of light."

The rockets continued to inch closer, but the carpet's alarm silenced. I left our speed and elevation alone, confident we were far enough away. My faith was rewarded minutes later when the burning dots sank into darkness.

"Too bad the carpet can't turn invisible," Amesh said.

"The carpet told me it can. It can do all kinds of things we can't imagine. It's just a question of unlocking its secrets."

"You said it's your mother who's been talking to you through it?"

I had told him a few particulars while we were shopping.

"She's the one who forms the words using the stars. But the carpet communicates with me in other ways."

Amesh shook his head. "I feel ashamed."

"Why do you say that?"

"For acting like it belonged to me as much as to you. From the start, it was obvious you knew how to handle it. I was jealous, I'm sorry."

"Don't be sorry, Amesh. You've been put through so much pain."

He nodded and hugged me tighter, not speaking.

The unmistakable glow of New York became visible in the distance. At Amesh's urging, I ordered the carpet to drop down to a hundred feet. I cut our speed to that of a small plane.

"Do you remember the name of the hospital where your mother was being treated?" Amesh asked.

"Hadley Memorial." I did not bother to point out that she was not being treated, but was merely being kept alive. Amesh was studying me.

"You look worried," he said. "Are you afraid you won't be able to find the hospital?"

"She was at Hadley Memorial years ago, but that's in Washington, D.C. Now she's under the control of the Anulakai. I'm sure they've got her stashed in some weird spot, probably some place that isn't even listed as a hospital. All I know for certain is that she's in Manhattan."

"How do you know?" Amesh asked.

"I saw the Chrysler Building when I was in Tracy's room."

"Is that a famous landmark?"

"Very. The only problem is, it looks the same from every direction."

Amesh studied the vast metropolis we were approaching.

"That might be a problem," he said.

Before we rescued anyone, we had to stash Amesh's chest of jewels. We hid them atop the Verrazano-Narrows Bridge, which connected Staten Island to Brooklyn. It was in a special spot only the birds could reach. We figured they would be safe there for as long as we needed.

"I'm going to circle the Chrysler Building from the air," I said as we flew toward the building.

"You said this air space is full of police and helicopters."

"It has been since 9/11. We'll just have to find her fast."

We circled the Chrysler Building several times and got nowhere. There were too many tall buildings in the area. Plus, from my brief vision, I couldn't tell if Tracy had been one mile or five miles from the building.

I needed a second landmark to narrow our search area.

We landed on the top of an office building. Getting off the carpet and stretching, I tried to imagine what altitude I had seen the building from. At thirty stories, I felt we were too low.

"What are we doing?" Amesh asked, standing beside me.

"Getting our bearings. I think we're too close."

"You're not too sure about this, are you?"

"I definitely saw the Chrysler Building. But I saw it while I was in the throes of hypothermia. My heart and lungs were not working. My brain had probably flat lined. I wasn't at my best."

"I think you should try talking to the carpet."

"I tried. But all it says is, 'Stay away.' It's my mom warning us not to take any risks."

"Maybe she knows what she's talking about," Amesh said.

"I don't care. I'm going to rescue her." I yelled at the carpet laid out beside us, "Did you hear that?"

It formed the words. "Go to Hawaii."

"What's in Hawaii?" Amesh asked.

"Nice beaches," the carpet said.

"She's teasing us," I said. "Ignore her."

I kept staring up at the moon. There was something about the moon . . .

Then I had it. I knelt beside the carpet.

"Mom, I know you think it's too dangerous for us to find you, but we're going to keep trying until we're arrested or shot out of the sky. So you may as well cooperate." The carpet did not respond. I continued. "Do you know the name of the hospital you're in?"

"I'm in a coma. When they checked me in, no one said a word to me."

"I know your eyes are probably shut, but is there a light on them?"

"It is dark. It must be nighttime."

"True. It is nighttime. But did a light begin to shine on your eyes, say, two hours ago?"

There was a long pause. "Nope."

"Wait a second! You're awake and sitting outside your body!"

"You weren't supposed to remember that."

"What are you guys talking about?" Amesh asked, confused.

"She can see through her soul. Her soul uses the carpet to talk to us." I turned back to the carpet. "Is the moon shining through your window?"

"It's too dangerous, Sara."

"We're not stopping until we find you," I repeated.

The carpet took a long time to answer. "The moon is shining through my window."

I clapped my hands together. "We've got our second landmark! Now we only have to search one side of the building." I grabbed my binoculars and studied the skyline and then pointed. "That building is in a perfect line between the moon and the Chrysler Building."

Amesh was impressed. "Sometimes you take my breath away."

"Really? Well, now it's your chance to take mine away."

"How?"

"The Anulakai were definitely afraid of Tracy. That means she's going to be guarded. Figure out a way to get rid of them."

Amesh nodded. "Find her room and I'll think of something."

We flew the carpet to a spot where the moon was angled toward the Chrysler Building. From there I simply backed up. There was only one building it could be. It was sixty stories tall and it had only one floor devoted to hospital beds—the forty-second floor. That meant it wasn't an ordinary clinic, probably just a place the Anulakai stashed their victims or wounded.

We flew alongside the building, peering in each window. We had a flashlight but tried not to use it. We didn't want to wake patients or sound any alarms. The moonlight helped and hurt us. It allowed us to peek inside and see if there was a man or woman in the bed.

But it also made us visible. I kept glancing down, expecting a crowd to form on the sidewalk below. *Look! Up in the sky! It's a bird! It's a plane! No, it's the Carpet of Ka!* I was worried a police helicopter would shine its light on us. Nothing would alert Tracy's guards quicker.

We found her fast—I was pretty sure it was her—in a corner room. Hooked up to a breathing pump, she had a needle in her arm shunt, a plastic tube running into her belly. The moonlight shone on her face.

A burly man sat on a chair by the door, his chin resting on his chest. He was asleep, but that gave us only a small advantage.

"Did you figure out a way to get rid of him?" I asked Amesh.

"There could be more than one guard. If she's that dangerous to them, they probably have another one outside her door."

"Just tell me your plan."

Amesh looked around. "It's pretty scary."

"I've already died today. What could scare me?"

"My idea." Amesh pointed to the railings that separated each floor. "Do you think you can stand on it and not fall off?"

The railing jutted out two feet. It appeared to be flat, a steel beam.

"Yeah. As long as I don't look down," I said.

"We're in an air bubble right now. Have the carpet drop it."

"No way!" I snapped.

"We have no choice. We have to see how strong the wind is up here. Grab the sides."

I grabbed hold of the tassels and commanded the carpet to drop its shield. Immediately, we began to sway in the breeze. He was right. I was scared.

"You still haven't told me your plan," I managed to shout.

"Tell the carpet to raise its shield." It did as I ordered. Amesh went on as the carpet settled back down. "My plan's simple but dangerous. First, we pull off the screen and open the window."

I nodded. "We're lucky this building's old. I don't think you can open the windows in most skyscrapers."

"I'll say we're lucky if we're still alive in fifteen minutes. But let me go on with my plan. We tell the carpet to drop us on the railing around the corner from this window. There's another window over there, covered with white curtains. If they turn on the light, we should be able to see inside but they shouldn't be able to see us. Then we send the carpet into her room, with instructions."

"What kind of instructions?" I asked.

Amesh told me. His plan was clever. I thought it might work if we didn't lose our nerve—or fall. That was the biggest flaw in his plan.

"Let's do it," I said.

"You don't want to think about it?"

"If I think about it, I'll chicken out."

To open my mother's window, we had to drop the carpet's shield again. That was bad enough. Fortunately, Amesh had a Swiss Army pocketknife. He popped the screen off and opened the window without making too much noise. The sleeping guard didn't stir.

Next the carpet took us around the corner from the open window so we could remain out of view while it carried out Amesh's final instructions. Now came the hard part. We had to step off the carpet and onto the railing. The carpet helped by lining us up perfectly with the railing. But the wind—God, if only it had been a calm night. If we lost our balance for an instant, it would be over.

Amesh went first, brave boy. He stepped on the railing and immediately flattened his back against my mother's side window. He stood with his arms pressed against the building.

"How does it feel?" I asked.

He was already shivering. "There's plenty of room to stand. It's just the wind, and being up so high." He swallowed thickly. "Sara?"

"What?"

"You don't have to do this. You can wait down below. The carpet can always pick you up when it comes back."

"Why don't we both wait down below until the carpet returns?"

"We can't move your mom without healing her. We have to be done before the carpet gets back."

"That's why I'm staying with you," I said. "I'm doing the healing."

Amesh did not respond.

How did I get off the carpet? I was too much of a coward to stand and step off like Amesh had. Instead, I turned my back to the building and wiggled my butt until I was sitting on the railing. Then I held onto the carpet while I slowly climbed to my feet. But the instant I let go of the carpet . . . well, let's just say it was every bit as scary as facing down bloodthirsty djinn and evil Anulakai.

Closing my eyes, I pressed my back against the glass.

"I hate this plan," I said.

"I wish I had come up with a better one," Amesh agreed.

The wind tugged at my hair, my legs, my pants, my coat. It seemed to make the whole building sway, although that might have been an illusion. It would have helped if I could have kept my eyes shut, but one of us, at least, had to know if the guards were falling for our scheme.

I opened my eyes and peered through the curtains that were supposed to be hiding us. I was pleased to see the light was on in my mother's room. The first guard was awake; good. The carpet had done what we had told it to do. Nudge the guy and then lie down on the floor and play dead.

The door to my mother's room opened. Another guard entered. Along with his partner, he stood and studied the carpet. No one seemed to care about the open window. Certainly, no one looked in our direction, toward the closed window.

"What makes you think they'll step on it?" I asked Amesh through a shaking jaw.

"It's human nature to want to touch a carpet that beautiful."

"When we found it, I felt the opposite. I didn't want to step on it because I didn't want to get it dirty."

"You're a nice girl. These are tough guys. They're guards, they carry guns. They won't care if they get it dirty. They'll step on it. Remember, the carpet just needs them next to it to raise its shield. Then it's got them."

"I wish they'd hurry up."

A guard went to the open window and peered out. But he didn't close it. Perhaps he was happy for the fresh air. I doubted the staff ever opened the windows. The room was probably stale.

His partner called to him. Then one of the men did the strangest thing. In the dark, I saw Amesh give me a knowing smile. The guy was taking off his shoes.

"It attracts him," Amesh said. "He wants to feel it under his feet."

"Did you feel that way when you saw it, tough guy?"

"Sure. Oh, look, the other guy is kneeling beside it. He's feeling it with his hands."

One got on it, rubbed it with his bare feet, then got off. Another got on it, on his knees. It was like they were doing a video workout. I wanted to scream for the two of them to get on the blasted thing at the same time . . .

Then it happened. The carpet raised its shield just as the men stepped on the carpet together. They were trapped inside an invisible bubble. Before they could cry for help, the carpet raced out the window.

Amesh and I heard their howls as they faded in the distance. They probably assumed they were doomed. They would have been if the carpet had followed Amesh's instructions and dumped them in the sea. But I had told it to take them to New Jersey and drop them off in the middle of nowhere.

CHAPTER TWENTY-SEVEN

M OVING AT A SNAIL'S PACE, Amesh
and I crept around the corner and climbed in the open window.
We shut and locked the door and turned out the light. It felt
good to be inside, standing on solid ground. But that joy didn't
approach the happiness I felt at seeing my mother again.

She lay on her back with so many needles and tubes in her.
Amesh was right; we could not move her without returning her
soul to her body. Not unless we were willing to cart a ton of
life-support equipment with us. What magic we were going to
do, we would have to do it now.

Undoing my pack, I went to take out Trakur's artifact.

But I couldn't find it.

"Looking for something?" Amesh asked, holding up the artifact. "Were you planning on using this to save your mother?"

I was angry. "Why did you take it from me?"

"Because it's not your turn."

"What are you talking about? This has nothing to do with you. This is between my mother and me."

"I could say my Papi and Mira had nothing to do with you. But when you were in Istanbul, you did everything you could to calm them down." He paused. "Now I have to return the favor."

He began to slip his right hand, his new hand, into the artifact.

"Wait! Amesh, you don't understand. This djinn's the most powerful one on the island. I've seen it with my own eyes. It doesn't even speak to you without taking some of your blood."

"Did you already ask this djinn for a wish?"

He had me cornered. "Yes," I admitted.

"One's not so bad. We both know that. But two is. You can't owe it anything. It would probably demand the carpet in payment. But if I make the wish, it can't ask for anything in return." Amesh paused. "You know what I'm saying is true."

I nodded. "Ordinarily I wouldn't argue with you. But this djinn is crafty, Amesh. I didn't plan on asking any wish from it. But it tricked me. First it got a taste of my blood, then it wanted more. When I wasn't looking, it let loose its hidden blade, which pops out from there." I pointed to the hilt. "It pierced my side and I had to make a wish just to stay alive. It'll probably try to do the same to you, or worse."

"You think you're smarter than me?"

I hesitated. "Yes."

Amesh shrugged. "I'm not insulted. You are smarter. But what matters is how many wishes you've made. And you've already made one. The next one should be mine."

"Not true. This burden's mine alone. She's my mother."

"Sara, since we met, you've made the right decisions and I've made the wrong ones. Forget about owing the djinn—I owe you." He paused and stared down at my mother. "Give me the name of the djinn."

"Is that why you came with me, to do this?"

"Yes."

"His name is Trakur Analova Ta. Can you remember that?"

Amesh nodded. "How do you want me to word the wish?"

"Wish that Tracy's health is restored so that her body is in perfect condition. So her soul can reenter her body and she can . . . live happily ever after." I stopped, frustrated. "That's not going to work. It sounds like two wishes."

"It is two wishes," Amesh said.

"How about this? 'I wish for Tracy's health—her physical, emotional, mental, and spiritual health—to be restored to how it was before she entered this coma.'"

Amesh nodded. "That's close. But you're not sure that she was healthy just before she went into the coma. We'd better back up the health date. But not too far. The djinn could turn her into a five-year-old."

"Okay, I've got it! Say, 'I want you, Trakur Analova Ta, to restore Tracy's health—her physical, emotional, mental, and spiritual health—to the level it was at on her thirty-fifth birth-day.' Repeat his name and the wish at least twice."

"Are you sure she was healthy at thirty-five?" Amesh asked.

"We had a birthday party for her. She was in great shape."

"How old is your mom now?"

"She's . . . I'm not sure. Forty. Another thing, keep that hilt pointed away from you. The djinn may move about the room to get you to twist it so it points toward your guts. Don't fall for that trap. That's how I got poked." I glanced out the window. "The carpet will be back soon. Are you ready?"

"Ready as I'll ever be."

"Trakur Analova Ta is ugly but he's charming. He's hypnotic—the less you talk to him the better. Invoke him with his name. When he arrives, expect the snake to bite your fingers and drink your blood. The worse thing you can do is try to shake it off. You'll end up tearing your fingers to pieces."

Amesh smiled. "I can handle him. Relax, Sara."

We moved so we were on opposite sides of the bed. Amesh began his invocation. He was fifteen seconds into it when the snake closed its fangs over his index finger and middle finger. To Amesh's credit, he didn't waver. He kept going and then, like a hurricane, Trakur Analova Ta made his entrance.

I could see him clearly, perhaps because I had made contact with him before. He was in a bad mood. His anger was focused on me, not Amesh.

"Sara!" his voice boomed inside my mind. "I have heard in detail the charade you played with my mate. Do not fool yourself into thinking you will play me the same way."

I felt weak addressing him without the artifact in my hand or the carpet beneath my feet. Plus, Lova had told him my first name, which gave him an even greater edge on me. Yet, I knew it was important that I not show any fear.

"Trakur Analova Ta," I said. "It's not I who has called upon you, but this man. He has a wish to make that only the great Trakur Analova Ta can fulfill."

Trakur Analova Ta bore down on me. "I'm not through with you, Sara. Take the sword from your friend, and let me drink of your blood, then perhaps we can see if your wish can be fulfilled."

"It's not my wish but his." I spoke to Amesh. "Time to take charge."

"Trakur Analova Ta, it is I who has summoned you," Amesh said in a strong voice. "Ignore her and listen to me. It is my blood you're drinking."

Trakur Analova Ta whirled on him. "Your blood is common and weak. It does not belong to a Kala. Why should I waste time on you?"

Amesh was thinking and I hoped he'd come up with something good.

"Your time with me is not wasted, oh great Trakur Analova Ta," he said. "Soon I'll mate with Sara, and when we're married, I, too, shall share in her power as a Kala. Drink deeply of my blood while you can. At the same time, listen to my wish."

Amesh's response was inspired! Never mind that he was talking about us getting married. As long as the djinn believed him, I didn't care.

I could see why the djinn would believe him. There was mountains of romantic tension between us. Well, at least I was tense—I was not sure how Amesh felt. He had said I was hot, but of course, that had been when I was about to die. People said all kinds of nice things to you when you were about to croak.

Trakur Analova Ta suddenly acted interested in Amesh, but he did not turn his back on me. He stood between us, so he could keep an eye on us both. Yet he kept moving and I noticed Amesh was having to turn to follow him.

"What's your name?" Trakur Analova Ta asked him.

Amesh did not answer. *Good*, I thought, *keep silent*.

"Your full name. You know mine. It's only proper I know yours."

Amesh went to speak. He had been staring at Trakur Analova Ta too long without a break. I knew he must be hypnotized. Yet I was afraid to interrupt at such a crucial moment. I had warned him . . .

"Amesh . . ." he began.

"Amesh is his name!" I snapped. I was giving nothing away. Surely Lova had already told her mate about Amesh, as well.

"Silence!" Trakur Analova Ta screamed at me. "You insist I speak to your potential mate, and now that we're talking you interrupt. Do not do that again. You have been warned. Once my blade has tasted your blood, it can always find a way to taste it again."

I decided it best to keep silent.

Trakur Analova Ta smiled and repeated my *fiancé's* name to himself. "Amesh . . . Amesh . . . Amesh . . . Tell me, is it your desire to be with Sara?"

"Yes," he said.

I bowed my head and remained silent. Amesh had already made a mistake. If he made another, we were doomed. I could only hope my interruption had broken the djinn's hypnotic spell. It was a pity the creature had Amesh's first name to play with. Each time he said it, Amesh twitched.

"Amesh," Trakur Analova Ta said. "Tell me more of your desire for Sara. I assume that's why you've summoned me. You wish to be mated to her for life?"

I held my breath for what felt like an hour before Amesh answered.

He smiled! "I do not need your help in that area, oh great Trakur Analova Ta. She desires me as much as I desire her. No, I have another task in mind. Listen. I, Amesh, wish for you, Trakur Analova Ta, to restore the health of the woman you see lying here. Her name's Tracy, and I wish for you to restore her physical, emotional, mental, and spiritual health to the level it was at on her thirty-fifth birthday. That is my wish, Trakur Analova Ta. Please carry . . ."

Amesh did not finish. The hidden blade had sprung out like before. Amesh had been wary, at first, to keep the hilt pointed away from his body. But with my interruption he had forgotten about it and the blade sliced his right side. The wound did not look deep but it was long and he started to bleed heavily. Of course, the blood was going nowhere but into the hungry sword, which was still stuck in his side.

Trakur Analova Ta smiled. "Are you sure there's not another wish I can perform for you first?" the djinn asked.

Amesh, God bless him, even with his side gushing blood, smiled again. "Oh great Trakur Analova Ta. I wouldn't waste your healing art on a scratch like this. I've made my wish clear." He repeated it once more, adding, "It is I, Amesh, who commands you."

Amesh had recovered nicely. Trakur Analova Ta drew back and frowned. It was obvious the djinn had no other choice but to grant his wish. The more time that went by, the more blood Amesh would lose.

Out of the corner of my eye I saw bandages. Tape and gauze.

Amesh stared up at the djinn. "Heal her now," he said firmly.

Trakur Analova Ta set about healing Tracy in a curious way. First he allowed his shape to dissolve, until he was a large glowing red oval. Then that oval shrank until it was less than three feet from top to bottom. Only then did he approach Tracy.

But he did not simply touch her.

He sank down into her.

Tracy's body began to jerk and her vital signs became erratic. The bedside computer monitoring her began to beep and I knew there must be a similar computer at the nurses' station going crazy. Grabbing the chair the first guard had been sleeping on, I wedged it against the door—even though it was locked—so no one could enter.

It was a good thing. A few minutes after the beeping started, a nurse began to pound on the door. "Hello? Is there someone in there? Please open the door."

I deepened my voice. "Nurse Palmer here. We have our hands full at the moment. Please come back later."

"I don't know who you are, Ms. Palmer. Is Dr. Landen in there?"

"He's working on the patient. Please, we're very busy. Leave us alone and come back later."

The nurse strode away but I heard her muttering under her breath. She was going for help. Probably for security, who would break down the door.

I turned back to Tracy. Her whole body was flopping on the bed. She was shaking so violently, it was scary. Amesh stepped to my side.

"What should we do?" he asked.

"I'm afraid to interfere. He's the king djinn. He should be able to heal her." I paused to examine his side. The djinn blade was no longer stuck in his side, nor were the fangs still attached to his fingers. He had set down the hilt. But blood seeped through his clothes. I reached for the gauze and tape. "You're bleeding pretty badly. Let me bandage you up."

He stopped me. "Don't worry about me. Your mother's trying to breathe. But that tube they have stuck down her throat is choking her. We've got to get it out."

"But what if she's not ready to breathe?"

"Listen to her lungs," Amesh said, and he had a point. It was as if she was trying to squeeze air past the tube. He set down the artifact and added, "We have to take it out."

Thankfully, Amesh took charge. He told me to hold her steady while he tilted her head back and grabbed the tube and yanked on it. I had no idea how he knew how to do this. From watching *ER* reruns?

There followed a horrible minute where Tracy turned blue and we worried we had made a terrible mistake. She was struggling to breathe on her own, but her diaphragm and chest muscles must have shrunk to nothing during her long sleep.

But hadn't we ordered the djinn to restore her to the health she had enjoyed on her thirty-fifth birthday? It appeared Trakur Analova Ta was working on refinements but they were taking time. Just as Tracy's color began to improve, we heard a loud pounding on the door.

"This is Dr. Landen! Open this door immediately!"

Amesh coughed and lowered his voice. "Dr. Landen, Dr. Spear here. We almost have the patient stabilized. Please give us two more minutes."

Dr. Landen did not buy it for a moment. I heard him order whoever he was with to break down the door. A cracking noise followed and it sounded like Dr. Landen had brought two NFL linemen with him. They smashed the door a second time.

The Carpet of Ka flew back in the window.

Tracy stopped shaking and relaxed on the bed. She was breathing peacefully, but her eyes were still closed. Trakur Analova Ta reformed into his usual shape and hovered above her.

"She has been healed," he pronounced. "What do you want for your second wish?"

Amesh picked up the artifact, without gripping the hilt. The blade had already vanished. Amesh went to speak. We had agreed on what he would say. He was going to tell Trakur we wanted nothing else.

Then I felt a strong pressure at the back of my skull.

Lova suddenly appeared beside her mate!

She stared at me!

"Sara," she said in a soft velvety voice. "Is there anything you'd like to wish for right now? Anything I or my mate can do for you?"

Her eyes were such a beautiful red, I could not help but stare back.

"Yes," I whispered. I loved the way she said my name, and it was odd because I had never found her voice enchanting before. The pressure on the back of my head increased. It seemed to move deeper inside.

"Sara," I heard Amesh say from far away.

Lova drew closer. "What wish would you like granted?"

"I want nothing from you," I mumbled.

"Not true. You know what you want. We spoke about it during your first wish. You asked for the carpet when you really wanted . . . someone else."

"Amesh," I said, remembering. What she said was true. I had asked for the carpet when I had been longing for Amesh to stop hating me. When I had wanted him to love me the way I imagined he had loved me before the craziness had come between us.

"You couldn't stop thinking about him, Sara," Lova whispered as she brushed her hand across my cheek. It felt like a physical hand. "What do you desire from Amesh? His love? His kisses?"

"Sara! Don't listen to them!" Amesh yelled.

"Both," I admitted. "But he's not—"

"He is not what?" Lova interrupted.

The words came out painfully. "The same as me."

"Who told you these lies?" Lova demanded. "Who is trying to keep you apart from the one you love?"

"The carpet. No, the one behind the carpet. She . . ."

"She has lied to you. You know in your heart you belong with Amesh." Lova spoke sympathetically. "You want the feeling you and he shared to return. The kindness and innocence you felt at the start of your relationship."

There was such truth in her words! It was why I kept listening to her. I didn't want to be separated from Amesh, or told that he was not good enough for me. I wanted to forget all our sorrows and just lie in his arms.

I sighed. "That would be so nice."

"You want a future with him. You don't care that he's not a Kala."

"I never cared."

"Sara!" someone shouted.

"Just say it, then," Lova ordered. "Just say, 'I want him the way he used to be! I want him to be as perfect as me! That is my wish!'"

"I want him!" I cried.

"Formalize your wish. Say, 'Oh great Trakur Analova Ta, I, Sara, wish I could have Amesh for my own forever. To love and to cherish as my equal.' Say the words aloud."

"Oh great Trakur Analova Ta, I, Sara O'Ma—"

Sara, I heard a faint whisper interrupt. I did not recognize the sound, and yet I did. It belonged to my past. I shook my head. It was hard to think of the past with so much pressure in my head. Or a future without Amesh . . .

"What?" I stuttered.

Stay silent, the voice whispered.

Lova's smile widened and her eyes bore deep into me.

"You hear the lies in that voice?" Lova asked. "That's the voice that wants to take Amesh away from you!"

It's a trick, Sara, the voice said. *Remember how she entered your head.*

I cried in pain. "But I want him!"

It's a trap, the voice persisted. *Remember how the tendrils attached to the back of your head.*

Suddenly the room was spinning and in the center of the storm I saw my mother's face. Mom! She smiled at me. She was the one who loved me! She was the voice to trust.

"Trakur Analova Ta," I mumbled. "I, Sara, say what my mom says . . ." I paused, confused. Was I still bound to Lova? "Mom?" I whispered.

I'm here, the voice spoke again. *Let the light come. Push against the tendril. I will push with you.*

I obeyed. The light came and I pushed. Again, I felt such love.

"Sara says Trakur Analova Ta is to leave!" Amesh said, taking charge again. "Her mother says it, too. You're no longer welcome here! Both of you, get out of here!"

I felt a hard snapping pain at the back of my head.

Yet the pressure inside vanished.

To my surprise, the djinn did not argue with Amesh. Both looked suddenly weary. With the pot destroyed, it must have taken all of Lova's power to appear to me and slip a tendril inside my head. Plus, Trakur had just used up a lot of energy healing my mother.

The djinn must have realized we were back in control.

They both began to slowly dissolve.

Yet I heard Lova say one last sentence inside.

One day, Sara. You will be mine.

Then they were gone, and Amesh was shaking me.

"Get on the carpet!" he said.

"My mother . . ." I stuttered.

There was more loud banging on the door. It splintered.

"She's already lying on the carpet! I've disconnected all the tubes and wires! We have to go! But I need you to fly the carpet!"

"You need bandages," I gasped, stuffing the gauze and tape I was still holding into my pockets. I grabbed some bottles of pills as well.

"Sara! Dammit! Fly the carpet!"

"I love when you curse," I said, and jumped on the front of the carpet. My mother lay behind me. Amesh climbed on the rear. "Where to?" I asked.

"Anywhere but here!" he yelled.

I smiled. "Carpet. Take us to where you think is best."

The door broke open at our back. But we were already floating above the bed and shooting out the open window. Fortunately the carpet understood me even when my mother was not speaking through it.

Just before we split, I caught a glimpse of the doctors, the nurses, and the guards. Their expressions were priceless.

EPILOGUE

THE CARPET TOOK US NORTHWEST, far out of the city, to an isolated home in the country, beside an unkempt farm. There were acres of grass and trees in every direction. The house itself was huge but old, made of red brick. It was four stories tall. A relic, probably, from the turn of the previous century.

Tracy told me where to find a key—under a pot on the wooden porch—and soon we were inside. Despite the home's neglect, the electricity still worked and we were able to turn on the lights. I still had tape and gauze in my pockets. I insisted that Amesh sit while I bandaged his side. He was a poor patient.

He kept trying to push me away. But I was able to stop his bleeding.

Tracy rested on a nearby couch. She said she could move her limbs, but it was as if her brain was not sure how to use them. She could not walk without help. But she was so thirsty, she drank three glasses of water without pause.

"I think I've been dehydrated for the last five years," she said.

I should have been in shock, overwhelmed at least. I guess I was both of those things, and yet, as I sat near Tracy, my mother—it was going to take time to get used to calling her that—I felt at home. Indeed, I felt as if I finally knew what the word meant. Maybe it was because I was with the two people I loved more than anyone else in the world.

I finished with Amesh's side. "How does it feel?" I asked.

He grumbled. "Tight. You used too much tape."

"You need pressure on the gauze to keep the bleeding from restarting. Later, we can loosen it. For now, take a pain pill." One of the bottles I had grabbed back at the hospital was Vicodin.

"I don't need any pills," he said.

"That sword cut like a razor. It stings now but it's going to burn later. You'll end up taking plenty of pills."

"How do you know so much about wounds?" Tracy asked.

"You should know. You were there when Trakur Analova Ta impaled me."

"Ah. I saw that through the carpet, yes. It was like watching a drama on TV."

"It didn't feel like TV to me," I said, sitting next to her. "How are you feeling . . . Mom?"

She brightened. "Is that hard for you to say? Would you prefer calling me Aunt Tracy?"

I shrugged. "It's up to you."

"No, the choice is yours." She turned serious. "I know you have a painful question to ask. And I know you're afraid to ask it. But there's no reason to worry. What I did, leaving you with my sister, I'd do it again."

"Why?" I asked. I felt a stab in my heart.

Tracy sighed. "You're beginning to see that the world we live in is much more complex than you imagined. There are many forces at work on this planet. Some are here to help mankind, others are here to destroy us. And others still . . . they haven't made up their minds."

"You're talking about the djinn," I said.

"I'm talking about many things you have no names for yet. Suffice to say we have a significant role to play in the days to come. I turned you over to my sister because I had work to do. And you would have been targeted and killed because of my work."

I struggled with her answer. "I guess you had to prioritize."

Tracy stared at me. "You were always my number one priority, Sara. You cannot imagine how devastating it was to give you up. To pretend you didn't belong to me."

"You were trying to protect her from the bad guys," Amesh said.

"Yes, Amesh."

"You never explained how you landed in a coma," I said.

"That's a story for another day." She paused and pointed a finger at me. "But let me make one thing clear. As important as my work is, yours is more important. Many people—and many who are not even human—are hoping you can help us."

I shook my head. "I'm fifteen years old! I have to go back to high school. I have to graduate. When we woke you up, I was relieved. I assumed you would take over now."

"I cannot 'take over,' Sara. I was never in charge to begin with."

"But can't I return to a normal life?"

"Is that what you want?"

"Yes. I mean, the last few days have been exciting, but I don't think I can keep it up. I'll crack."

"No, that's one thing you'll never do. You can have a normal life, but it will mean turning away from your destiny."

"That's what the carpet said."

"That's what I said." She studied me. "This isn't a decision you have to make tonight. I merely bring it up because you need to start thinking about it. But understand one thing—you cannot go home to my sister. Your father will be waiting for you."

"What about me?" Amesh asked, worried. "Can I go home to Mira and my Papi?"

"If you do you'll put them in danger. They'll use your family to get to you, and the Anulakai will use you to get to Sara. Either way, there's no going back."

"But, Mom, you just said I can have a normal life if I choose."

"If you want it, you can choose it right now. You can decide once and for all never to find the carpet."

"I found the carpet by accident," I replied. "I was just sitting there, at the edge of the pit, and I saw it sticking out of the mud. It was not a decision on my part. I didn't even know what it was."

"No one finds the Carpet of Ka by chance. It only comes to those who are led to it. And the person who leads them to it is always the same."

"That woman at the pit?"

"Yes."

"She was strange. Who was she?" I asked.

"You."

I blinked. "I don't understand."

"Time is not a constant. It will take more time for you to fully understand the meaning of that phrase. And when you do you will take the carpet and travel back through time and give it to yourself." She paused. "You see, you can decide whatever you want. But destiny is more powerful than our personal desires. You were that woman who led you to the carpet. At some point in the future—I'm not saying when—you will lead Sara to it again."

This was so hard to understand, to accept. If I couldn't go home, I would never see my mother again. And even though she's not my real mother, she loves me. And I love her. To just disappear on her seemed so cruel. How could I do that?

Tracy sat silently, watching me. "I'm so sorry," she said.

I lowered my head. "So am I."

She moved closer to me. "Sara, look how much you've accomplished already. I, for one, am grateful. You rescued me from my endless sleep. You have given me back my life." She reached out and squeezed Amesh's hand. "You were very brave to face such a powerful djinn."

He blushed. "I'm just glad I was able to help."

"But will you stay with me?" I asked, suddenly panicked. I needed at least that to survive.

"I'll stay with both of you as long as I can," she said.

"What about Harry? Your boyfriend? Do you know where he is?"

"I know where Harry is. You do, too."

"I do? I don't think so. He's my father, isn't he?"

"Harry is your dad. But you might know him by the nickname I used to call him—Hara."

It was my turn to smile, and to cry.

"Who is Aleena?" I asked.

For some reason, my mother burst out laughing.

She hugged me and pulled Amesh closer.

"I'm afraid the answer to that question will have to wait," she said.